Dr. B.

Dr. B.

Daniel Birnbaum

Translated from Swedish by Deborah Bragan-Turner

4th ESTATE • *London*

4th Estate
An imprint of HarperCollins*Publishers*
1 London Bridge Street
London SE1 9GF

www.4thestate.co.uk

HarperCollins*Publishers*
1st Floor, Watermarque Building, Ringsend Road
Dublin 4, Ireland

First published in Great Britain in 2022 by 4th Estate
First published in the United States by Harper in 2022
Originally published in Sweden in 2018 by Albert Bonniers Förlag

1

Copyright © Daniel Birnbaum 2022
English translation copyright © 2022 by Deborah Bragan-Turner

Daniel Birnbaum asserts the moral right to be identified
as the author of this work in accordance with the
Copyright, Designs and Patents Act 1988

A catalogue record for this book is
available from the British Library

ISBN 978-0-00-837448-8 (hardback)
ISBN 978-0-00-837449-5 (trade paperback)

Set in Adobe Jenson Pro
Printed and bound in the UK using 100%
renewable electricity at CPI Group (UK) Ltd

MIX
Paper from
responsible sources
FSC™ C007454

This book is produced from independently certified FSC™ paper
to ensure responsible forest management.

For more information visit: www.harpercollins.co.uk/green

Cut off the supply of iron and you will force Hitler to capitulate.

Fritz Thyssen, Paris, 1939

CONTENTS

Dr. B.

PROLOGUE

Immanuel's face showed no sign of blushing. It would have been superfluous anyway, for the shame he bore ran deeper than that. He stood with his back to the corridor wall and felt the chill of the plaster against his head. The light of a bulb hanging from the blistered ceiling fell on his colorless face. So this would be where it ended.

He would have liked to withdraw, and yet he remained in the brightly lit corner, right by the turn in the east corridor on the first floor of Kronoberg Prison. From here one had a view in both directions. He noticed immediately when the guards brought a new arrival to the cell or wheeled along the clattering soup trolley. Moreover, it was here the detainees could meet briefly on their way to the linen closet, where they had to leave their bedding at daybreak and collect it at nightfall.

Why they let him stay here he didn't know; the guards came and went, passing him as if he were invisible. Yet it was right here in the corner that the publisher caught sight of him. It was obvious he recognized Immanuel instantly as he came walking down the corridor, holding his sheets.

In the light from the bulb Immanuel saw the publisher look at him coldly. At the man who had been the recently appointed editor, the journalist with the byline Dr. B., the new member of staff who had quickly become known by all as Immanuel. The publishing house lawyer cautioned strongly against all contact with him now. He had offended in a way that could only be viewed as unforgivable for a Jewish immigrant. The lawyer had apparently emphasized just how unforgivable.

He had asked for help in making contact with his wife and family. Concern for them had overcome the stranglehold of shame that seemed to render him powerless. His family were living in complete limbo, a situation that must have been unbearable for his wife. His own anxiety kept him awake at night.

Gottfried Bermann Fischer did not even pause. Nor did he turn when Immanuel addressed him.

"Gottfried. Listen to me."

No, what he was guilty of was patently impossible to forgive. And what would happen to them now, to his family and the publisher's? Avoiding deportation looked hopeless. Stockholm had rescued them. They had managed this far. But what was left now? The world was divided. There were places where Jews couldn't live. And there were places they couldn't enter.

Immanuel saw the publisher's back disappear into the gloom of the corridor in the direction of the linen closet.

It was too dark in the cell to study the report and all its long-winded appendices. But he had read them so many times that certain of the passages had lodged in his mind. Some of the sections he could recite verbatim. The letter around which it all revolved had been transcribed and translated, including the invisible lines. Now the thick sheaf of papers lay on the cold floor beside the bunk. From time to time he groped for one of the pages, held it up to his eyes, and with a struggle managed to decipher it. After the search of the house, typescript from the Weil family's typewriter had been analyzed by a tireless gentleman from the Secret Service, the same tall, thin inspector who conducted the interrogations. Immanuel made it out, letter by letter:

```
This specimen was typed on a Rheinmetall machine:
A s d f g h j k ö ä y x c v b n m , . - q w e r t z u i o
ü ß ß ß ß ß ß
= e 9 8 7 6 5 4 3 2 1 " - ) ) ) ) ) § § § § § § § § §
/ / / / / / / / ˆ + + + + + + + +
+ + + + + + + + + + + + + + + + + + + + + +
```

```
The serial number of the machine is 161732.
It is reportedly the property of Weil.
2 3 4 5 6 7 8 9 é ` =
q w e r t z u i o p ü ß
a s d f g h j k l ö ä
y x c v b n m , . - - - -
```

This machine is quite distinctive in that, inter alia, it lacks the letter A with a ring on top. It is reasonable to assume that the person in custody used such a machine, since I have noted that in certain correspondence he added rings above the letters by hand, including in some cases on the wrong letters. Of course the Jewish family Weil say they did not lend anyone their machines, but that information cannot be trusted. In addition it would be useful if it did prove to be the machine on which the letters were typed, for

then we could have a crack at the Weils as well.
14 April 1940 / O.D.

It was as if the inspector's own speculations surfaced here, without being clarified or conforming to the strict format of the report. The report itself was introduced with a list of all the visas and stamps in the suspect's passport, which Immanuel could recite like a litany. There followed an account of his racial origin: "Despite the fact the detainee's passport is not stamped with a J, the detainee maintains he is Jewish." As he read this section for the seventh or perhaps eighth time, he was overcome by such weariness that his eyelids gave in to the weight, and the half-light of the cell gave way to the gentler darkness of his closed eyes. In this internal night, syllable by syllable, he made his way through the text he now knew by heart: "His father was without question a full Jew. However his mother's descent has not been established."

161732. O.D. All those numbers and abbreviations bewildered him.

He leaned back on the hard bunk. Was it just his imagination, or could he hear the sound of a typewriter through the wall? Or was it coming from above, through the ceiling? He might be mistaken, but hadn't someone said that the investigation records were typed out in rooms located in the same prison block as the cells, but on a different floor? Whatever the source, the sound increased in intensity, only to fade away. Then it came back, even more distinctly. *Clickety-clack, clickety-clack.* It was a vehement, sharp tapping. Perhaps his arrest warrant had been hammered out on that machine.

He had always liked listening to his wife working in the evenings as she typed up the articles he had dictated during the day. But in comparison that was a gentle hum, broken only by the *ping* at the end of the line and the swish of the carriage return. The boys didn't mind it either, even referring to the noise as their lullaby. This industrious clatter, on the other hand, had something metallic about it, rather like the sound of crickets or a distant choir of voices emitting a harsh, rhythmic dissonance. It seemed clear to him now that it was the staccato rattle from several machines. The noise seeped into the room as a distant babble trickling across the floor. His eyelids were so heavy now, he couldn't open them.

There appeared to be something burning high up outside the window. It must be the fire in the tower of St. Gertrude's Church, spreading heat and light as far as the prison, he thought, the fire that had made the tower collapse and the spire with the golden cockerel come crashing to the ground. Without, thank heavens, injuring anyone on Tyska Brinken, the street below. The rooster itself was undamaged, as he had ascertained on a recent visit to the church. That was when he had seen the boy disappear up into the tower. Should he be worried about the fire?

But what if it was arson? he could clearly hear a friendly voice whisper. Now the noise of the typewriters had completely receded, and instead he heard the repeated whispering. *Yes, you must understand, it was definitely arson.* He recognized the voice, but how could it possibly be heard in here? It was quite plainly Rickman. Alfred Frederick Rickman, the laughing Englishman. Arson or not, now the flames were very close indeed. But it wasn't the heat of the fire in St. Gertrude's he could feel; he should have known that at once. No, it was the offices of the newspaper *Norrskensflamman* that were burning. It was obvious it was arson, that was evident to everyone, and it was as clear as day that it was the editor of their rival in Luleå who was behind it. They might have been in league with the cabal around the German consul, the one who invited the arctic explorer. How strange. Suddenly he was unsure whether it really was Rickman's voice he could hear, or could it be that of the German polar explorer? In any event, now the man's voice was drowned out by the tolling of bells. Was it the church outside the prison, or was it once again the chimes of St. Gertrude's in Gamla Stan that he had heard distinctly earlier in the day? The sound reached a crescendo. The melody was hard to follow. As a matter of fact there was no tune at all; it sounded more like the heavy hammer blows in a smithy.

He sat up in a cold sweat. He must have dozed off and begun imagining things. What he had heard was nothing more than the sound of the cell's door being opened with customary lack of care. There had been no bells, only the jangling of keys and the deafening noise of the weighty bolt being pushed upright and banging against the doorframe. There were no more flames to be seen, only bright sunlight streaming into the cell through the tiny window.

He had fallen asleep properly for the first time in several days. His nightshirt was wet, and he could feel his heart pounding with fear. As he placed his feet on the cold stone floor, the door opened, the food trolley was wheeled in, and a plate of porridge was unceremoniously set down on the nightstand. The trolley was wheeled back out by the tight-lipped guard, the door slammed shut, and he was alone once more.

It was now sufficiently light in the room for Immanuel to gather up all the documents scattered over the floor. At the top of the pile he placed on the bunk was the report about the glass bottle of invisible ink and the German fountain pen he had hidden in the bureau. Lucia had sensed all along that nothing good would come of it. It should be out of the house, she had said. And she was right: they had deciphered the letter to Kutzner, the editor in Berlin, and uncovered the lines about the Englishmen and their plans.

He read:

> On 19 April 1940 the National Forensic Science Institute received the following material from the National Criminal Police third division with a request for investigation: A glass container with ca 25 cl of pale yellowish-green liquid. The container bears a label with the letter T. A fountain pen of the brand Tintenkuli. The purpose of the investigation was to establish the type of liquid in the container.
>
> Hereby solemnly declared that chemical analysis of the liquid found it to consist of a 0.4% solution of yellow prussiate of potash $(K_4Fe[CN]_6)$.

All was revealed, nothing kept secret, even from the prisoner himself.

This, then, was where it would end, what had begun just a few months earlier in a time that was turbulent and yet full of light. A time of prospects and breaking with the past. A time so bright it was dazzling. A time when Immanuel could still see a way out.

SUNFLOWERS

Immanuel knew nothing about the island. But he was sure the light that morning was more golden than anything he had ever experienced and the pale woman on the jetty the most ethereal creature he had ever set eyes upon. He could barely make out her shape. She was almost diaphanous, her hair translucent, the breeze giving it life. The sound of the engine grew louder, and he could see the boat approaching, although the reflections on the water made it hard to focus. This morning was nothing but sun.

Now she was already standing in the bow of the motorboat that had come to fetch them. In her white dress her body could only be described as a shimmering light. Helios was the god of the sun, but of the seas too, he thought, as he stepped aboard, firm-footed but happy nonetheless to hold on to the strong arm of the boatman. Helios gave us something priceless, the gift of sight. He dwelt in a light-filled palace on the great river at the eastern ends of the earth.

Thoughts flitted across Immanuel's mind as if he were not really up and awake, but still lying in relative comfort on the sofa in Mittag-Leffler's mathematical library. A slim volume with the puzzling title *On the Motion of a Rigid Body about a Fixed Point* was the last thing his eyes had rested on for a few seconds before the shifting images of sleep displaced it. He had slept badly and woken repeatedly with a gnawing sense of unease, as if misgivings concerning the immediate future were already confirmed.

He was still in this state of mind, and the monotonous drone of the engine heightened the sensation of riding through a dream, but not a dream that belonged in the night. From his slumped position on a white leather bench right at the stern he could make out the boatman's muscular back ahead of him, but the impression this gave was of traveling under the glistening water and not on top of it.

Impatient shouting from the bow interrupted his thoughts. The athletic boatman appeared to be doing the splits, with one foot on the deck and the other on the lowest of a flight of stone steps that was surprisingly grandiose for a little island of otherwise frugal wooden structures. Immanuel's gaze followed the steps up. A series of small terraces could soon be seen, lined by statues and enormous rhododendron bushes. The young woman, who had been friendly enough but of few words when she met him on the jetty and had then stood bolt upright in the bow throughout the short journey, seemed to have disappeared into thin air. For a second he thought he saw her figure flash past behind a railing quite a long way up the steps.

Or maybe it was reflected light, tricking him into seeing things that weren't there. He found it hard to clear his vision, his eyes still slightly dazzled after the boat ride. But suddenly he caught sight of something unexpected. High up, amid the huge treetops, stood a gray stone building of almost ridiculous dimensions. It was partly concealed by leaves, which had already turned to flaming red. It was autumn, but still as warm as high summer. In front of the castle, for a castle it was, were Norway maples and laburnums.

"You'll have to wait here until Miss is back from the house," the boatman said, with no great warmth. "Madame doesn't want the guests to go up by themselves, under any circumstances." He turned away with a gesture that clearly implied he had said what he was going to say and now was going to mind his own business. Silence fell, an oppressive silence.

"Thank you for the ride. It was quick. Smart boat, by the way," Immanuel said, in an attempt to lighten the atmosphere. That his Swedish was less than perfect was not going to stop him making casual conversation. It was something he had resolved to do from the moment he arrived in his adopted country.

The boatman seemed little interested in chat. They were both now standing firmly on the quay, with the terraces at their backs and the pale-green water in front of them. On the other side of the bay the leafy gardens of Djursholm were visible, and behind the rich autumn reds was the hint of one grand villa more stately than the rest. Somewhere it must be possible to make out parts of the Mittag-Leffler Institute, where Immanuel had spent the night so he could walk down through the wooded neighborhood at dawn and be on the jetty at the allotted time. Unusual for a breakfast meeting to require a motorboat journey, he thought, turning to look back in the other direction, up toward the villa that seemed now, in the wavering morning light, to be floating among the treetops. He followed the elegant lines of the Louis XVI–style building, and for a second he forgot his uneasy feeling; a feeling that in fact he was to have every reason for, given the deception the trip would demand of him.

The house stood on massive foundations. They must have transported huge quantities of stones here on barges, he was thinking, when a sudden metallic noise roused him from his musings. The boatman, his blond hair swept back, had dropped something heavy and compact onto the quay, making them both jump. In a split second the man had bent down and picked up the object, before hastily slipping it inside his blue sports jacket. It was a pistol, small and hard, black as tar. A piece of coal, hard, absorbing all the sunlight, it was so black.

The whole thing happened so quickly, it was difficult afterward to be totally sure it hadn't been a figment of Immanuel's imagination. It hadn't occurred to him that the man piloting the boat that had picked him up from a wooden jetty in the tranquil setting of residential Djursholm would be armed. There was silence, apart from a dull thud every so often when the boat moored several meters below them hit the quay. The engine was turned off now, and with some curiosity Immanuel gazed down at the elegant craft. He was familiar with these neat, speedy wooden boats from his visits to friends at Lake Garda, but he hadn't seen a single one since arriving in these latitudes.

"Has it been imported from Italy, maybe?" he asked aloud, to break the silence.

The boatman turned to look at Immanuel, blinking nervously into the sun, but still said nothing, as if he hadn't heard the remark, or deemed it irrelevant. Perhaps he had found the incident with the pistol embarrassing. Or perhaps he was unaware that the guest had seen the handgun that had dropped to the ground momentarily, only to be just as swiftly slipped into the holster in all likelihood concealed under his jacket.

Seagulls landed close to the bow of the boat, unperturbed by the presence of the two men. They fought over a small, shiny fish jumping around on the stone surface.

"Everyone knows it's a copy that Kassman had built of the old boat, the one that went up in flames," the boatman said suddenly, almost reproachfully.

"Kassman? Who's Kassman?"

"No problem for the likes of Gunnar Kassman to find a new engineer and a new gardener," the boatman went on, as if he hadn't heard the question. "Who wouldn't want to work for a boss like him? Especially if you're not that fussy about the true source of the money. No, Director Kassman entertained women with champagne and caviar, and men as well. The motorboats were moored here at the quay until midnight, before heading back to town. Who cared if one of the boats went up in flames at daybreak, and a young engineer and a groundsman vanished into the deep? Who cared about it, except for Karin, who was to have married Axel a few days later? She was only nineteen, too young to marry maybe, but that's how it was. Her life was over then."

He stared blankly across the water, now an even deeper green, until the sound of light footsteps could be heard approaching.

There she was again, in front of him. Delicate, gossamer, as if the rays of the autumn sun could shine through her. It came as a surprise when, with a gesture up toward the castle, she began speaking, her voice soft yet firm.

"Miss Lorentzon knows you're here. She's working with Madame in the salon but wants you to wait on the grand terrace."

"The grand terrace." Immanuel repeated the words hesitantly, unsure why he felt the need to do so.

She set off up the steps without checking whether he was

prepared to follow. But follow he did, of course. He could barely keep pace with her as they climbed up the steep stone ledges, and he was already regretting his decision to take with him the weighty tomes from Mittag-Leffler's library. He could perfectly well have collected them on his way back into the city, but now the massive leather briefcase his wife had purchased on one of their final days in Warsaw was as heavy as if loaded with the same flat slabs that were under their feet. They hurried up the gravel paths that zigzagged between the flights of steps leading them toward the increasingly imposing mansion.

The young woman—he guessed she was the same Karin about whom the man with the gun had been speaking, and into whose destiny he had been given an unwarranted flash of insight—almost flew along the balustrade ahead of him. Panting, he managed to catch up with her, and for a few seconds they walked side by side. He turned to her and, with a boldness, an impertinence even, that surprised him, breathlessly asked a question he hoped would instigate a conversation.

"So you were working here in Mr. Kassman's time?"

Whatever had got into him? This woman's sad fate was none of his business. Not in the slightest. She had nothing to do with the task ahead, which was already quite complicated enough, nor with the subtle game that formed the purpose of the entire visit and should undoubtedly be his focus.

As it turned out, his impertinent question had no effect. The luminous figure had increased her lead and now disappeared through a glass door standing open on the object of their climb, the grand terrace. He mounted the last step and, gasping for breath, put his heavy bag down on the ornate flagstones, set in a lavish mosaic the likes of which he had never seen, even in villas he had visited in northern Italy.

He dropped into one of the chairs on the terrace and was aware at once that behind the white curtains moving gently in the breeze something was happening. He heard the dulcet tones of a woman's voice, apparently reading from a script, and another slightly deeper voice interrupting in Russian and then making comments on the reading in what seemed to him to be very broken Swedish. Sometimes the more pleasing voice delivered long pages without intervention. It sounded flat and slightly forced, as if they were in a hurry to work through a large body of text.

"But who is this new independent woman? She is a child of the large-scale capitalist system. She is not a rare apparition, but as an everyday phenomenon she was born simultaneously with the infernal din of machines and of factory sirens summoning the workers. The independent woman, of whom our grandmothers and even our mothers had no idea at all—she exists, she is a real, living person."

She was interrupted by a testy comment in Russian. There was a clatter of china and the sound of other voices chiming in with questions about entirely different matters, followed by silence. The mellower voice resumed but was obliged to repeat the phrase "real, living person" several times. After a short pause, the reading continued.

"Independent women are a million gray-clad figures, pouring out of working-class quarters in an endless stream, and at daybreak, when the dawn sky still battles with the dark of night, they set off for the mills and factories and railway stations."

At this point the reading was cut short by prolonged throat clearing.

"Right, right. That's enough. Thank you, Emy. Thank you. We'll continue this afternoon." Silence fell, and it sounded as though the women had left the terrace room without noticing Immanuel's presence.

From this position he could gaze out over the fountains in the garden and the lush vegetation of rhododendrons and exotic trees, and he thought how out of place they looked in this Nordic archipelago. He leaned forward to inspect the sunflowers growing nearest to the villa. Their extraordinarily long stalks reached up to the terrace. They seemed to be staring him in the face, like huge black pupils.

"They turn during the course of the day and follow the sun, as if they have no choice but to look straight into the ball of fire," a woman's voice behind him declared suddenly. "Madame loves them. They're one of the reasons she rents the villa. She'd really like to buy it, but who knows what the future will bring? We tie the sunflowers back with string so they don't collapse under their own weight. But they'll wither soon anyway, now it's autumn. Do forgive me, my name is Emy Lorentzon, Madame Kollontai's secretary. You're extremely punctual. Did you have a comfortable trip across?"

Immanuel nodded to the young woman who had appeared beside him, but there was no time for even a pleasantry in response before she carried on with her account of the flowers' daily rotation around their own axis.

"Heliotropism, a tendency Madame has taken an interest in, as something with potentially profound significance for social movements. It's hardly surprising if that intense mass of light creates the right conditions for a completely different type of politics, is it? Pavel Dybenko, who spent many white June nights on the Baltic Sea, introduced her to these ideas. You know the story about the Lapland sunflowers that grow so far north they never have the chance to turn their heavy heads back at dusk?"

Miss Lorentzon gave him a searching look, like a teacher with high expectations of her student, and continued without waiting for a response.

"Because there's no dusk, ever, nor is there the essential respite dusk brings. For the twelve longest days of the year the flower twists in a spiral until it finally strangles itself. And in exactly the same way the stalk of north European socialism is threatened by the optimism of its own blooms, or ought we say, extremism?"

She smiled serenely at him, as if her words were the most natural thing in the world, so self-evident they hardly needed voicing. He looked closely at the young woman, utterly convincing in her gray suit, thoroughly proper and exemplary. A secretary, a typical secretary at an embassy in a north European capital. Behind her he glimpsed the indistinct shapes of the dark-centered heads in a sunflower sea, motionless in the morning calm.

Nebulous thoughts flashed across his mind without really taking shape. Dybenko, the naval officer, the Ukrainian giant in the Baltic Fleet. The love affair that nearly had the woman he was about to meet expelled from the party. He recalled the words the irreproachable Albert Oeri earnestly and repeatedly pronounced: *She is an authority, perhaps our greatest authority, on the field of carnal love.*

He was roused from his musings by a booming voice.

"And you've been sent here by Albert Oeri, editor of *Basler Nachrichten*, a man my Swiss friends hold in such high regard they overlook his political stance, by and large."

Her appearance was so sudden, he didn't quite grasp what had happened, but there she stood in all her splendor, wearing a long morning gown of dazzling silk.

"I presume you see yourself as a liberal voice in the continental darkness. You're a journalist, I understand. And you wish to ask about the woman question. Or, as you wrote in your letter, 'so-called feminism'—is that so?"

Madame Alexandra Kollontai gave him a piercing look. Under the arched brows her gray eyes appeared lit from within, their luster truly uncommon. And now this warm iridescence was directed at him in a way that made abundantly clear it would be difficult to hide anything from this woman. Had he been far too rash in taking on this project? Had he overestimated his own ability?

In any event it was too late to change his mind. Now he was standing in front of this formidable person, with no possibility of beating a retreat or holding anything back. Or more accurately: *she* was standing in front of him with such a clear advantage that the notion of him staging any kind of subtle maneuver was ridiculous. Of course he had heard about her charisma and her unfading beauty. But he could never have foreseen the authority she commanded physically, the aura of absolute power surrounding her. He pulled himself together and took the plunge.

"Your Excellency, that is correct, I arrived here in the city some time ago after many years in Warsaw, and I continue to work as a correspondent for *Basler Nachrichten*. I am first and foremost German, and my mother tongue is German. I am delighted to hear that in your circles too the esteemed journalist Dr. Oeri enjoys the respect he deserves in these dark times."

"So you're the one with the pen name Dr. B. I was only reading you yesterday. You wrote about our problems in Finland."

"Yes, that's right," Immanuel answered, unsure whether her remark held any criticism.

"*Basler Nachrichten* has another correspondent here in Stockholm," she said.

How could she know that? Gabriel Ascher, for years the Vatican City correspondent, had been in Stockholm for a while now, an awkward situation in several respects. Immanuel had never liked Ascher, and there would obviously be stiff competition for space.

But he had no time to expand upon that. Kollontai continued, in a more conversational tone, "You spent the night at Mittag-Leffler's villa on the other side of the water, my secretary tells me. Isn't that what you said, Emy?" She turned to seek the younger woman's confirmation, but Miss Lorentzon had quietly withdrawn.

With a gesture into the light-filled room, Kollontai invited Immanuel to take a seat in one of the two gray armchairs, relatively modern for a palace. "Another splendid house I've considered renting as a summer residence in the past. I suppose the famous library is still there, but I heard that plans for the mathematical institute itself were put on ice after the bankruptcy. Anyway, I prefer spending weekends out here on the island, and I hope we'll be able to move in properly next summer. I'm contemplating bringing some of the legation over—at the moment I'm getting help from Kassman's old staff. You've met Karin, poor girl. She's working for me now, and her brother pilots the boat."

So the man with the gun was the gossamer woman's brother. That explained his vehemence, and his despair. But aloud Immanuel said, "Yes, the library is still there. Thousands of mathematical treatises on mahogany shelves stretching up to the ceiling. Excuse me, but who is this person Kassman who builds a palace on an island in the Stockholm archipelago?"

"Of course, I'm sorry. You don't know Director Gunnar Kassman, do you? I'd forgotten you're new to the city. A great friend to Russian culture, a financier with connections on both sides of the Baltic Sea. He hit problems around the same time as Mittag-Leffler was declared bankrupt. And now both villas stand empty. Speaking of which, you will of course be aware that Sonja Kovalevsky, our first female mathematician, was awarded her professorship thanks entirely to Mittag-Leffler. A forward-looking scholar, an exemplar. Higher education wasn't open to women in Russia, and under Professor Weierstrass in Göttingen, who naturally saw her talent, only private study was possible. You've heard of Kovalevsky?"

She must have realized that wasn't so, because without waiting for a response, she carried on with her account, as if everyone needed to be informed of the Russian mathematician's fortunes. She spoke as if delivering a lecture, or possibly a welcome speech to a full delegation.

"She devised important calculations concerning Saturn's rings and subsequently wrote *On the Motion of a Rigid Body about a Fixed Point*, which at a stroke made her famous in scientific circles across Europe. But the Royal Academy of Sciences here in Sweden drew the line at accepting a woman member. On the other hand, apparently the academy did preserve her brain in alcohol as an example of something that violated the laws of nature, something that really ought not exist, genius in female form. We're touching on our topic now, aren't we?"

"I beg your pardon? I'm not sure I follow your train of thought."

Her expression when she looked at him was hard to determine. But when she continued, her tone was markedly less friendly. "Kovalevsky did not publish only mathematical research into cosmic rings. I suppose her autobiographical novel might be of interest, if it really is so-called feminism that concerns you. But perhaps it's now time for *you* to explain to *me* what we're going to talk about. I see you've made notes and picked out some quotations, which I presume are from my writings. But first a question for you: What does the year 1905 say to you, if I give you the clue 'Halle'?"

He had not imagined the conversation unfolding like this. It began to smack of an examination, and that even before it was properly underway. To extricate himself from this uncomfortable situation he answered in a tone he hoped would convey a certain levity.

"That isn't the story I wished to speak about with Your Excellency, but instead, more specifically, your view on woman's position today, as expressed in the novella about Vasilisa Malygina, the knitter. Vasilisa is pregnant, she forgives her husband and his mistress, and she makes a life for herself, devoted to the party. How should this be read in the light of your critique of marriage today?"

His hope was that a reference to the only book by Alexandra Kollontai he had actually read from cover to cover, *Love of Worker Bees*, would provoke a lively discussion and obviate the need for him to confess that he had no idea what might have happened in the small university town of Halle in 1905. He gazed at her with an expression that probably betrayed a certain hopelessness.

At once she seemed to take pity on him, answering in a kinder voice, "As I'm sure you know, I usually do argue that marriage, the modern-day compulsory union of two individuals, is still, for all its shortcomings, the mainstay of woman's affluence in the middle bourgeoisie and obliges her to cling to this institution. Are you married, sir?"

He nodded cautiously, welcoming the invitation to move on to something personal, but before he had a chance to mention his wife's name, they were interrupted by a sliding door opening almost soundlessly, and a trolley with tea was wheeled up to them. Two steaming cups.

She broke off her exposition with a short, "Thank you, Emy," without so much as a glance at her secretary. Just as soundlessly the latter vanished from the large room, the wide glass doors still open to the sunflower terrace. They were already bathed in warm morning sunshine.

They remained silent as both attempted to drink the piping hot tea. What then followed was nothing short of a lecture on the economic plight of the single woman in the Soviet Union. As though to demonstrate his intense interest, Immanuel made assiduous notes in one of the pads he had brought, interrupting occasionally with a brief question or to request further clarification. The literary examples came thick and fast but were far from familiar to him, and the language became steadily more high-flown.

Finally, after a prolonged pause, she arrived at what he took to be a kind of summary. "The transformation of the female psyche, adapted to the new conditions of its economic existence, is not achieved without dramatic self-delusion. You understand that, of course. And this conflict playing out inside the female soul gradually draws the attention of writers. By degrees woman is transformed from an object of the tragedy of the male soul to the subject of an independent tragedy."

To indicate his awareness that at this point an official person of her rank would probably judge she had spent enough time with her guest, and other duties beckoned, he cleared his throat and rose to his feet. Was this the right moment to thank her humbly for a fruitful discussion and then, without in any way revealing how important this was to him, progress to other questions and observations about the diplomatic world? He had been mulling over this move for days, but now it seemed out of the question. Suddenly openings to the kind of conversation he needed looked highly unlikely. How could he ever have thought otherwise? However, when he nervously cleared his throat again to offer a few pleasantries, she remained seated and continued gravely:

"If it's the situation in the new Germany that interests you, there's clearly much more to be said. You will obviously understand what National Socialism means for these issues. But let me remind you of a bit of history here. German feminists worded their bourgeois concerns very precisely at the women's congress in Halle. On the one hand they demanded that society should recognize one single morality for men and women and that the state should be prevented from interfering in personal sexual morals, while on the other hand they insisted on measures for the protection of social morality from that same state. Do you follow me?"

He really didn't know what he should say to this. There was no point pretending he knew what had been discussed at a women's congress several decades before. Instead, with forced enthusiasm, as if she had never posed the question, he said, "I'm convinced this will be a fascinating portrait, and your views will attract much attention. As you know, initially it will be published in *Basler Nachrichten*, a free voice in the German-speaking world, but naturally the hope is that we can place the article in a number of newspapers, in all probability *De Telegraaf*, and why not in a paper in a Nordic country too? Has *Uusi Suomi* or any daily paper in this country talked to Your Excellency about these subjects?"

There was no reply. She gazed out through the fluttering curtains at the sea of sunflowers swaying gently in the breeze that had now sprung up, as if she hadn't heard the question. A shadow play came to life on the wall behind her, gray veils moving back and forth.

When she finally resumed her monologue, it was obvious she was reading from one of the sheets of paper lying in front of her on a low table. "'When the woman of old left love behind, she buried herself in darkness and gloom to lead the life of a helpless wretch, whereas the new woman has liberated herself from the thralldom of love and stands proud.'"

She turned to the shadow play on the wall. For a moment it seemed she had forgotten Immanuel's presence in the room. Whenever he looked back later on the lengthy silence that ensued, it always struck him that it had cast them both, him as well as her, out into another sphere, as if they had embarked on a voyage to quite different places, which in some strange way manifested themselves as the salon in the gray palace on the leafy Swedish island. Did they visit the bright halls in the country house of her childhood on the Karelian Isthmus, or was it the exhilarating tumult of the revolution? The Young Workers' Party's bustling headquarters, or the colorless maze of power in later years? Their journey couldn't have lasted more than a minute or two, but it was more real than anything else that had happened to him that day, despite being impossible to explain satisfactorily. He would never forget it.

Then they were back in the salon, the white curtains dancing ever more merrily in the sunlight flooding the terrace. She turned slowly, but only halfway, so that her famed profile could be seen to full advantage, and explained in the most casual of tones, "These are the ideas with which Miss Lorentzon and I engage in the mornings. When you arrived we were working on a translation of some of my lectures. But tell me now: Why have you actually come to see me?"

He felt as though his entire body had turned into something alien, something that didn't quite belong to him. His legs couldn't decide whether to remain straight or bend at the knee, and as a result his stance was only semi-upright, leaning against the back of a gray armchair.

"What does Your Excellency mean?"

"I'm simply wondering what your business is here. You can't persuade me that the conversation we've had was the real purpose of your visit."

He heard himself reply in a voice that didn't sound like his own. It came from his lips, but who was technically speaking, he didn't know. "Your Excellency, what makes you think that?"

Now she turned to him so that he could see her face. The beautiful gray eyes, not in the least threatening but absolutely steady, inspected him from top to toe, while she spelled it out, point by point. "I'm not generally mistaken. You introduce yourself as 'first and foremost German,' but let me say this: I think I can recognize Jewish intelligentsia when I meet it. The fact that you're trying to establish yourself at the present time as a journalist for a daily newspaper openly critical of Hitler doesn't exactly preclude my hypothesis. But be that as it may, it's plain you haven't mastered the subject you claim you want to discuss."

In a whisper she added: "You want something else from me."

Without noticing how, he found himself back in the gray armchair, in a crumpled heap opposite Madame Kollontai. It was all up now, his failure complete.

With the feeling of resignation came something else: amazement at his own plan, the fundamentally incomprehensible and totally unrealistic idea that he, a journalist in exile, could hoodwink one of the diplomatic world's most experienced negotiators, a renowned tactician, in the way he had supposed. Would the woman who had miraculously escaped all physical reprisals from the party leadership, despite being regarded as a counterrevolutionary, be so easily deceived? What insane arrogance! Would the woman who negotiated with ministries and embassies and under whose firm direction the Soviet legation operated be duped by him, a man for whom the present situation was so complicated that a cool head was out of the question?

It all obviously came down to the absurdity of the whole plan. Though it had to be said, when he looked back later, that in principle it could have worked. If only it had involved someone other than Alexandra Kollontai, former People's Commissar for Education, now a minister and the Soviet Union's first female envoy to Europe. Had it not been for her, it would have been feasible. But she was the one sitting in front of him now, waiting for an explanation. Why had he *really* come to see her?

It occurred to him that the situation was an outright disaster, and a series of realities sprang to mind like a flurry of icy gusts to the soul. First of all: he was on an island and had no control whatsoever over his departure. He recalled the tight-lipped boatman's less than cooperative body language, his powerful physique, and above all the sports jacket that evidently concealed the fact that he was armed. In fact the villa was probably guarded by other representatives from the Soviet legation. He was effectively a prisoner on this island.

Once again he had the feeling someone else was speaking through him, in a strong, clear voice: "It concerned a visa question."

A faint murmuring was heard from other parts of the villa, but here in the sunlit room everything seemed to stand still. He filled the void with an account to strengthen her suspicion that the conversation hitherto was basically a pretext for broaching other subjects entirely. "As I said, a visa question. More precisely, a transit visa needing to be extended. I'm sure you'll know the publisher Gottfried Bermann Fischer, who relocated here to Sweden with the assistance of Tor Bonnier of Albert Bonniers Förlag. Bermann Fischer spent the last weeks of the summer with his wife and children in a large wooden house belonging to the Bonnier family south of the city, more precisely on Dalarö. The other week they were visited by Katia and Thomas Mann, who should have been the keynote speaker at the PEN Congress, which was naturally canceled because of the outbreak of war, but Bermann Fischer's press wants to publish the speech now and distribute it in Germany. You'll be familiar with his publishing house, now fifty-one percent owned by the Bonnier family and forty-nine percent owned by Bermann Fischer himself. He has found a number of very capable coworkers in the city, and miraculously he has resumed publishing at a level many thought was impossible these days, with the press's authors spread all over the world. But Zweig, Werfel, and Hofmannsthal are back in print despite the German censor. And Mann as well of course, and Ève Curie, whose successful book about her mother actually provided the financial footing for the company's recovery."

He tried to meet her eye to gain some sense of how his explanation was being received. She was still sitting in profile, which made it impossible.

"German literature is at stake, and now Bermann Fischer is convinced that the next step requires him and his family to get to America, where Mann has already settled and will provide assistance. The journey will be difficult, of course. I saw the family's passports yesterday, all five stamped full of transit visas, every one of which has to be renewed on a regular basis to enable international travel. I don't need to tell Your Excellency what this journey involves. Naturally you're aware that one has to fly from Bromma to Riga, then on to Velikiye Luki and from there to Moscow. From Moscow one takes the Siberian railway to Vladivostok and then a boat to Yokohama. Finally across the Pacific Ocean to San Francisco in one of the famed passenger ships and onward over the new continent. Not something accomplished in a hurry. But forgive me, are you acquainted with Bermann Fischer, the illustrious publisher of Nobel Prize winner Thomas Mann?"

The reply came immediately, scornful and not exactly oozing goodwill. "Gottfried Bermann Fischer, publisher of Leon Trotsky's mendacious book *My Life*—yes sir, I am well acquainted with him. Did he really send you here? Is this the reason for your visit, the travel plans of the Jewish publisher and his family?"

He was going to point out that Trotsky's autobiography had nothing to do with Bermann Fischer, that it was his father-in-law, Samuel Fischer, who had published it, but he stopped himself, recalling that Bermann Fischer had predicted this reaction. Publishing Trotsky would not go unpunished, of that he had always been convinced. Yet he had knowingly backed the proposal. Some had suggested it boiled down to Jewish solidarity being stronger than any ideological differences. It was widely known that Trotsky described Comrade Kollontai's obsession with sexuality, especially her own sex life, as offensive. In Trotsky's opinion, probing into matters of sexuality, despite the uninhibited and wild impression it gave, in the end indicated a fundamentally bourgeois disposition. Those were the very words he used: *she probes into her own sexuality*. Then again, their mutual antipathy was also widely known, and Kollontai had later prevented Trotsky's entry to Sweden by simply refusing his visa application, which in turn had earned her one of the Soviet Union's greatest political distinctions, the coveted Order of Lenin. Perhaps her triumphant report on how she stopped Trotsky's admittance was what saved her from Moscow reprisals. Whatever the case, clearly Bermann Fischer's publishing house, no matter how crucial to German literature it was held to be, was for Alexandra Kollontai essentially part of Trotsky's infernal network, possibly even a central part. That the Jewish publisher and his family would receive aid in their plight from her of all people was unlikely.

She repeated the question, her voice now betraying a degree of impatience, not to say antagonism: "So this was the real reason? Your implied interest in the issues explored in my writings was nothing more than a false pretext, and your famous editor Oeri, our great liberal journalist in Basel, nothing more than a smoke screen. Thus your visit is exposed as an attempt to fool me, lull me into a feeling of intellectual consensus in order eventually, almost *en passant*, to broach the matter of a visa, as if merely a bagatelle. I believe we have said all we have to say to one another, sir."

She rose to her feet and left the room. Immanuel's heart was pounding in his chest, thoughts racing through his head. The awkward thing was that her version wasn't far from the truth, even if it had been expressed with a brutality he couldn't have articulated even to himself. But it was true, he had hoped to raise the subject of the Bermann Fischer family's predicament at the end of their meeting, after the interview had been concluded. Anything to impress the publisher who had given him relatively well-paid commissions and had actually hinted at the possibility of a permanent position. Nothing could be more pivotal to his current situation, and the whole idea of sorting out the visa problem for the publisher was one of the reasons he had pressed ahead with this visit. Now she had found him out before they had even finished their conversation about the woman question.

He heard firm footsteps, and Madame Kollontai appeared at the wide sliding door leading to the villa's inner recesses. He saw his last chance of putting things right.

"Your Excellency, you exaggerate, or rather, you misjudge the entire situation. Firstly, of course I'm here to discuss your view of society and the issues to which you have devoted a large part of your life. Believe me, Dr. Oeri will be delighted to publish this portrait should you give the newspaper permission. Naturally Your Excellency will be able to read the article in its entirety and have every opportunity to correct any errors or potential misunderstandings."

Suddenly she no longer seemed annoyed or even slightly upset. "From my perspective the conservatives mark a pause in history. For all his urbanity in Swiss salons and his self-professed liberalism, Dr. Oeri himself represents just such a pause. A conservative is, as we like to say, a person who admires radicals centuries after their death. A conservative is a person who believes quite simply that nothing really big should ever be undertaken. Nothing new should ever be done. I have no time for such men, and history will prove me right. Thank you for coming. Miss Lorentzon will take you down to the boat."

Without further ado she turned and disappeared from view. In her place appeared the smiling young secretary in the immaculate gray linen dress. She showed him out to the terrace, and together they began the climb down to the water.

The sun was in the southwest of the clear blue sky as they quickly descended one level after another, passing the sunflowers and the huge rhododendron bushes lining the terraces and railings. He broke the silence by asking a few questions about the villa and its irrefutably dramatic past. To his surprise the prim secretary's account picked up precisely where the boatman's had ended that same morning. Once again he heard the story of the boat that had caught fire and sunk in the bay, claiming the lives of a groundsman and a young engineer who was about to be wed. This was in Director Kassman's time, when the house was known for the most sumptuous of society parties. The bride, the translucent woman who had met him that morning, and her brother, the young man in the sports jacket, still worked on the island, carrying out all manner of services for the Soviet delegation.

"Yes, all manner of services," she repeated, as if there were some inner meaning to the words. "And not just for the Soviet legation, but for the German one as well. And doubtless for others too," she added.

They were close to the water now and could see the boat approaching at full speed. They could already hear the muffled engine noise, which seemed to emanate from somewhere beneath the shining surface.

"I have informed Madame of my concerns," she went on, "but she can see nothing strange in it. Everyone needs work these days, she says. But I'm wary of that man and want as little as possible to do with him. We all feel a fondness for the poor girl, but her brother's hiding something."

Why Miss Lorentzon of the Soviet diplomatic mission felt the need to share these suspicions with a journalist who was a complete stranger was a mystery to Immanuel, and at that moment it didn't preoccupy him, for now the boat was along-side and the boatman was once again straddling the boat and the jetty. As if to avoid having to greet the young man, Miss Lorentzon said goodbye, but just as she set off back up to the house, she turned to Immanuel with one last message.

"Madame would like you to know that the publisher Bermann Fischer may collect a transit visa for all members of his family at the end of the week. If he hands in the passports to our consular department on Thursday morning, she will make sure they are stamped the same afternoon. The embassy is at 17 Villagatan, as you know."

THE BOY IN THE TOWER

Immanuel strode briskly toward the German church. St. Gertrude's was in the Juno district, circled by Prästgatan, Svartmangatan, and Tyska Brinken. It was on the uneven cobblestones of the latter that he was now striding forth, with a sense of purpose that was in no way matched by any clear idea of what awaited him. Light drizzle had made the cobblestones shiny and somewhat slippery. He passed through the massive black gates, which were standing half open, and glanced up at the gilt letters gracing the top, which left no doubt that he was entering German territory: FÜRCHTET GOTT! EHRET DEN KÖNIG! Interesting use of exclamation marks, he thought, before noticing that the church door was also partially open. He hadn't prearranged his visit or even checked the parish office hours. But might he be fortunate enough to meet an appropriate person, maybe even the priest himself? Had they taken his letter seriously?

The church had an airy, almost square nave. The arches rested on half columns of limestone. The floor was of marble. Black, white, and brown. Despite the half-light he could admire the patterns surrounding his wet shoes. In front of him was the pulpit in ebony and alabaster. But his attention was drawn to something quite different: a group of young seminarists gathered in a tight cluster in the darkness. They were being led around the vast nave by an elderly gentleman who was describing in ringing tones important aspects of the works of art in the church interior. They reflected in a striking way, he explained, the riches that characterized the church community in the Baroque era. The students, presumably all theologians, turned their faces in the direction the teacher indicated. He gesticulated enthusiastically toward the black eagle wings standing out against the golden base of an epitaph.

"How might this be interpreted?" the teacher asked, but allowed no opportunity for his audience to respond. He was already on his way toward the pulpit, where he paused for a few seconds before turning his gaze up to one particular window, representing Saint Gertrude herself, the church's own saint, the patron saint of travelers all over the world.

"The window was gifted in 1887 by a merchant from Brandenburg. It was the year after the great fire, when the spire collapsed. We'll probably never know with any certainty whether the fire was the result of arson. But back to the window. As you see, the design dutifully follows the style of the parish seal, featuring our Belgian saint holding a church in her left hand and a chalice in her right. We know very little about Gertrude, save that she lived in Nivelles in the seventh century, and while we know rather more about her cult, we don't know what decisions led to the creation of this particular window. But given the donor's own occupation, it's reasonable to assume he had a hand in it."

Scenes formed in Immanuel's mind. Quite where he had

viewed them, he couldn't recall, but he remembered pictures of the church, in particular a dramatic woodcut showing the great fire: flames engulfing the spire, already disintegrating far up high, close to the sky; the water jets helpless against the mighty blaze; the tower growing more slender and graceful until it was thin as a pen stroke. The image had made so strong an impression that he remembered every detail. At the very top, above the flames, he fancied he could see the weathercock, floating in the gray clouds. The golden weathercock, as he now realized, because that was what the group had gathered around. Everyone's attention was on the metal object. The cockerel glittered with gold and was almost unscathed, despite toppling through the flames from the clouds.

The lecture resumed.

"Eyewitnesses recount that the fire was a spectacle of rare beauty. A report issued the day after the monumental tragedy tells of the spire swaying majestically and then sinking soundlessly into the depths, leaving a towering column of fire to shoot up in its place. Coal-black smoke hung over the city, and the penetrating smell of fire lasted for days."

Immanuel, now hidden by the shadow of a column, was standing only a few meters from the group of listeners. As the little troupe tacked this way and that around the church, no one appeared to pay any attention to the stranger in their midst. On closer inspection the golden cockerel wasn't especially impressive; on the contrary, it was cut roughly from some kind of gilt metal. But of course its fall from the skies had been all the more spectacular, and the tail feathers as well as the rooster's comb were slightly damaged. It was now installed like a museum exhibit on a discreet pedestal in the narthex, which had been built after the fire. The light streamed in through the magnificent window onto the metal cockerel. The folds in the saint's clothing had a strange sheen, as if they were made of copper. Sure enough, she was holding a chalice in one hand and a miniature church in the other.

Immanuel was intrigued, forgetting for a moment that important matters were at stake, perhaps even matters of life and death. The priestly teacher—could it be the reverend himself?—guided his party to the font, and from there to one of the organs, where they remained for a few minutes. His explanations demonstrated a passionate interest in the art of emblematics. They passed the royal box without stopping before finally positioning themselves before the resplendent altar.

"As you know, many important figures in the expanding Swedish empire were German-speaking. Let us take this glorious altar as an example. It was in all likelihood a gift from one of the kingdom's wealthiest men, Magnus Gabriel De la Gardie."

The topic seemed of particular interest to the verbose church historian, judging by the length of time the group stood in front of the intricate golden centerpiece, so long, in fact, that the attention of some of the young theologians wandered. The manner in which they were leaning against the altar rail was not exactly devout. They looked as if they were slouched against a fence, Immanuel thought, seizing the opportunity to slip past them. He sat down on a pew at the back and felt exhaustion overwhelm his body. The lighting in the church was subdued and the monotonous voice soporific.

That was when he saw something that aroused his interest. A burly figure, stout but scarcely taller than a schoolboy, passed behind the organ screen and slipped into an opening in the wall, which in all probability was the entrance to the tower. It all happened so quickly, he wasn't quite sure if he had imagined it.

Could the person he thought he had seen hurry past be a product of his overwrought mind? The last few days had certainly not been restful. Since the trip to the island, his sleep had got worse, his dreams more ominous and his hallucinations more frequent.

Behind him he heard the venerable teacher's never-ending lecture, which now revolved around the famous church bells. He recalled hearing the bells ring "Nun danket alle Gott" when taking his first walk through Gamla Stan with his wife and sons. It had been evening, and they had looked up at the spire, which frankly had something eerie about it in the twilight. The winged dragons projecting from the tower at two levels reminded them of similar ornamentation on churches they knew in Warsaw, and the sound of the bells in the narrow streets around the church was so shrill, the youngest son had put his hands over his ears.

"Johann Crüger's 'Nun danket alle Gott' and four other melodies are played automatically," the tireless teacher explained to his now visibly weary and hence somewhat inattentive audience. "But the bell ringing can also be done by hand," he added in a tone suggesting that this was of the utmost interest. "In the middle of the room right at the top of the tower is a clavier. It's reminiscent of a piano, but with oversize keys. The bells are controlled by wire ropes connected to the piano. And playing it requires serious strength. It's not for softies!"

When Immanuel tried to explain afterward what had happened, he couldn't, but suddenly he found himself halfway up the tower. He had stolen into the same doorway through which he had seen the small thickset figure disappear, convinced that the pack of seminarists had noticed nothing. They had probably not registered his presence in the church at all. He climbed the first flight of stairs fast and paused on a stone landing. Up above he could hear the sound of hurried footsteps, he was sure. They were intermittently very faint, like soft thuds, and then louder, almost like hammering. Resolutely, he carried on up the steep staircase. When he stopped again to catch his breath, he was already at the height of the roofs of the surrounding houses. The acoustics in the tower were playing tricks on him, and at times he fancied the steps he could hear so clearly were very close. Then suddenly everything was silent, apart from the sound of his own increasingly labored breathing.

The ascent was hair-raising, more vertiginous than he could have dreamed. A narrow staircase turned like a spiraling funnel, steep and confined, before opening into a tower room so large and bright that its ceiling was just an impression high above, like the heavens. The next flight of steps led on, even narrower and more winding, straight up into the unknown. He felt a cool draft and realized he must be approaching an opening. And sure enough, to his left he could look straight out into the gray light. It was still drizzling, and when he stepped onto the tiny balcony he could look down across the array of Gamla Stan's rooftops. He let his eye wander over the labyrinth of little streets before resuming his cramped climb inside the tower.

He passed the huge bells that rang out for worship, their heavy shapes now so still it was hard to believe they could suddenly spring into action. Their earsplitting peal at such close proximity would surely have sent him toppling headlong into oblivion, he thought. But they were already below him, and next he faced a maze of narrow passageways with dark alcoves, sharp turns, and steep wooden ladders. He gripped the thin uprights on the ladder so hard his knuckles turned white, flinching every time the rungs creaked under the weight of his feet. At last, when he had given up trying to fathom how the tower could be so high, his head finally emerged into the small oval room where the bell ringer could sit at his keyboard.

But *sit* wasn't the right word, as he soon realized, because in front of him lurched a figure making jerky, almost mechanical movements, like a crewman on an ocean steamer pulling levers in a wild jig to keep the engine parts going. He heard a scraping noise that seemed to come from the steel strings vanishing upward into the top of the spire. The bells, hung from beams that were only a few meters above their heads, had come to life. Now they were all in motion, obviously controlled by the frenetic dancing of the boy's limbs, as if they were part of the machine. The vibrations took possession of Immanuel's body with such force that he almost lost his footing.

It was truly astounding. The bell ringer's dance was terrifying but also beautiful. It was like nothing he had ever seen before and difficult to describe in a way that did it justice, as he later became aware when trying in vain to recount the strange incident. And yet he could remember the convulsive movements of the mechanical ballet in detail and with an almost hallucinatory clarity. There was no question but that the gestures made by the bell ringer's limbs in astonishing symbiosis with the pedals, steel strings, and bells themselves was one of the most wondrous things he had ever witnessed. And the music coming from the twenty-four bells in the tower was of a kind that he could only compare to the great organ concerts in the temple of his childhood. It wasn't the bells' usual chimes—no, this music was exuberant and intricate, captivating and complex. The largest bells rang out in unison in a single harsh rhythm, intersected by the quicker, more playful melodies of the smaller bells and the high-pitched trill of the smallest.

As if bewitched, he was following the swaying bells in the top row when he suddenly noticed they were playing on their own. The bell ringer had disappeared.

Where had the boy gone in such a hurry? Had he carried on farther up into the spire, beyond the beams, or down the steep wooden ladder Immanuel himself had just climbed? It must have happened while he was absorbed in the sound of the bells, which was decreasing in strength now and fading completely. In the ensuing silence he could hear the wind, strong enough to make some of the steel strings swing to and fro. A flock of pigeons frightened off by the deafening noise returned and made themselves at home among the beams. The sound of their flapping wings filled the room when they collectively changed places. He wasn't totally sure, but he thought he could hear the thud of footsteps somewhere below him, perhaps where the near-vertical ladders met the top landing and the stairs started. As he began the dizzying descent, he couldn't believe the speed with which he had managed to climb up these slippery ladders with their far-from-steady rungs. At every creak he was reminded of the dark abyss beneath him; the alarm that gripped him was very different from the feeling he had had on his way up, when his eye had been fixed on the light above, admittedly gray, but light nonetheless. The way down was into darkness.

Eventually he reached the first stone floor. Now that he was on a firm footing his breathing slowed, and he made much easier progress down the spiral stairs, making it to the bottom of the tower with a sense of relief before stepping through the little door back into the nave.

The church was now in total darkness and silence, and with great effort he managed to grope his way forward without walking into any of the pillars or pews. He sat down, his legs shaking, in the same place on the back row from which he had first caught sight of the bell ringer.

He could see the flicker of candlelight by the font, presumably from some of the altar candles. The church was empty, the young seminarists had evidently left, but in front of the altar was a shadow. If he wasn't mistaken, it was moving in his direction. Yes, it was definitely coming toward him. He heard footsteps, of that there was now no doubt, and he could soon see that it was the elderly gentleman, the church historian, who was approaching. "There you are, my son. I wondered how long it would take," he said in a friendly but slightly challenging voice, as if he had had to wait a tad too long.

By now Immanuel could see the cross resting on his chest. "I'm sorry, Father, but we haven't been introduced."

"I've been waiting for you since I received the letter. There's a lot to set straight, Immanuel. God is with you, as your name attests, but there are questions that need to be answered."

This didn't make any sense. How could the priest know his name? The same old man who earlier on, before the adventure in the tower, hadn't even been aware of him and certainly hadn't noticed when he vanished up the winding stone staircase. Or perhaps he was wrong; maybe the priest knew very well he had climbed the church tower without permission.

His reply was brief: "I was looking around in the church. An exceptional altar."

"Don't digress, my son," the priest said. "Have you gathered your thoughts? What we must talk about is the Jewish faith."

Immanuel's letter, addressed directly to the reverend, in addition to setting out the case for the family's admittance to the evangelical congregation, had encompassed some possibly unwarranted thoughts on the relationship of enlightened Judaism to Protestant belief.

"Your father was cantor in the synagogue in Königsberg, and if I'm not mistaken he composed a number of the Jewish hymns sung today in temples all over the world, including the synagogue here on Wahrendorffsgatan. Your letter gives me to understand that as a child in Königsberg you were part of the Jewish community but that you gradually distanced yourself from Judaism, and the reasons you cite are unusual. I really must emphasize this: they are unusual."

It was true that, in what was admittedly a rather lengthy appeal to St. Gertrude's, he had given details of the approaches made by the Jewish community in Königsberg to the evangelical churches in the city. It was common knowledge that the city's Jews had even declared their willingness to convert en masse to the evangelical faith. Progressive Christianity would soon jettison all obsolete doctrines anyway and become an enlightened religion indistinguishable from that of any reasonable Jew. Clearly the old priest had taken these views seriously and wanted to discuss their deeper meaning.

The man looked at him searchingly. "Your argument is worthy of consideration and is certainly also historically correct. But is it sufficient reason for our evangelical church to admit the son of a Jewish cantor and his family into our congregation? I am not sure that Reverend Ohly, our minister, would be convinced. But let me reassure you. Reverend Ohly hasn't read your letter, and it is the church council whose task it is to decide on these issues. So let us please develop your ideas a little."

It was almost totally dark inside the church. Immanuel could barely make out the features of the old priest's face, although they were both now sitting in the pews at the back, with just one row between them. But he could hear every word the priest said distinctly, as if whispered straight into his ear.

"I regard such ideas as important, especially these days. I wish to remind you of the opposition to Orthodox rabbinical teaching, to Jews dancing in joyous piety. We Christians had Pietism, but its equivalent for Jews was undoubtedly Hasidism. And after orthodoxy on both sides came the joyful dancing. We should be talking about Messianism. But you know all this, Immanuel, and what you are urging now is basically the next step: Haskalah, the Jewish Enlightenment. Isn't that true, Immanuel; you consider yourself enlightened, and you expect the same of your church?"

Later this exchange would seem as unreal as the scenes in the tower. It took Immanuel back to the rigorous examinations he'd faced before his bar mitzvah, to long, tedious conversations in the gloomy library, harsh comments. But also to the happy walks through Warsaw with his father, who would explain enthusiastically the difference between the various Hasidic groups living in the city. They would meet them everywhere in the street, the corners of their shirts adorned with uniquely tasseled fringes, the traditional knee breeches, the long coats, and the fur hats. He recalled the curled sidelocks that looked so strange on small boys. Childhood images flashed through his mind, together with the tunes his father had been so fond of humming, wild and rhythmic. His father had loved those songs, working them into his own hymns.

He recalled how he and his brother used to hide in the tight corner behind the piano. High up in the stack of books on the floor was the beautiful volume *Der jüdische Kantor*. He remembered maarib, the evening prayer, and his father's voice softly singing the Hashkiveinu to a melody he had composed himself.

He was brought abruptly back to the present. Other considerations forced their way in, thoughts that had completely dominated his working day for the last few months. Did he have his passport with him? Yes, everything was in order. It wasn't stamped with a "J" either, something he had managed to avoid by cultivating his contacts at the German embassy in Warsaw. With the assistance of the helpful envoy at the Swedish legation, Joen Lagerberg, all his travel documents had been issued in time. It had been a journey with more stopovers than they had foreseen when they left Warsaw at the beginning of July. They had left their home in the Żoliborz district and their furniture and other household effects. First came the summer months in Latvia, in the peaceful seaside resort of Majori. The boys had bathed in the Lielupe River in the mornings and spent the light summer evenings roaming along the sandy beaches of the Gulf of Riga. Despite this being the start of their life as refugees, it felt to the family like a summer holiday. After that were several weeks in Helsinki, where they would like to have stayed. The train journey to Åbo should have taken a few hours, but because of all the military exercises and controls a whole day was required. As luck would have it, the boat had also been delayed. Crossing the Baltic Sea in the comfort of the white ferry had seemed like an exciting holiday trip. The boys had been alarmed by all the No Anchoring signs, scared they might have something to do with "Jew." But they were soon reassured and their good humor restored by the time they landed, right next to the hotel on Skeppsbron where Lagerberg had booked rooms for them.

Thank goodness their visa was valid for a year. Had it not been for his friend Lagerberg, he would probably never have been in Stockholm. It is questionable whether he and his family would have managed to leave Poland at all. But they were here now, and their passports were valid and adorned with the right stamps. It was Lagerberg who had stressed the importance of the family enrolling at once in the German church. Absolutely crucial for any permit extensions in the future, he said.

Immanuel had converted when he was a student. The deliberations that had led to the decision had been difficult, for his parents too. But all of that felt very distant. He and Lucia had already been members of the evangelical church in Warsaw. Why raise religious ruminations that belonged in the past? He had even proposed the suitability of his father's hymns to render Christian music in the evangelical cathedral, as if that had anything to do with it. That was a real blunder.

He checked his breast pocket. Sure enough, his wife's passport was there. Born in Częstochowa in 1900, German citizen. Like his own, her passport was stamped with Border Recommendation 825 from the Swedish legation in Warsaw, valid for single entry to and residence in Sweden. Twelve months from the date of the stamp. This litany of numbers, always there, even in his dreams, the secret codes of hope and despair. Someone might have woken him in the middle of the night to question him about them. His elder son Karl's passport was there too, next to his chest. Henrik, the younger one, was included on his mother's. It was all correct, his friend Lagerberg had assured him.

Complete silence had fallen on the church, and the old man's breathing, so palpable before, seemed to have stopped. Had he vanished into the darkness like the boy in the tower?

"We are Germans, and this is the German church."

He could hear nothing except his own breathing and the

sound of his own shoes scraping impatiently on the footrest under the pew in front.

Finally the answer came. The voice had grown stronger, and the words were articulated with a new emphasis.

"Immanuel, if you think the angry waves of regional and racial strife don't sweep over the walls that surround the church, you are wrong. The Jewish Enlightenment that underpins all your thinking appeals to me. In all respects it is convincing. But Reverend Ohly has raised the swastika flag on every national holiday for the last two years. A colleague on the church council has resigned in protest and has announced he is leaving a church to which he no longer feels he belongs. You need to know that. You need to know what this church is today."

On their first walk along Skeppsbron, the family had seen the swastika flying over the German embassy on Blasieholmen, to which they would soon be obliged to go in order to have their residency permits validated. He hadn't realized that it was also raised outside the church. Someone had said the priest refused, but evidently he must have changed his mind.

"Naturally you all have admission to your church. The fact is, you and your family have already been registered. You sent us all the required details, with one exception: we have no postal address."

Had he heard correctly? Everything was actually in order, and they had been admitted to the church. Could he breathe out? He chose to withhold the fact that they were living at the Hotell Reisen, just a few streets away. Fortunately they had been promised rooms with the Weil family on Frejgatan, and obviously that sounded more convincing, more stable. So his answer was quite matter-of-fact. "I am grateful to you for this fruitful discussion and ask that I might reply to you in writing so that all the particulars are accurate. I will send the information to the parish office tomorrow. It is evening already, and I must hasten home to my family."

He gave a brief bow. Since he still couldn't see the priest, whom he presumed to be somewhere in the darkness, it was an odd gesture. He looked around and discovered that there was in fact a faint light coming from the far corner of the church. He cautiously took a step in that direction and felt his way toward the shaft of light that appeared to be coming from the door. Was the priest, whose name he hadn't asked, still sitting on the pew behind him, or had he also withdrawn? The only steps he heard were his own.

As he had thought, it was the gray band of light under the door he had seen, and with a firm hand he pushed the door open, allowing the evening light to filter into the church. He let it close behind him and hurried across the paving stones. He didn't know where he was—this couldn't have been the same door through which he had entered the church—but he managed to come out onto a street running along one side. He felt slightly uneasy, full of questions that he couldn't properly formulate. He looked up at the street sign next to a lamp illuminating a small three-cornered square with a solitary chestnut tree, and he spelled out the letters. Svartmangatan. It meant nothing to him. He turned left by the little square and hoped it was the way back toward the water where the hotel was.

This area of the city was like a labyrinth, and he remembered the warren of narrow streets his gaze had wandered over when he stepped out onto the tiny ledge high up in the church tower. The streets were empty, but he glimpsed an unsteady figure a stone's throw ahead of him, keeping close to the buildings and then disappearing around a corner. He turned the corner too and thought he could see the short figure again, casting a long shadow on the wall opposite. The light must have come from a low window, but to his surprise all was in darkness when he reached that part of the street. He wasn't sure he was going in the right direction, and again he was filled with a sense of disquiet. The feeling intensified at the thought that he had recognized the outline of the figure that was walking in front of him a moment ago and was now no longer to be seen. It must surely be none other than the small boy from the tower, the bell ringer. Or was he chasing his own shadow?

Getting lost in a forest isn't difficult, but losing your way in a city is an art that has to be cultivated. He recalled this maxim, formulated by a friend on the *Frankfurter Zeitung* in the days when they were both contributors, and he laughed to dispel the consternation he felt at finding himself back at the three-cornered square. The friend from his youth had displayed a philosophical mind quite different from his own, an entirely distinct gift for speculation that did not go unnoticed, in particular by their shared teachers. But politically he had always been clueless, a point on which Immanuel never wavered. Their only dispute had been over Immanuel's patriotism, which his friend dismissed as ill-judged and fundamentally incomprehensible in a Jew. But that was all a long time ago. It was about a different war, and a different Germany. Since then the friend had made a name for himself with quirky radio programs and pithy commentaries on urban walks, with streets and alleyways like arcane manuscripts for people to wander through. Where Walter Benjamin was now, if he were still alive, Immanuel had not the faintest idea. In that narrowest of streets he had thought of his introverted old friend for the first time in several years.

Without any effort to acquire the art, he had now managed to get lost in this maze. He was back under the same chestnut tree, illuminated by the same streetlamp. Or was it a different square with a different tree and a different lamppost? He hurried on and turned left. He hoped that at the end of this backstreet he would see one of the boats that was moored by the quay, and behind it would be the hotel containing his waiting family, who by now had good reason to be wondering where he had gone. But there was a bend in the street, and it looked as though he was back at the German church, where the whole exercise had begun.

He decided to follow a straight course this time and not deviate in any direction. The medieval district, which actually formed an island, wasn't very big. If you didn't walk in a circle, sooner or later you had to reach the water. Eventually the quay would appear.

The sensation created by unintended repetition can sometimes resemble the desperation of a dream state. To banish his thoughts and not fuel the seed of panic growing inside him, he tried to recollect what he had recently read about the psychological effect of repetition. It must have been in one of the many texts his editor at *Basler Nachrichten* had recommended. Maybe an article by a Swiss psychiatrist, he was thinking when, incredibly, he saw the square and the solitary tree in front of him once more. He stopped and leaned against the stone wall of a building that seemed to have no openings whatsoever onto the street. What was the force drawing him toward this peaceful square in the middle of the city? Then he saw the silhouette again. This time he was quite sure; it was the boy from the tower, disappearing into a door facing the square. It opened quickly and instantly closed behind him.

The odds against what happened next must have been high, but on the other hand he had suffered far stranger experiences that day. He actually knew very few people in this city. But coming toward him in the narrow street was the librarian Josephson, the thoroughly obliging mathematician from the Mittag-Leffler Institute who had allowed him to stay overnight in the villa to facilitate his meeting on the island early the following morning. And this despite the fact they had only just become acquainted. The librarian's oval spectacle frames reflected the light from the streetlamp on the little square to shine in the dark like two crescent moons.

"Good evening. What a pleasant surprise!" he said, giving Immanuel a slap on the shoulder. "This is where I live, on Själagårdsgatan, next door to the old synagogue. If you have a look in here you can make out what used to be the women's gallery. Today our temple has been turned into a police station, so in some ways it feels doubly reassuring to live here."

He smiled good-naturedly. "An evening walk in the new city, I assume?"

Immanuel nodded. It was comforting to meet Josephson after all that had taken place. It was through Bermann Fischer, one of the first people he had sought out in Stockholm, that he had been introduced to the likable librarian, who was helping one of the publisher's authors with information about the subtleties of chess from a mathematical point of view. And here he was, next to the solitary chestnut tree, whose leaves had still not started to fall despite the arrival of autumn. He pointed up to a number of windows from which a warm glow lit up the leaves outside.

"My family and I organize quite a few concerts here. We have excellent musicians performing. My son plays too, and he's not at all bad, though I say so myself. It might be of interest to you and your family. The Katz family usually drop by. I heard about your father's great contribution to music from Viktor. No one today has the same overview, he says. No one's demonstrated the historical connections between what's played for us in church and secular music like he has."

Immanuel didn't have the faintest idea who this Viktor could be, but the favorable words about his father cheered him up, so he just gave a friendly nod. He did know of the Katz family, however, very well. David Katz, the German psychologist, had become a professor in Stockholm, but the appointment had attracted criticism from National Socialist quarters, and his inaugural lecture had been interrupted by young nationalists. Immanuel had heard about all of this in his first few days in the city, and he would have liked to carry on talking to the librarian, but he felt almost dizzy with tiredness, and it was getting late. He had no desire to enter the warren of little streets again only to end up back at the three-cornered square where the synagogue had once been. Enough of this; the day had provided quite enough twists.

He gave a nod of farewell as affably as he could. "You don't happen to know the quickest way to the Hotell Reisen?"

Instead of the simple directions he was expecting, Josephson said with a new gravity in his voice, "You need to be very careful of the Reisen. The Germans eat all their meals in the dining room there. You must have seen the little flags set out on the tables for official meetings. That's no place to make friends. We call the hotel the Little Embassy."

Immanuel had indeed noticed the flags the hotel staff placed on the tables on certain occasions. The small pieces of shiny white fabric were decorated with black swastikas, the same as the ones fluttering in the wind on the other side of the water. The German legation was located opposite the Hotell Reisen, somewhat hemmed in on either side by the National Museum and the city's one true luxury hotel. Presumably the legation supplied the table decorations.

One day soon after they had arrived at the hotel a large group had assembled in the dining room to hear a lecture and award some kind of academic distinction. That was the first time he saw the swastikas appear. The noisy gathering was patently composed of Germans, and Immanuel had asked the people in reception what it was about. His two boys, both teenagers, had been curious because it clearly involved a widely known arctic explorer, a Mr. Pantenburg, who was to give a talk about his adventures in the very north of Lapland and on the other side of the Russian border. They had heard applause and enthusiastic shouts from the dining room. The pictures projected onto a plain white cloth hanging on a metal stand didn't serve to lessen the boys' interest. They showed icebergs and glaciers, bears and packs of wolves, and sledges pulled by huskies. It had quite simply been too much to resist, and without asking their parents for permission, they had crept into the dining room and sat down at the back. The parents had retired to their room on the third floor and didn't realize where the boys had gone until the lecture was over and they came racing in, full of the arctic explorer's stories of polar seas and vast snowfields, and of mysterious spy planes with bases east of the Finno-Russian border.

Immanuel was discomfited by the memory but had resolved that no great damage had been done. That his teenage boys saw this as something exciting was no surprise. He nodded his agreement with the librarian in the street. "No, that's quite right, the Reisen is no place to make friends these days. But we have managed to rent three excellent rooms with the Weil family on Frejgatan. We're moving in next week. This evening I have no choice, though, and my family will be wondering where I am. Which is the quickest way, would you say?"

Josephson indicated with an oddly crooked arm that Immanuel needed to go around the corner a few meters ahead, walk toward the water, and then left at the quay. He added a few jocular parting shots in Yiddish before he turned away and disappeared into the shadowy doorway that a few minutes earlier had swallowed up the boy from the tower. Just as Josephson stepped over the doorstep and his face was no longer discernible in the dark, he said one last thing. It sounded like a warning.

"*Zay gezunt!* He works in mysterious ways. Take care of yourself and your family."

CAFÉ OGO

The windows were misted up and the air thick with tobacco smoke. The coffee shop on Kungsgatan had quickly come to feel like home. Immanuel behaved like one of the regulars, nodding in recognition to the tables by the window as he stepped inside and closed the inner glass door behind him. There were always people here he recognized, many of them sitting alone with a book in front of them or a newspaper spread out on the table. At the far end of the café sat Ascher, writing. Immanuel pretended he hadn't seen him to avoid being drawn into a conversation about how they should split assignments for *Basler Nachrichten*. The fact was, Immanuel felt uncomfortable with the whole situation. It was really unfortunate that Ascher had ended up in Stockholm too, after being forced to leave his post in the Vatican. No one found him a likable person. He was always the injured innocent, and often ill-tempered.

As usual the café was full. Every day small groups of people would meet, speaking languages of which Immanuel had a better command than his adopted land's. He gleaned fragments of their stories. Two Russian men, one bearded and rather portly, the other bald and wearing high-strength spectacles, were always sitting deep in conversation at the same table. Now and then they would glance around, as if they were actually keeping watch on the place. There were Poles, in exile for months or years, on their way to the next city, with worn-out suitcases and leather briefcases bursting at the seams with the thick sheaves of papers inside: passports so crowded with stamps they were illegible, visas and testimonials grubby with thumbing and anxious fingering. Large numbers of German speakers were here, some of them well-dressed office workers but others stranger characters with furtive eyes, on the run or perhaps with business best kept to themselves. And then groups of Swedish women, young and all dressed up, as if they were on their way to some festive soirée, although it was early afternoon on a very gray weekday in the autumn of 1939.

He had almost an hour to read the newspapers. Rickman wasn't due at the café until three o'clock. Bermann Fischer had asked him to get together with the Englishman. Preferably not at the publishing house but somewhere else, on neutral ground. An agreeable fellow, a man with a past in the world of musical entertainment, thoroughly charming, the publisher had assured him. The purpose of the meeting was unstated, but the publisher had implied it had something to do with deliveries to Germany and had added that his secretary Miss Stern would be pleased to assist with the practicalities.

Bermann Fischer had already given Immanuel a number of minor editorial commissions, and he naturally hoped for more. He wondered how he could broach the subject without appearing either too forward or too desperate. To show his willingness to meet with an unknown Englishman was one way of demonstrating his keenness. Unfortunately it was becoming ever clearer that he needed several sources of income. He was finding it more difficult to have his articles accepted. His work was published very infrequently in *De Telegraaf* now, and he didn't understand why. When he applied for a residency permit in Sweden, he had listed the Dutch newspaper as though it were as obvious a revenue stream as *Basler Nachrichten*. On the other hand he hadn't mentioned the provincial German-language newspapers where his items regularly appeared; it had been too complicated to explain the press agency's somewhat special function in Berlin. In the long run that couldn't be counted on as a given either. It was only a question of time before it ceased entirely. He hadn't heard from the editor, Kutzner, for months. Nor from Ilse Stübe either, who was supposed to be the new contact person.

Immanuel sat down by one of the windows and placed his briefcase on the chair next to him and *Basler Nachrichten* on the table in front of him. As usual it was a two-day-old newspaper. One of his own articles, an attempt at summarizing the reactions in the Nordic countries to the outbreak of war, was at the top right corner of page 1. That was gratifying. Albert Oeri, the increasingly renowned editor in chief, had recognized the importance of a staff writer in this little metropolis in the far north, a place that until recently had been completely peripheral but now suddenly was the scene of vital decision-making. In fact it was the city in which Europe's future might be decided this very autumn, maybe even within the next few weeks, if Immanuel had interpreted accurately the precarious situation that had developed concerning the transport of iron. If its transportation were to be disrupted in the slightest, German occupation wouldn't be far behind. Dr. Oeri had understood this and encouraged him to write regular reports, giving his articles a prime position in the newspaper. He didn't need to worry about Ascher. Clearly Oeri preferred Immanuel's pieces to Ascher's, which more often than not concerned obscure topics from the Catholic world and were generally placed near the back of the newspaper. And yet it was a difficult situation to have a rival who made no bones about his readiness to fight for space.

Immanuel's article, the third longest from Sweden, was extremely well placed. Although the remuneration left much to be desired, this was the ultimate incentive, a validation greater than that generally bestowed by money, even if it was the money he needed at the moment more than anything else.

It had been a time of constant disruption. For a number of weeks now he and Lucia and their sons had been lodging with the Weil family in Vasastan. They had three adjacent rooms, which in reality felt like their own apartment. And furthermore, the Weil family were almost never at home. But if they were going to stay in this city for several years more, another solution would be required. Yes, he would have to talk finance with the editor. It was clear from the positioning of the articles that his cooperation was appreciated. It's unwise to pay too much, Oeri had said the last time they met and the question of fees was raised. But thankfully he had added that paying too little could cost even more. There was clearly room for negotiation, even if he could also recall another of the Swiss journalist's less promising axioms: Money won't help on Judgment Day.

Judgment Day or not, vital decisions for the progress of the war would be taken by his adopted country's government this autumn or winter. Though perhaps in the long run it would be the family of the industrial tycoon who decided, or so it sometimes seemed to anyone trying to follow the negotiations.

Lagerberg had promised to arrange an audience for him with Marcus Wallenberg.

It was evident that the whole scenario could change radically over a matter of weeks. And if the Germans entered the country, what would happen then? What help would an increased fee from *Basler Nachrichten* be when that day came? How would they be able to leave Stockholm without a visa for any other possible country? Deportation to Germany would be equivalent to a death sentence. Perhaps the boys should stay here if flight became the only option. But the mere thought was unbearable. He had the same suffocating sensation he had experienced so often since their arrival here, an increasingly frequent reminder of the seriousness of their plight. The relative calm could end at any moment, he knew it, his body knew it. It wasn't just the swastika in the window of the German travel agency around the corner, or the growingly sympathetic articles about National Socialism in one of the city's evening papers. No, the signs were visible everywhere for anyone who wanted to see, and he wasn't one of the blind masses.

Basically he and his family were stuck here. As he looked around, it occurred to him that many of the people gathered in the café would undoubtedly be in the same position. They had nowhere to go. Many were waiting in vain for travel documents and transit visas that would enable onward movement from the northern metropolis in which they found themselves in their escape from worse fates.

He could hear German being spoken behind him, and the exchange was such he couldn't help following what was said. Two middle-aged gentlemen were in lively discussion about a disastrous voyage across the Atlantic. It was as if the whole room was buzzing with similar tales.

"Apparently certain people were offered entry if they paid five hundred dollars. You can imagine the chaos onboard!"

"How long is the crossing from Hamburg to Cuba? Two weeks, or more? Over nine hundred people tried to disembark. My sister said she received a letter from one of the few who managed it. It might have been one of those who paid. Others tried to throw themselves into the sea in sheer desperation. An entire family went on hunger strike."

"Naturally it didn't do any good."

"Of course not."

Immanuel had seen some newspaper reports about a passenger ship full of refugees from Germany who had been denied entry permits to Cuba. After futile attempts to stop at a port in Florida, the captain had been obliged to return to Europe with almost a thousand refugees. It had been a veritable hell onboard. Shortage of food and other essentials. Psychological mayhem, mutiny attempts. If his memory served him correctly, they were finally allowed to disembark in Antwerp, hundreds of people without homes to return to. He must have read the story in *De Telegraaf*. The ship was called the *St. Louis*, that was the only thing he could remember with certainty.

Immanuel immersed himself in his newspaper but found it hard to concentrate on Albert Oeri's editorial about the German steel magnate, the greatest of them all, who was in exile in Switzerland. There were too many causes for concern. His wife's persistent dizzy spells were getting worse and worse. She needed to be seen by a doctor, but would he be able to get her to Sophiahemmet Hospital, as Lagerberg had promised? Another worry was his brother, Gerhard. Right up until the journey to the Latvian resort in the summer he had been a cherished family member, loved by the boys and a true support to Lucia. Immanuel cursed the fact that he had treated his brother's decision to remain in Poland so lightly. An ingenious young bachelor like him would always find a way to get by, he had said cheerfully. On that warm evening at the beginning of July when they had all set off in a comfortable Russian sleeping car, Gerhard had stood alone on the platform. The boys had hung out of the open window, waving and laughing, as he ran alongside and tried to keep up with the train. Since that time all contact had been lost.

After Immanuel fell asleep, his brother often appeared in obscure fantasy scenes that he couldn't fight. Recurring dreams churned on, monotonous and disquieting. Now and then he woke in the night, thinking he could hear him shouting. In the dreams his brother was imprisoned. He was threatened and intimidated. His cries were desperate.

It was difficult to escape these thoughts. To break the vicious circle, Immanuel concentrated on his article on the outbreak of war. It had been abridged somewhat but nevertheless made very clear the vulnerable position of the Swedes. Had the people of the capital realized what was at stake, what was happening in their country? Did they register the level of curiosity with which reporters from all over the world followed every tiny hint coming from government or industry?

Apart from some rather unsavory characters he had learned to recognize, more and more women had sat down at the tables. Most of them were in their early twenties and elegantly dressed. All the same he could sense something rather gauche and provincial behind the sophisticated facades, as if they had just arrived from the country and adopted a worldly attitude with the help of a few quickly acquired props—cigarette cases, satin gloves. They sat in small chattering groups, animated and noisy. Had the cigarette smoke not been so thick, the scent of cheap perfume would have made him queasy.

He tried to take a sip of the piping hot tea the short-haired girl behind the counter had been kind enough to bring to the table for him, the girl who always greeted him with the familiarity of someone who had known him for a long time. There were two women behind him now, sitting so close he couldn't focus on the newspaper article about growing Finno-Russian tension and the Åland Islands question. Instead he was drawn into a matter of an entirely different kind.

"And you went home with him just for a new brooch and a few glasses of champagne at the Riche?"

"What would you have done? You can't pretend to be Little Miss Proper. I can guess what goes on when you invite someone from the German legation over to the boardinghouse. Like the one with the posh car with a chauffeur that you went swanning around with all night. Him with the necklace."

"I have absolutely never invited him in. What are you talking about?"

"No, you don't need to because he had his own suite at the Reisen, didn't he, and took girls like you to the Grand and then back to his hotel room. He was one of the swanky ones."

"You're only jealous. Next time he comes, he's going to introduce me to his friends at the embassy and the people he knows in high society, he's promised. And when he comes next time he'll be divorced, for my sake."

"Hahaha! And you'll soon be having dinner with a Berna-dotte?"

The conversation was interrupted by a paper airplane sailing across the room from another table and landing in front of them. When the piece of paper was unfolded, it evidently revealed a message so comical, the two dolled-up women burst into laughter in unison before subsiding into whispers and giggles. They behaved as if they were in their own living room. All these foreign people from other countries immersed in reading didn't appear to bother them in the least. They gaily greeted women at other tables, who for their part came over to borrow cigarettes.

Every so often the young women changed places and formed new groups, as if there was a secret format familiar only to those in the know and to which they adhered without deviation. The two chatty ladies had found a new place farther inside the café. The two Germans who had been discussing the disastrous passage to Cuba were now in their old seats.

"Yes, of course one feels hard-pressed! Trapped, even. To a certain extent I am trapped."

Immanuel glanced in their direction. The two gentlemen were engrossed over a small chessboard and a notebook that appeared to have a great number of sections. In the mutual mumbling it was difficult to catch any complete sentences. But there was a sudden commentary from the other man, perhaps in delayed response.

"The white rook must get to the *a* squares via g8 to capture the black bishop and the black queen without losing time. Since the black rook will be needed later, it can't be taken but must retreat to the only square from which it can come back and block b1, namely h1. Then, my friend, the coast is clear!"

A young woman Immanuel thought he recognized came in to collect some confectionery that had clearly been preordered. It was on the counter, already wrapped to be taken away. On the way out she nodded discreetly to him, and he recalled where he had seen her. It was Miss Stern, the woman from Vienna whom

Bermann Fischer had appointed as secretary and who was, he had said, privy to the questions Rickman wished to talk over with Immanuel. Indeed the Englishman might appear at any moment, as it was almost three o'clock. Behind him the chess players continued to air possible alternatives.

"Trapped or not, you missed that. The black queen begins by taking the piece guarding the superfluous knight on the checkmate square, so that the black king can go there on the second move."

Another person had joined the conversation. His shrill voice was familiar, and Immanuel gathered immediately that it was Ascher who had taken a seat at the adjacent table. He was obviously sufficiently knowledgeable to be able to follow the game analysis. Ascher was speaking loudly, as if he wanted Immanuel to hear his every word.

"The white rook must go to the *a* squares via g8. Exactly so. That's how simple it is to remove or cut off all the black pieces that can come in between, while covering all the squares around the black king. Anyone who gets blocked in like this hasn't exploited the rook's potential. Each piece has its own rules, its own possible escape route."

Ascher then fell silent as he turned to Immanuel with little more than a tap on the shoulder in greeting. He had probably seen Immanuel enter the café and decided not to forgo this opportunity of resuming their generally quite strained discourse. Immanuel had never shown much bonhomie, but Ascher wasn't deterred. Now he slid over beside his colleague and left the two chess players to themselves.

"Frankly, I see my own situation in the same way. I have the church, my friend. The Curia. I might have cut off the road to the temple; I've been criticized for that too. But anyone called

Ascher is never completely cut off from the words of the proph-
ets. What else? I have socialism, which for the time being I regard as no great asset. And we have certain new movements in
the homeland that might be less than fruitful for the likes of us,
but I'm having a number of talks at the German legation that
have, surprisingly, opened some doors. Into a future where all
exits might not be closed after all."

What sort of admission was this? Immanuel, who hadn't
been listening very attentively and didn't follow the religious
turns at all, had no desire whatsoever to confide in this man, of
whom both he and Lucia had felt vaguely suspicious. In reality
he had tried to avoid the man for as long as possible. But now
Ascher was sitting next to him and clearly intent upon a conversation about the predicament that, when all was said and done,
they shared. For in a way, of course, they were both trapped.

Although disagreeable, Ascher was far from narrow-
minded. There was always some new theory or doctrine he
wanted to quote. This time was no different. Immanuel had felt
it coming when he saw Ascher holding an opened tract by a
contemporary zoologist, which he proceeded to place on top of
the pile of newspapers.

"Have you heard of Hedinger, my young friend in Bern who
runs Dählhözli Zoo? Didn't I tell you about him and his ideas
about escape response in animals, specifically so-called higher
mammals, including man?"

Immanuel said nothing, but he had indeed come across the
biologist's name, and that had been entirely attributable to Albert Oeri's curiosity regarding all kinds of eccentrics and mad-
caps. There was no shortage of them in the German-speaking
part of Switzerland, and notwithstanding that Oeri's expertise
was in the field of politics, he was keen that they should be given

a voice in the newspaper he published. The whole world was on view in Basler Nachrichten, and the whole of Switzerland, Oeri would repeat at every opportunity. And sure enough, one day it would be about the strange psychiatrist who declared he had lost his childhood faith when he had a vision in which the golden sunbeams shining down on the cathedral roof in Basel were suddenly transformed into turds. Oeri had himself profiled this singular mind doctor, a friend of his since childhood. The next day it would be some wayward theologian or indeed the young zoo director in Bern. Immanuel even remembered an inspired article on the psychological life of animals by that original young man, but he didn't have a chance to mention it before Ascher carried on.

"Hunger and sexual appetite may be important drivers for all life-forms, no one can deny. But it is the ability to flee that is paramount, from a biological point of view. All animals, even the largest and most powerful, have enemies, and that makes escape capability pivotal. And in man, Hedinger says, escape routes are forming all the time. They aren't visible, but they exist."

Immanuel nodded as if he understood the line of thought. They remained side by side with their teacups before them, neither of them saying anything. Ascher was frantically flicking through his newspapers as if searching for an article that had mysteriously disappeared. In the end he gave up and with an impatient movement folded the newspapers and ostentatiously placed the slender pamphlet about animals on top of the pile. He took a deep breath.

"Our behavior is developed at an abstract level; animals find a means of escape more instinctively. But look around you here, and you'll be reminded of scenes you've experienced in front of an enclosure at the zoo. An animal nervously walking back and forth, again and again, as if driven by something mechanical. Emitting the same sound, time after time, an abject expression of frustration and resignation. Tossing its head to and fro, with no purpose and no possibility of an outcome. Licking frenetically at one spot and starting to bite the bars of the cage in a mixture of aggression and apathy."

Reluctantly Immanuel looked up. He had no wish to be drawn into Ascher's flights of fancy in this way and intended to extricate himself from the situation by fetching more tea and sitting down at a now empty table beside the counter. Rickman might appear at any moment. Immanuel made it perfectly clear he wasn't interested in engaging in deeper discussion, packing his things into his briefcase and turning to the entrance. He folded the newspaper and put it in his jacket pocket. But Ascher didn't appear to pick up the signals.

"Take a look around this café, and you will see the same mixture of resignation and aggression in people's eyes, pleading and at the same time ready to attack if the opportunity arises. They are prepared to do whatever is necessary if a means of escape presents itself. I myself am prepared to do whatever is necessary. Aren't you?"

Immanuel had risen to his feet. Just as he took a step toward the counter, he felt a draft from the door. A man was walking toward him with his hand outstretched, wearing a gray overcoat that had been thoroughly drenched by the heavy rain. As he removed his hat, which was also soaked, he revealed a head of slicked-back brown hair. The whole impression was one of casual elegance. With a truly winsome smile spreading over his entire face, he was the first to speak, embracing Immanuel in an astonishingly familiar way, considering they had never met.

"Marvelous! There you are! I do apologize for being a tad late. I have been so much looking forward to making your acquaintance. Gottfried has only the very best things to say about you—he commended your know-how and skill in conveying the right message in the written word. What is required is a professional, he said. A real professional. A man with proper expertise. Yes, in a word, he insisted that I meet you."

They sat down beside the counter. Rickman kept leaning forward across the table, his face so close it made Immanuel flinch.

The conversation that followed was conducted alternately in English and German, and now and then in a strange mixture, interrupted regularly by Rickman's guffaws. In place of a letter of introduction he had brought a thin book, practically a pamphlet, published in Britain by Faber & Faber. With a degree of pride he passed the little booklet across the table, and with some surprise Immanuel noted the title *Swedish Iron Ore* beneath the publisher's well-known logo, and at the bottom the author's name: Alfred Frederick Rickman.

"Yes, that's me," Rickman said, pointing to his name. "I thought it might make an impression on a literary individual like you. Gottfried said he was greatly impressed by my choice of publishing house. The fact is, I didn't have much to do with it; it all came about on commission, and it's the only thing I've ever had in print in all my checkered career. I suppose Gottfried mentioned that I'm now a businessman. My office is on Näckströmsgatan, right by Kungsträdgården. Dental Materials Ltd. I run the firm with my fiancée. I suggest we meet there when you've had a look at the information. It's not suitable for perusal in public, if you know what I mean."

He winked in a slightly affected way, as if they were sharing a secret, and then pushed a thick envelope across, addressed in capital letters to Verlag Bermann Fischer. In pencil someone had added the address, 19 Stureplan, and in fainter writing the name Immanuel. No surname, no title.

Immanuel left the envelope and instead opened the little pamphlet on Swedish iron ore, which proved to be a book about the mines in the north of Sweden and associated transport routes and port facilities. It was complete with maps and diagrams, adding apparent authority to its review of the recent growth in Swedish iron-ore mining. The book, which had no literary pretensions despite the distinguished imprint, had been published in London the previous year and therefore must be judged to be a current report. By no means without interest, thought Immanuel, who only over the last few days had himself tried to examine the political significance of iron-ore export more thoroughly. But in truth he was bewildered by the direction the conversation had taken. He was mentally forming a question that he hadn't yet managed to articulate when Rickman rose to take his leave, patting him on the shoulder and adding some final words while glancing out at the street.

"We have a 'grand opening' to think about, but as soon as it's all settled, you'll hear from me."

"Pardon. A what?"

"Oh, sorry! We're expecting a gentleman from London by the name of Grand. Laurence Grand. A very important gentleman. When it's over you must meet Biggs, my one-legged friend. The fellow from PUB, as we call him. A war hero. He's the one who wrote the material. The idea is that Gottfried can include it in the distribution of a political publication by a writer who has evidently distanced himself from the German universities. A polemic, he says. The author's called Mann, lives in the United States now."

"Mann? You mean Thomas Mann?"

"It's possible. I can't say for certain. But it's conceivable, perfectly conceivable," Rickman said breezily on his way to the door. "In any case, please keep the material to yourself for the time being. We'd like you to go through the actual language. Forget all about Mr. Grand, he has nothing to do with our conversation. Thank you, it has been a real pleasure to meet like this. See you again!"

He disappeared into the rain, whistling. Immanuel stared at the envelope bearing his name. The meeting had been concluded in under half an hour. During their conversation it had all seemed fairly clear, as if he had been lulled by the Englishman's charm. But now, afterward, he was baffled. What did they expect of him? The book about Swedish iron ore appeared to be a gift, since it had been left on the table next to his empty cup.

He put it in his briefcase and looked around. Ascher had apparently given up and drifted off without a fuss. That was a relief. The café was no longer as full, but a number of the women were still clustered at the back and seemed to be getting ready for the night's exploits, touching up their makeup and adjusting their hair. Occasionally they were escorted out into the street, usually one at a time, and collected by men who entered the café only to immediately go back out and depart in a car. At that moment, for example, a burly man was waiting in front of the entrance. He was walking restlessly back and forth, darting urgent glances inside at the group of women. Now he was standing with his feet apart, staring straight into the café. With a start Immanuel recognized his face. It was the man who had taken him out to the island in the motorboat on that sunny morning. The one who worked for Madame Kollontai and maybe others too. Immanuel couldn't remember his name and wasn't even sure he had heard it. He did remember his sister's name, however. The sister, that translucent young woman who had waited for him on the jetty at daybreak and then stood in the bow illuminated by the sun. Karin.

No sooner had he silently said her name than he felt a waft of air as a light-footed figure hurried past. The nervous young man who had scowled into the café didn't even need to come in to collect his sister. She appeared to know what was expected of her. Yes, it was undoubtedly Karin who stepped out into the street and approached a black car parked directly in front of her. She must have been inside the café among the other women without Immanuel noticing her. Perhaps she had been there all afternoon. She got into the car with her brother, the man who had informed him on the quay that her life was basically over. A moment later, and they were gone.

THE OPERA BAR

He had a wide, rugged face, and his eyes, which were quite close together, were kind and radiated sincerity and calm. That he had trained as a doctor was something Immanuel had read in the newspaper obituaries when his father-in-law, the patriarch Samuel Fischer, had died. There had been intense discussion in the press at that time over the future of the publishing house. Immanuel could instantly picture this man in a white coat and was sure his patients would have had great faith in him. The obituaries had not failed to note that the heir, on whose shoulders contemporary literature now rested, in a manner of speaking, had hastily renounced surgery for literature. Rilke and Hölderlin had made him lay down his scalpel, joked his young wife, Brigitta, whom everyone called Tutti. Admittedly the publishing house had little to do with those particular poets, but Tutti's comment was avidly quoted. Nor had the newspapers been slow to point out that Samuel Fischer's daughter would also be joining the board with her husband, Gottfried Bermann Fischer, who had added his wife's name to his own, in the same way she had adopted his.

They were both called Bermann Fischer now, and this was the name gracing the book covers too. Tutti was a delightful young woman in every way, as deeply committed to the company as her mother had always been, and passionately interested in design matters. Their books would be the most beautiful in Europe, she proclaimed, proudly turning to two novels by Franz Werfel and a new edition of Ibsen's plays. Ibsen's *The Lady from the Sea* had once been the publisher's most outstanding success, alongside Gerhart Hauptmann's *Before Sunrise*.

Gottfried and Tutti became acquainted at the home of Bruno Cassirer and his family. They had both been invited to make music with Cassirer's daughter Agnes and her friends, and had quickly become close. Only a few weeks later they were engaged. What happened next was a shock to many. It didn't take long before the father-in-law, who was concerned about the future of the firm following the early death of his only son, invited the young doctor to join them with the aim of taking over at the appropriate time. He had barely any qualifications, but those were different and quieter times. Little did Samuel Fischer know that his books would soon be piled high and burned, that they would be devoured by flames on Opernplatz only a few moments' walk from the firm's offices on Bülowstrasse. He didn't know that the publishing house was doomed if it remained in Berlin, nor that before long his daughter and son-in-law would have to sign contracts with authors and translators in Switzerland. Soon they would be forced to find offices in the Austrian capital in order to resume publication of Mann and Hesse, von Hofmannsthal and Zuckmayer.

Despite all this they had been busy years filled with enjoyment. The offices they found on Esteplatz were excellent, only a few minutes' walk from the city center. Vienna's colorful literary figures had all become involved in the firm's activities in one way or another, including in their increasingly uproarious events. They were swiftly joined in the life of the company by leading lights from the world of theater and music. The home of the young Bermann Fischer family on Wattmanngasse soon became a natural meeting place, on a par with the Herrenhof and Zartl cafés. Their daughters, Gaby, Gisi, and Annette, settled in the district well. Writers and musicians would come and go as if they were part of the family.

Until suddenly it was all over.

Now the publisher was sitting at one of the tables by the window in the Opera Bar in Stockholm, the new city, with a thick sheaf of manuscripts and a cup of tea in front of him. He had managed to set up the publishing house in Sweden and had again begun issuing the most important of the works that were banned in Germany. He had invited the German columnist to meet him here to discuss a manuscript about Queen Christina and—provided the meeting went well—to establish a relationship with the company.

Bermann Fischer was engrossed in his papers and didn't notice that Immanuel had entered through a side door and hung up his coat. Now he was standing so close he could see the wrinkles around Bermann Fischer's eyes and the slight sheen on his brow. The publisher was wearing a gray suit of heavy wool, a pale blue tie, and a matching handkerchief in his breast pocket. His hair was neatly combed, with the parting surprisingly far down on the right side of his head.

Opposite him sat a young man in a light-colored linen jacket and orange tie, his legs crossed. His brown hair was slicked to his head. He had a soft, melodic voice exuding goodwill. His German was faultless, but his intonation almost comical. He sang out his sentences as he read aloud from some kind of contract, suggesting deletions and amendments. He was clearly Swedish.

"Paragraph four is superfluous. I pointed that out the last time we went through this draft, didn't I? We'll simplify things for ourselves and delete it. The translator's rights are covered in the sections that specify the editions relative one to another. It's the same book after all, regardless of language and regardless of the size of the edition. Besides, we have standard contracts that were drawn up for Bonniers decades ago. As I understand it, they can be adapted for translations into German. There's no difference. What difference would there be?"

Oddly, the young man talked on without waiting for a reply from the publisher, who barely seemed conscious of his colleague's painstaking reasoning and pedantic remarks. In pencil he underlined names and sentences on a typewritten manuscript. It was uppermost on one of the thick bundles of papers that were spread out across the table in such a way that the teapot and especially the china cups had been nudged alarmingly close to the edge. Now and then the publisher gave a barely perceptible nod as indication of his awareness that work was being done.

Immanuel was on the point of trying to interrupt the conversation, which was essentially a monologue, when the young Swede stood up and strode briskly toward the staircase leading down to the foyer and cloakroom. He caught sight of Immanuel and held out his hand in quick greeting.

"There you are! We were waiting for you." Without further explanation the man hurried down the stairs to the gents.

Immanuel surmised that this must be the Bonnier family lawyer, Ivar Philipson. The shareholders would naturally have to be consulted if Bermann Fischer was intending to add to his editorial staff. It was a good sign he was there, although Immanuel endeavored not to pin too much hope on the lawyer's presence. Perhaps it had nothing to do with him. Either way, Bermann Fischer looked up in typically calm fashion, met Immanuel's eye, and said affably, "Do sit down. Here, let me move Mr. Philipson's briefcase. So good of you to come. I'm sitting here with an almost endless list compiled by Thomas Mann and some members of the Swedish Academy with whom he's kept in touch. It's all been done with the best of intentions, but it makes no sense to me at all. Silfverstolpe. Who is Silfverstolpe?"

"When the sun of culture is low even dwarves cast long shadows," Immanuel said with a lighthearted laugh, but instantly realized the aphorism didn't go down well. This was entirely the wrong occasion to be sarcastic. He handed back the list of authors' names, regretting his attempt to show off in an area he knew so little about, and added contritely:

"It's barely three o'clock and it's getting dark already. What a strange country we've found ourselves in." He looked out of the window facing Kungsträdgården and observed that the oblique sunlight that had just now imparted a golden glow to the large elms in the park and thrown long shadows onto the pavement from passersby had dimmed and assumed a colder shade of blue. He had never known such a light, not even in the northerly cities of Breslau or Warsaw. Definitely not in Munich, where the afternoon light made one think one had already crossed the Alps to northern Italy.

No, this light existed only in his new city. It was November 30, 1939, an uncommonly clear afternoon in Stockholm.

The fact was he hadn't read a word of the writers mentioned, neither Gunnar Mascoll Silfverstolpe nor any of the other intimist poets who were without doubt held in very high regard by the country's renowned, albeit to the outsider extremely arcane, academy. The truth was, he wasn't conversant with any of the young Swedish writers with whom he had just feigned familiarity. Nor did he know anything about the esteemed Finnish author Sillanpää, who in a few weeks would be receiving this year's Nobel Prize in Literature. He was basically a political reporter with literary interests, not an expert.

"Have you heard that the Nobel Banquet has been canceled?" Immanuel said to change the subject. "It's perhaps just as well. At least they won't have three empty seats in the concert hall, now that Hitler has prohibited German prizewinners from attending."

The publisher gave an absentminded nod, but it was unclear whether he had grasped what was said. He seemed to be absorbed in his manuscripts again.

It was hardly surprising that Bermann Fischer was interested in finding new literary voices in the city in which he had chosen to seek refuge, given that the book stock had been moved to Amsterdam and plans to relocate the business to London completely scrapped. Even if they did manage to set up in America, the publishing of books in German could continue with Sweden as the base. Suddenly he looked up, his expression more alert.

"Of course you're aware of the role of Scandinavian authors in our publishing house. Admittedly I don't share my father-in-law's taste for Ellen Key's visions of family life—they feel outmoded now—but think of Jacobsen and Brandes! Not to mention Ibsen."

As he lifted the teacup to his lips, he came out with a final name, like a fanfare. "Bjørnstjerne Bjørnson!"

He swallowed a mouthful of tea. After an unduly long

silence, and in a quieter voice, came the real matter to which the whole conversation was leading.

"Our Nordic library was probably my father-in-law's most lucrative venture. And I understand the enthusiasm for Ellen Key's *The Century of the Child*. Thirty thousand copies sold in two years. Not bad! Why not have a shot at something new, new voices, new books for our times? What's your view—is it something you could work with?"

They didn't know each other, but nevertheless, wasn't Bermann Fischer aware that the man he was about to employ had arrived in the city that autumn, and thus had only a rudimentary command of the language of his adopted land? He had indeed written articles for Swedish newspapers, not least *Dagens Nyheter*, but surely Bermann Fischer didn't think he could instantly pass judgment on the latest literature?

Perhaps Bermann Fischer could read the apprehension in his thoughts, because he added, "Let's forget Silfverstolpe. We don't want to publish poetry anyway, others do it so much better. I know nothing about him, but naturally Mr. Mann has excellent contacts in the academy here and has put me in touch with several of the members. We don't need to affect interest; everyone must understand that we're principally looking for prose writers. And new drama, of course. Unbelievable that Brecht is one of us now. He's hiding here in Stockholm. I'm sure you know that, on Lidingö."

"Hiding? Far from it, he makes his presence felt every day. We saw him recently in the city hall at the reception put on by the council in honor of Thomas Mann, didn't we?"

It was Philipson's melodious voice again. He had approached without a sound and sat down at the table. "His articles appear in quite surprising places. He has offered his services to the

Communists at the *Ny Dag* newspaper under the pseudonym Sherwood Paw. Don't ask me what that's supposed to mean. And he has already made connections here that might bring his work to the theater. There are going to be lectures and soirées, there are whispers of a small symposium at the Royal Theatre. His wife, the actress, was spotted at a premiere. And Tor Bonnier has promised to bring forward the publication of a collection of his poetry in a translation by Johannes Edfelt. A fine young poet himself."

Philipson turned to Immanuel and quietly asked him a string of questions that, had they not been couched in such a friendly manner, would have sounded like an interrogation.

"You're also a socialist, I've heard, sir."

"No, a Social Democrat."

"Are you numerate—I mean, can you add up? Can you deal with simple bookkeeping? The proprietors are in total agreement that our editors can't walk around with their heads in the clouds, even if they are socialists."

They were alone with the two unruffled but reasonably attentive waiters, apart from a middle-aged British gentleman peacefully reading his newspaper. Immanuel could make out the headline about seven shells detonating in the Soviet village of Mainila, by the Finnish border, and realized it must be yesterday's edition of the *Times*. Radio Moscow's report of the Finnish army opening fire on the Soviet unit and killing four soldiers had been worrying him all day. It could only mean that war was inching closer.

"Philipson will help to formalize a brief we sincerely hope you'll find attractive enough to accept," Bermann Fischer said. "Now that Viktor Zuckerkandl is leaving us for America, we'll seize the opportunity to change procedures to suit us both. Everyone in the company appreciates your rather more pragmatic approach, your desire to understand the political situation. Yes, we identify with your values and are delighted to have you on board."

Bermann Fischer took a bundle of documents from Philipson, who without further ceremony bid them goodbye and left by the side entrance opposite St. Jakob's Church. Relieved that the meeting had ended so positively, Immanuel followed him with his eye until he disappeared behind the elm trees in Kungsträdgården. When the publisher resumed speaking, his voice had a different, easier tone.

"Philipson has many good points; you must forgive those foibles about socialism. There is a great deal of irritation over your predecessor's excesses, and Philipson has been under considerable strain. The practice where until very recently he was a partner has disbanded because their main client, a subsidiary of a German firm, suddenly demanded the dismissal of all the Jewish employees. Tor Bonnier has reported pressure from the Germans. He has the utmost confidence in Philipson. They are united as advocates for the Jewish cause in this country. Yes, at heart he is a very good person."

Bermann Fischer calmly returned to his cup of tea. As he leafed through a bundle of letters, something obviously bothered him. He sighed deeply and pushed the letters away with an exaggerated gesture, before exclaiming, "It was delirium tremens. As a doctor, I can say that with some certainty."

"I beg your pardon?"

"I'm sorry. It's an old story that has dogged me since long before Roth died."

"Joseph Roth, the writer?"

Once again the publisher flicked through the letters. He cleared his throat and took another sip before explaining.

"Precisely. He hounded me with all manner of accusations, all founded on misunderstandings. Now he's dead, and we'll never be able to clear it up."

"What a pity! A great pity," Immanuel said dutifully.

"Yes, it's awful," the publisher went on, still leafing through the correspondence. "We're reissuing his *Radetzky March* jointly with Allert de Lange and Querido Verlag. Exile publishers have helped us with another of our authors too. I'm told that Stefan Zweig is gathering material for a novella he calls symbolic, whatever that might entail. It has something to do with chess. Zuckerkandl has devoted his days to ceaseless research into the subject instead of concentrating on his own job."

Immanuel recalled the heavy books he had been asked to bring from Mittag-Leffler's mathematical library.

Bermann Fischer put down his cup and continued.

"But it is largely to Zuckerkandl's credit that Zweig is now one of our authors and he did in fact complete his first novel, *Beware of Pity*. As you know we published it jointly with Querido, but whether there'll be a novella, I don't know. Have you read it?"

Immanuel hadn't even held Stefan Zweig's novel in his hand. He hadn't realized that Zweig was one of the writers of whom he was expected to take charge if he worked for the publishing house. As luck would have it, he didn't have to admit to this, as they were interrupted by one of the waiters clearing the table in so methodical a fashion, it could only be a sign that after several hours it was high time they left or placed another order.

For the first time in weeks Immanuel actually felt content. He looked around the bar, whose decor surpassed anything he had seen in Warsaw; it was even more elaborate than the dining room at the Savoy on Ulica Nowy Świat, where for many years he used to meet colleagues. He raised his eyes to the splendid glass roof with its ornamental motifs reminiscent of flowers, berries, and fruits. The profusion of color was remarkable, as if every little leaf had its own shade. *Stile floreale* was the term for art nouveau in Italy, he remembered, and this really was a prime example of how the organic suppleness to which it aspired could be achieved in cast iron and glass. The curved lines were continued into the bar itself and its light-brown wooden paneling, with elegant arabesques here and there ending in pine-cone wreaths. The small interior windows separating the tables were crafted with loops and winding strips of iron. The publisher's heavy head, with his neatly groomed, slightly graying hair, was outlined against the blue glass mounted in the wood.

The sedate English gentleman in the corner had been joined by a young man, wearing a bow tie and a checked jacket. Probably another Englishman, Immanuel thought. He was about to stand and express his thanks when the publisher addressed him again.

"You'll be aware that the Bonnier family will not permit me to publish more than eight books a year initially. But I've already found ways to extricate myself from this straitjacket, and we're seeking new joint editions. Cooperation regarding the Scandinavians is a chance to expand publishing significantly. Tor Bonnier fully agrees with these ideas. Apropos of cooperation, have you had a look at the Cassirer?"

Immanuel had of course carefully studied the manuscript about Queen Christina that the publisher had given to him at their last meeting. His concerns that it would be too specialized a piece for him were quickly dispelled. As a matter of fact, it was a scholarly but accessible cultural history of the Swedish queen's life and work, and an attempt to understand her declaration that

Descartes's private tutoring had contributed to her conversion and that she had his teachings to thank for her first step on the road to Rome. The publisher had asked him to work through the manuscript, which he had handed over with a sigh and a word or two about having managed hitherto to avoid the philosopher's insufferable prose, but in this case having found no opportunity to decline. Professor Ernst Cassirer's open lectures in Gothenburg were extremely popular, and now Tor Bonnier had decided on a Swedish translation before a German original was anywhere near completion. It was therefore a matter of urgency, but Zuckerkandl had botched the job.

In short, it was time for a change, and Bermann Fischer had decided to do something about it. The new editor would take over both titles forthwith. Enough of in-depth studies into the mysteries of chess: Cassirer's manuscript would be edited with a light touch, as rapidly as possible. He had underlined a number of passages that in his opinion rendered the text cumbersome.

Immanuel had taken a closer look at these, but he hadn't finished the whole manuscript. He read aloud one of the passages with his suggested amendments.

The publisher nodded his approval. "Then we had the section about the soul and sex; how does that bit sound?"

"I'm letting those lines stand, by and large; I think it's perfectly clear. It sounds like this now: 'Such a strong and one-sided rationalism, seldom encountered in men, is expected even less in a woman. But this is a preconception that must be overturned in response to Christina. The soul, she observed, has no sex: *l'âme n'a point de sexe.*'"

The publisher nodded in a way that could only be taken for agreement. The main thing was to get a move on with the publication, he said. Zweig's symbolic novella might also materialize one day, if only the firm's editors would stop distracting the author. It had reached the point where Bermann Fischer had quietly discarded a number of the postcards with notes about the philosophy of chess that Zuckerkandl had addressed to Zweig in England.

"The dwarves casting long shadows at culture's sunset must be a quotation from Nietzsche, I suppose. I think we should steer clear of that sort of thing, however brilliant it may sound. No one else in the publishing house has a taste for the exaggerated rhetoric our colleague Zuckerkandl cultivates with such finesse."

Immanuel nodded, choosing to interpret the words purely as criticism of his predecessor and thereby curbing the impulse to explain that Nietzsche had nothing to do with it. With some mundane comments on the best way of traveling around the city, the publisher said his farewells and paid the bill at the bar. With a hearty handshake he thanked Immanuel for coming and for declaring his willingness to report to the office the following week. "It will be a great pleasure for the staff to have you with us. There's quite a jovial atmosphere in the office, despite the difficult times. Miss Stern, my secretary, has proved to be a veritable rock. You'll work together very well."

He packed up his manuscripts and donned his hat and coat before hastening down the short staircase. There was a sudden need to be at one of the family's musical soirées, and naturally he wanted to get home before the first guests arrived, even though Tutti was handling all the practicalities of the evening and would be ably assisted by their daughters.

After the publisher had disappeared into the twilight, Immanuel debated whether to leave or stay for some peace and quiet to read through the day's articles on the Finno-Russian conflict, which appeared to be escalating into war. He looked around and observed that a lively little group had joined the Englishman. There were two other men and an elegant young woman who looked like a Swedish actress. She was dressed as if for a party and had kept on her wide-brimmed hat. There was no doubt that the man with the slicked-back hair, the one sitting with his back to Immanuel, was dominating the conversation. He was gesturing wildly and evidently had a string of such enthralling tales that the others listened without interrupting. Now and then they burst into laughter, the young woman repeatedly tossing her head back so violently, it was a wonder the hat didn't fall off. The previously staid gentleman in the checked jacket was in extremely good spirits and raised his glass to each of them in turn with a theatrical flourish. He slapped the man with the raft of stories warmly on the back and then turned to the waiter by the bar, demanding attention.

Immanuel, who had decided it was time to go and was looking forward to telling his wife the reassuring news about the job, put his papers back in his briefcase. It had become too noisy in the bar to concentrate on reading, anyway. The jolly gang were sitting around two small tables immediately adjacent to the stairs, and as Immanuel approached, the man with the slicked-back hair appeared to sense something happening behind him. He twisted round and looked briefly over his shoulder.

How strange! This truly is a small city, Immanuel thought, having immediately recognized the man's profile. There was no mistake: the man in the gray suit entertaining the party with such aplomb was the British businessman whose acquaintance he had made only a few days earlier.

Alfred Rickman was plainly just as quick to recognize who was coming toward him. He turned, stood up, and held out his right hand.

"Well, good evening! So nice to see you! Let me introduce my friends. I've told them about our conversation and that you're prepared to help us. They're all very grateful for that. And here's Biggs himself!"

He flung out his arm in a grand gesture in the checked jacket's direction, as if introducing an artist.

"This is Ernest Biggs, an advertising mastermind of the highest order. The very same Mr. Biggs I was talking about. I intended to introduce you to each other in my office on Monday, but this way was quicker. Excellent! Excellent!"

With some difficulty Biggs stood up, and Immanuel remembered Rickman saying something obscure about a one-legged war hero. Was he hiding a wooden leg behind the impeccable crease in his trousers? Immanuel had scarcely finished shaking hands with him before attention moved to the slightly older gentleman as Rickman continued with the introductions in a style worthy of a music hall.

"And here we have Sutton-Pratt! Needing no further introduction. We call him the ambassador—to us he will always be the ambassador."

The middle-aged man looked rather embarrassed. He held out his hand and explained apologetically that he wasn't an ambassador at all, but he did indeed work for the embassy. Rickman was an aficionado, and to him all the officials in the legation were ambassadors, he said. Everyone laughed merrily.

"And lastly my fiancée, Miss Johansson." Rickman raised his arm to the woman in the hat. "I met her at the reception desk at Belfrage's guesthouse. What a godsend, what a godsend! Didn't you say you were staying there?"

Immanuel knew the guesthouse on Blasieholmen; it had actually been recommended to him before the rooms with the Weil family were arranged. It was a mere stone's throw from the Grand Hôtel.

"No, we've never stayed there. You're confusing me with someone else. But it's possible that one of the others at the publishing house has had a room there. Maybe Miss Stern? Bermann Fischer was here, by the way, but he had to go. You've only just missed him."

"But do sit down! This is a wonderful coincidence." Rickman moved along to make space for another chair by the small round table. He added, "Miss Stern, yes, she has already been extremely accommodating. Kindness itself. A very helpful woman. But won't you sit down and drink a toast to our future collaboration?"

Immanuel remained on his feet, searching for the right words. He had opened the envelope Rickman had given him when he was alone in the kitchen at home and Lucia was out. It contained anti-Nazi leaflets composed in such poor German that they needed to be completely rewritten. And somehow that task had fallen to him.

He had no desire whatsoever to join this exuberant group of people, who were behaving as though they had something to celebrate. No, it really was high time he was on his way home. But he didn't want to appear awkward or to offend Rickman.

"We're in a festive mood here. Our 'grand opening' looks as though it's going to work," Rickman added, with a meaningful wink.

Immanuel recalled something about a Mr. Grand. "That's good," he said. "But I regret my family is waiting, and unfortunately I have to rush away."

Rickman didn't look particularly disappointed. He called on everyone to raise their glasses in a symbolic vote of thanks. Immanuel nodded with as much grace as he could muster and turned to the stairs down to the foyer, his heavy briefcase under his arm.

"To our German friend, who has shown himself to be most helpful," Rickman said, clapping Immanuel heartily on the shoulder. "And incidentally, I've forgotten to introduce you to Fraser here, but there'll be other opportunities. We all look forward to the meeting in the office. Cheers!"

LOOK AT THE WONDER AND BEAUTY

B ad-da-bum, dum-da-dum."
Viktor Zuckerkandl's curly hair was even wilder than usual.
One might have imagined he was a young student with big
dreams, not the author of *Wort und Ton bei Mozart* and until
very recently one of the most feared arbiters of musical taste in
Vienna.

"Bum-bum, da-da-dum."

He had a habit of humming to himself in a way that got on
his colleagues' nerves. Wordless song elevates the soul to God,
he would say to anyone who asked what the point of the humming was. A quote from a rabbi in his family. Occasional words
might be interspersed in the humming.

"Dum-da-dum. *Schpil a Nigndl mit Harz und mit Gefil.*"

Always in Yiddish. The others had to put up with it. The
songs were often mournful and slow, but they could be cheerful
and catchy.

"Da-da!"

Today he was in a good mood, and so was the rest of the
office. Everyone was waiting for the new member of staff who

would present himself in the course of the afternoon. The door might open at any moment, and there he would be, the new chap.

Work as an editor at Bermann Fischer's publishing house had expanded into a full-time occupation, and Zuckerkandl couldn't deny that contact with the writers brought him pleasure. Essentially the firm had also saved his life, and now he was safe and sound in central Stockholm, but once more with his bags packed. He was to be replaced by the new recruit. This was his last day in the office. He had only a few weeks left in Sweden.

"Intelligent people are never so astute as when they're wrong," he said sarcastically. To illustrate his argument he delightedly read out an aphorism about chess.

No one else in the office understood the point, for once again it was a question of some metaphysical subtlety that only Zuckerkandl could appreciate. His bantering tone reflected an irrepressible schadenfreude characteristic of his disposition. The unruly hair reinforced the impression of uncompromising intelligence; at least, that was what Zuckerkandl thought.

Everyone was agreed. He was insufferable.

Dr. Zuckerkandl always knew slightly more than anyone else, and dressed it all in a philosophical language that had once impressed but no longer inspired the slightest admiration. Quite the reverse: by this stage his colleagues were sick to death of him, his humming and his rantings.

"If mathematics be the music of reason . . ."

The front door opened without a knock, and everyone's eyes turned to the doorway. Even Zuckerkandl fell silent for a moment. Would it be Dr. B. at last, whom many of them had read in *Basler Nachrichten*?

Miss Stern, Bermann Fischer's secretary, entered the room, and Zuckerkandl continued his monologue.

"If mathematics be the . . ."

He was interrupted by Miss Stern, who had retrieved her new coat and was inquiring on her way out about her colleagues' preferences as to cakes for the coffee.

"Swiss roll or biscuits?"

Her main objective may have been to foil Zuckerkandl, because without waiting for an answer she was already halfway down the stairs. It was nearly three o'clock, and it would soon be time for afternoon coffee with cakes, which Miss Stern collected from Café Ogo.

Cakes had become important to them all in their new city. Their considerably more spacious premises on Esteplatz in Vienna had accommodated more people, and sometimes coffee had indeed been consumed in the office, but congregating like this wasn't a routine event. In those days a number of the editors had taken to having lunch at Café Herrenhof on Herrengasse, where they would bump into people in the press, or one or two of their authors, or colleagues from other publishing houses. It wasn't unusual for them to remain at a coffee table with their manuscripts for several hours in the afternoon. It wouldn't have occurred to anyone to buy a whole strudel for sharing in the office.

In Vienna they had a constant craving for something sweet, and Zuckerkandl was no exception, always at Café Zartl just around the corner, at the crossroads between Rasumofskygasse and Marxergasse. In addition he could be assured of a chat with Robert Musil, who could be found there almost daily, working at his regular table with a long-emptied coffeepot and a glass of water. Musil lived only a few doors away. Both Zuckerkandl and Bermann Fischer would take a seat at his table and exchange everyday observations until they sensed they were disturbing him. Zuckerkandl would generally find the time to order some well-chosen pastry. The publisher was distinctly less interested in Viennese delicacies, and always had been. In Berlin he had developed no such habits, even if coffee and cake were sometimes laid out on one of the desks in the office on Bülowstrasse. But that would only be on Fridays. Actually the publisher preferred tea.

Here in Sweden coffee and cakes had evolved into a ritual that brought the little group together and helped them familiarize themselves with the customs of their new country. They had worked their way through Swiss rolls and vanilla hearts, princess cakes and sponge cakes. Bermann Fischer loved a Swedish sponge cake. He did not subscribe to the criticism some of the other staff directed at this confection, which they judged inferior to the offerings of Vienna cafés. On the contrary, the range of a Swedish bakery suited his rather abstemious character perfectly. One or two pieces of sponge cake was all he really wanted to have with his tea.

Zuckerkandl, on the other hand, was by and large unfailing in his condemnation of the cakes, especially the so-called Danish pastry adapted from Viennese recipes. "Danish pastry? How can anyone have the nerve? A mockery. Nothing less than a mockery." His prattle filled the office. After Miss Stern had set out on her daily trip to the café around the corner on Kungsgatan, there was no one who had the strength to stop him.

There was an unusually high-spirited atmosphere in the publishing house because today's coffee break was a farewell party. Zuckerkandl was going to leave the country, and it was a relief. No one could deny that he had a unique way of combining musical and literary knowledge with a sense of what a demanding readership hungered for and for which they were therefore prepared to pay. But there was no doubt his company was trying.

Zuckerkandl turned his attention to the newly arrived books. "If mathematics be the music of reason, what is a game of chess if not a duet in a minor key that ends with the monarch's death? What drivel! Why a minor key? There are some amusing games, isn't that what François-André Danican Philidor says in *Analyse du jeu des échecs?*"

With his hair standing on end, Zuckerkandl was eagerly leafing through a book whose cover appeared to be in imminent danger of coming apart. The door opened with a loud noise, and everyone looked up inquisitively. This time it had to be the new man.

Great disappointment: it was only another delivery from Zuckerkandl's friend Josephson, the librarian at the Mittag-Leffler Institute, home to Europe's greatest private collection of mathematical literature, which included books about games, primarily chess. That was how Zuckerkandl had met Josephson, a thoroughly likable Jew in his forties who had the unusual task of running a research library without researchers and without opening hours, because all research had ceased following the founder's bankruptcy. The library was locked away in a magnificent villa in the city's most affluent northern suburb, which was easily reached by train from Engelbrektsplan, right by the National Library. They had become very good friends and regularly attended concerts together. Such good friends, in fact, that Zuckerkandl didn't even need to travel out to the villa, but could instead place his orders by telephone and have them delivered forthwith to the office on Stureplan.

The door had swung wide open with a violent shove, and a small, ungainly figure appeared. It was the librarian's rather odd son who had brought the books, a taciturn boy of indeterminate age. He was small in stature but wasn't a child.

Everybody sighed.

"Ho hum," could be heard from one of the desks.

The boy, if he actually was a boy and not just extremely short, possessed among other talents perfect pitch. He was far from a common lackey. This mysterious gnome was called upon to undertake a wide variety of tasks in the musical life of the city, a fact of which his father was very proud. He tuned grand pianos and upright pianos in the drawing rooms of the bourgeoisie and was a self-taught expert on all kinds of instruments. In a highly original twist, given his family's religious affiliation, he was responsible for the church bells of St. Gertrude's, whose tower for many years after the fire had been the highest in the city and whose evangelical congregation had financed its splendid carillon, equipped with twenty-three fine-sounding bells. These involved operating pedals with hands and feet in a manner requiring an excellent level of fitness in the carillonneur up in the clouds. The young Josephson climbed up and down the Lutheran tower every day. No one in the congregation seemed to care that he was a Jew, and equally at home in the synagogue on Wahrendorffsgatan. He was simply referred to as Der Kleine in the parish office, where everyone had become used to him coming and going as he wished. He always reported for bell-ringing with exemplary punctuality.

As Miss Stern was stepping out into the street to fetch the pastries and run a few errands, the sturdy boy had been doggedly trotting up the stairs to the publishing house office, directly above one of the city's busiest pharmacies. There was always a queue stretching down the street, even on days when a thin layer of snow settled on the customers' smart woolen coats. It was just a stone's throw from the Sturehof restaurant, one of the enlightened establishments that provided a setting for the city's increasingly international social life, no matter the day of the week. Sharply dressed representatives from the embassies of Germany and Great Britain dined there side by side or back-to-back with their highly official if also somewhat clandestine guests. It was not unusual for travelers to find a way of combining business with all that the Nordic metropolis could offer in the way of entertainment. That very afternoon the British military attaché Reginald Sutton-Pratt would assemble a motley crew around him at one of the window tables. In the course of the afternoon this talkative group of Brits, a gathering that included not only guests flown in from London but also Rickman, the cheerful businessman for whom Bermann Fischer had taken a liking, would graduate from drinking tea to sampling the restaurant's impressive array of white wines. Rickman had provided generous assistance with the innumerable visa applications that would permit Bermann Fischer's entire family to move to Great Britain. They had in fact been granted, all of them, but now would not be put to use because their travel plans had changed. Thomas Mann had got his own way; America was now the destination.

Bermann Fischer was, however, still indebted to Rickman, and now they exchanged documents of a different kind via Miss Stern. Rickman himself had popped into the office with his fiancée to collect address lists and envelopes. But today it was Miss Stern who would stop briefly at the Sturehof to pick up some of the specially printed material that was to be distributed with the company's next dispatch. Light snow was falling on the new Swedish coat she had bought for a very favorable price at PUB, courtesy of Rickman's friend, the one-legged adman.

Rickman gave her a nonchalant wave through the window when she left for Kungsgatan.

Stureplan, the square over which the rather cluttered offices of the German publishing house looked, was the heart of the none too large city that in the last few months had been transformed into Europe's most densely populated and frenzied hub for all manner of information exchange. Here every conceivable bugging method and decoding device was deployed, sometimes before anyone had worked out what they were trying to discover. Soviet and French press attachés dined with close confidants of newly appointed desk clerks from the German embassy and from the office being set up by self-assured gentlemen from the military intelligence service, the Abwehr, on Nybrogatan. It was obvious that the host country's security services had no means of establishing what actually took place at these tables and who in fact was monitoring whom.

"Dum-da-dum. *Schpil-she mir a Lidl wegn Scholem.*"

Perhaps Zuckerkandl was never able to keep quiet because he was bored. True, he had enjoyed all the conversations, especially the lively ones with Werfel, whose idea it had been to move the publishing house to Stockholm rather than Amsterdam. And with Zweig, of course. But it was his own theories on the realm of tone, music as a meaningful space without a relationship to worldly things, that claimed his attention. He wanted to get on with writing and escape the demands of friends such as Zweig.

As usual Zuckerkandl had perched himself on a bench behind the book table where Bermann Fischer left stacks of publications of all kinds, until no one in the office could remember why they had been purchased. He was browsing through François-André Danican Philidor's chess book, occasionally bursting into loud laughter. He certainly had particularly good reason to be in a cheerful mood. Against all probability his visa application had been successful. His wife, Mimi, had all the necessary papers and stamps ready too, and they would soon be crossing the Atlantic by boat. He didn't know whether it was Klemperer or Furtwängler who had been of most help to him, but he had made use of all his old contacts in the music world. And now he was almost as euphoric as when, twelve years earlier, he had been first entrusted with conducting the philharmonic choir in Vienna, and as relieved as on the joyful day Bermann Fischer let him know that all the necessary travel documents were in order for the journey to Stockholm, and there was absolutely no need for him to give up his editorial work just because the publishing house was forced to leave Vienna.

It had been a good time in the Swedish capital, better than he could have imagined. In the librarian Josephson he had found a kindred spirit, a music fanatic whose powers of association served to demonstrate that he must deepen his own study of mathematics. This was made abundantly clear on his first visit to the villa on Djursholm, when they had an initial conversation about the fugue and music's total autonomy from the outside world.

Josephson's son, the curious dwarf, was evidently in good physical shape. He had run up the stairs to the office despite carrying an exceptionally heavy load of mathematical books and papers. Just as Zuckerkandl was starting to declaim another aphorism in sarcastic tones, the stalwart lad staggered in and without any word of greeting dropped the pile onto the already full book table. They landed with a thud in front of Zuckerkandl, who was studying the spate of mathematical logic currently all the rage in Vienna's progressive circles. He liked to see himself as something more than an amateur mathematician and was by now very well versed in all the fashionable literature about chess, in which one of the publisher's most distinguished writers had developed such an interest.

Taking no notice of the boy, Zuckerkandl picked up the publication at the top of his heap. The youngster immediately departed without so much as a nod of recognition from Zuckerkandl, who felt slightly uncomfortable in the presence of this strange apparition.

Zuckerkandl waved the book around, addressing both Bermann Fisher and the rest of the room. "Of course you know Savielly Tartakower, the chess genius, don't you? He wrote *The Hypermodern Game of Chess* that I want Zweig to read, even though he'll never understand the technical subtleties. As you're aware, he's working hard on his symbolic novel, despite the dark moods. A few examples of the style, perhaps?"

No one said anything, which Zuckerkandl took as an invitation to continue. "Mistakes are there waiting to *be made*. Victory goes to the one who makes the *next-to-last* mistake. It's always better to sacrifice your *opponent's* men."

No one reacted in the slightest. The company's little band of workers were all absorbed in their tasks.

"These now fashionable Tartakowerisms are not especially clever," Zuckerkandl said. He memorized several of them nevertheless and wrote them on little cards to send to Zweig. "And the excessive use of emphasis doesn't improve them stylistically, quite the reverse."

The look on Bermann Fischer's face suggested that he had never heard of Tartakower and wasn't aware that the state of the game's play had entered a hypermodern period. Zuckerkandl was used to the publisher wearing this rather inert expression and was undaunted by any absence of enthusiasm or lack of encouragement from his unwilling audience.

The outside door opened again.

The same sigh of disappointment echoed around the room. It was Miss Stern, with the cakes. She placed a Café Ogo paper bag containing an unusually large carton in front of Zuckerkandl. "I bought extra, since we have something to celebrate. Biscuits and Danish pastries, and sponge cake for the publisher himself."

But Zuckerkandl was not one to be silenced by such simple means.

"On purely stylistic grounds," he said, "Tartakower belongs to the same school as Nimzowitsch and Réti, but he has a weakness for phraseology so paradoxical, not to say reckless, that the thoughts of the attentive reader who is given to conjecture are elevated to a giddy sphere far beyond the prosaic physical reality of the board."

Bermann Fischer buried his head deeper into his manuscript. He was all too aware that the editor, whose knowledge of diverse philosophical areas could only be described as original, had for months been exchanging ideas with the intermittently depressed and currently exiled Zweig, who had fatally misjudged Hitler and talked of Nazism as a little bump on the road to European unity. The continent's fundamental aim is to be as great as Switzerland, Zweig had said. This same Zweig had for some time been promising a novella set on an ocean liner, just like a previous story about a physician, the one who ran amok. The new story, which was going to be even more powerful, addressed the German tragedy and was based on an idiosyncratic understanding of chess. Not just idiosyncratic, but also erroneous, according to Zuckerkandl, who wanted to advise Zweig against the whole plan unless the premise were to be reframed. That was why he assailed him with musings and quotations.

The fact that Zuckerkandl and Zweig were no longer able to quarrel over a coffee table but instead had to elaborate their disagreements in increasingly delayed correspondence between Stockholm and Bath, where Zweig had settled with his new wife, meant that time dragged on. The former Miss Altmann, who just a year ago had been his secretary, was the one who had originally contacted Zuckerkandl to inform him that Zweig was deeply impressed by one of his essays, which he had stumbled upon by chance. Over the years the friendship had grown, and now Zuckerkandl was in fact one of the reasons Zweig had decided to cut ties with his previous publishing house and accept Bermann Fischer's invitation. By this time Lotte Altmann had married Zweig and was living with him in the English city. Zuckerkandl thought it very likely that she was filtering out certain of his communications. At any rate several of his postcards never reached Zweig.

"What is appealing in this game, everyone must agree, is that it is a match between *two* brains," Zuckerkandl continued.

Miss Stern heaved an irritated sigh. She pushed the cardboard box so far toward the editor, it nearly fell onto his knee.

"Biscuits or Danish pastry? You can have both, Viktor—it's your party, after all."

"As I was saying, two brains."

Zuckerkandl emphasized this in letter after letter. But now his Austrian friend had taken into his head that the story should be about a man who discovers a previously unknown split in his personality, an inner double life. A double persona knowing everything and at the same time nothing about himself and able to play a game of chess against himself. Zuckerkandl had warned against building a narrative on a paradox that has echoes of the man who tries to jump over his own shadow. He suggested as an alternative a story about particular moments in Alekhine and Lasker's matches, a kind of political allegory.

In vain. Instead of focusing on the drama building in a truly great match, Zweig dwelt upon his two grand masters: two players occupying the same brain. Time and again Zuckerkandl stressed the absurdity of one and the same person being capable of such a retaliatory attitude with regard to his alter ego, but his stubborn friend remained firmly convinced of the literary effectiveness of his idea.

The cakes were now being laid out on the large book table. It was time for coffee. Bermann Fischer leaned forward to take a piece of sponge cake.

The publisher had grounds for feeling irritated at Zuckerkandl for wasting time. Of course, it was thanks to him that Zweig had finally been persuaded to become one of their authors. It was a splendid achievement, and his first novel, *Beware of Pity*, had been a best seller. But why pander to Zweig's never-ending demands with a constant stream of new suggestions instead of working with some of the manuscripts that were actually ready? A particularly embarrassing case was Ernst Cassirer's book about Queen Christina, which was more than a little late.

It was unfortunate for several reasons. Not least because Ernst Cassirer, for a number of years professor in Gothenburg but now also about to leave the country, was the patriarch of a family that had links with Bermann Fischer's own. In Berlin he and Tutti had socialized regularly with members of the family as if they were close relatives. It wasn't just the remarkably carefree Agnes they treated like a family member, but her father too, the earnest publisher of lavish art books. The family had recently managed to move their company from Berlin to Oxford, where they now lived in safety, albeit isolated from the intellectual milieu that had been their lifeblood. They had briefly considered Stockholm as a possibility as well. There had even been some talk of a merger between their publishing houses, which, thank goodness, had never happened.

Bermann Fischer had been concerned that the editor would offend the learned Cassirer. Thomas Mann had warned him: Zuckerkandl often went too far. But on this occasion the editor had barely opened the manuscript.

No, the new editor would have to concentrate on finalizing Cassirer. Every day Tor Bonnier asked if the manuscript would soon be ready for translating. In any case it was pointless sending more material about openings and endgames, because basically Zweig didn't make use of Zuckerkandl's copious research. If truth be told, his questions about Tartakower and other grand masters such as Nimzowitsch were just a diversion, and the long article about Réti that Zuckerkandl had had translated from the Polish to cheer him up didn't seem to have made any impression.

Had Zweig even read it? No, it was increasingly obvious that the whole exchange with the agreeable mathematician at the Mittag-Leffler Institute was frankly leading nowhere. Perhaps it was primarily a kind of party game for Zuckerkandl, who had found an area in which to show off.

Any moment now, and Zuckerkandl's successor would be coming in. Bermann Fischer knew very little about him, but he had read him many times in the *Frankfurter Zeitung*. That was quite a few years ago now. He appeared every day in *Basler Nachrichten* under the byline Dr. B. By all accounts he lived with his wife and two sons with the Weil family, friends of Miss Stern. The work he had done for the publishing house thus far had been faultless. He also made a congenial impression, which was the crucial thing.

The publisher was woken from his ruminations by the sound of the door opening.

It wasn't Dr. B. at all, but Rickman's fiancée, who had come for the German stamps Miss Stern had forgotten. She left immediately, but only after a friendly nod to some of the people in the office that she recognized from her time working at Belfrage's guesthouse on Blasieholmen, where a number of them had stayed on their arrival in the city.

For once Zuckerkandl had broken off his tiresome humming. After some moments of silence came a few lines from a Jewish hymn that sounded familiar. His singing voice wasn't particularly good. "*Sieh', wie lieblich und wie schön ist's . . .*"

Even this was preferable to the interminable chatter. They all knew the melody, and to his own surprise Bermann Fischer chimed in with the next line. He had a beautiful voice, and his colleagues looked up from their desks in astonishment.

"*Wenn Brüder in Eintracht beisammen wohnen.*"

Evidently it was the new editor's father, the cantor in the synagogue in Königsberg, who had written the hymn. Naturally Zuckerkandl knew more about his successor than anyone else in the office and of course took advantage of the situation. No one could prevent him from delivering a lecture about the cantor, with whose unique collection of musical manuscripts Zuckerkandl was clearly well acquainted.

"In a sense he has been pivotal to the understanding of Jewish music. Everything you heard in the temple and sang as a child without understanding, he has collected together in one place and organized. Not just *chazzanut*, cantorial singing, but street music too."

This didn't bode well. Now there would be no way to silence Zuckerkandl for quite some time. The employees at Bermann Fischer's publishing house were indeed all Jews, but they had no great interest in sacred song. They wanted to eat their Swedish cakes in peace and quiet and wait for their new colleague.

Miss Stern did her best by loudly distributing the profusion of pastries. Patently there would be cakes left over. Outside the office windows the snow was falling heavily now. It settled on the pavements and the square, where people were sheltering from the snowfall under the rounded roof of the mushroom-shaped pavilion.

There were large numbers of people out and about despite the weather. The first Christmas decorations could be seen in shop windows. Their neighbor in the east was at war with the Soviet Union, as all the newspaper placards proclaimed. In Sweden the threat of a government crisis loomed. Yet it was remarkably calm on Stureplan in the heart of the capital. It was as though the snow formed a soothing white blanket over everyday life.

"Sieh', wie lieblich und wie schön ist's . . ."

Was it Bermann Fischer himself who struck up in song to quieten their insufferable colleague? Everyone appeared to remember the hymn from their childhood and joined in, *"Wenn Brüder in Eintracht beisammen wohnen . . ."*

The door had opened again, but no one noticed the new editor standing on the threshold. It was a remarkable sight that faced him: a group of grown-ups around a large table laden with cakes, singing one of his own father's hymns.

INVISIBLE INK

"Horst here."

It was all he said before asking to speak to her husband.

That was how the fateful day began.

"There's a Mr. Horst asking for you, darling. Why do you think he's ringing so early?"

It was indeed early; the boys were not even up. They had an hour of Swedish before their normal teaching began, so they rose at the crack of dawn, before it was light.

She heard Immanuel speaking in an unusually low voice out in the hall. For a few weeks now they had had their own telephone and no longer needed to disturb the Weil family. Calls usually came in the evening, and they had therefore looked at each other in surprise when the room filled with a loud ring so penetrating it would surely wake the boys, even though the door to their room was closed. Out in the corridor Immanuel was whispering into the receiver, but she heard every word.

"Yes, Mr. Horst. Of course. That's agreed then, seven o'clock this evening at the Strand. Thank you for the call. See you later."

It was an important day for Immanuel, and he tried to push

aside any thoughts about what this Mr. Horst from Berlin might have to propose. Today was submission day for the whole Cassirer manuscript. And today he would also be introduced to the principal owner, Tor Bonnier, who planned to publish the book in Swedish. Immanuel only had the morning in which to go through the last amendments. After lunch he and Bermann Fischer would walk over to the parent company's offices on Sveavägen.

But before the working day could begin, the boys had to be woken, and simply sending them off in time for their Swedish lesson every morning was an effort. They didn't exactly look forward to the teacher's stern interrogations. Henrik in particular was so anxious about these lessons that he would often throw himself back into bed, sobbing, and for as long as possible would refuse to put on his coat on the grounds that he didn't feel well. Once or twice Karl had had to go on his own, but Henrik could generally be persuaded in the end, often with the promise of a reward that very afternoon. This morning, the same day that the early call from Horst shattered their moment of peace before the boys had to be woken, was one of those mornings filled with darkness and sleet and fear of the Swedish teacher's morning mood.

When the children had left, Lucia sat down opposite Immanuel at the kitchen table.

"Is he a friend of Gerhard's? And what sort of name is Horst? That's not a person's surname."

"Wolfgang. His name is Wolfgang Horst."

Lucia sighed heavily.

Immanuel hadn't wanted to say any more about the telephone call, but it was obvious his wife wouldn't let the subject drop. "To be completely honest, I'm not really sure who he is.

He says we met briefly a few summers ago in Kaunas and that he's part of the set around the Berliner Zeitung press agency, so it's quite likely that he knows my brother. I didn't have a chance to ask, but it wouldn't surprise me if he'd been sent here by Gerhard. Or it might have been by Scheliha, you remember, my German friend in Warsaw."

The truth was, he hadn't had any contact whatsoever with his brother for several months. But his wife knew that. For a long time Gerhard had performed the role of secretary of sorts, typing up articles and helping with the accounts. He had been there every day around lunchtime in their villa in Żoliborz. They had developed an excellent way of working together, he and Lucia, who was also an excellent stenographer. For some months he even lived with them in Warsaw. But since the summer holiday in Estonia, Immanuel had had to manage without his brother's support.

It had crossed his mind many times that the best scenario would be if Gerhard could join the family here in Stockholm. But he had heard nothing from his brother since the summer, and, all things considered, anything could have happened to him. Could one even be sure he was still a free man?

"But why are you so upset?" Immanuel asked when he saw his wife's worried face and tear-filled eyes. "It's not the first time in Stockholm I've had calls from people I'm not absolutely sure I know, or even want to know."

This was quite true and didn't just apply to telephone calls but also to meetings with individuals from various countries who sought him out, sometimes with a letter of recommendation from a mutual acquaintance. Like the Englishman.

It started with Biggs, the man with the limp, to whom he had been introduced at the Opera Bar and who had later met him at Rickman's office, and continued one rainy morning with a whole delegation of them at his home on Frejgatan. The same Biggs again, now accompanied by Rickman himself and the latter's elegant fiancée, and another gentleman whose name he had forgotten. Biggs had positioned all the copies on the kitchen table. The material was hardly sophisticated, but that wasn't the objective. The leaflets functioned on the level of cartoons and were intended to illustrate how Hitler was being hoodwinked by the Russians. National Socialism wasn't being called into question, but the focus was on the führer's inability to keep his promises. The recurrent theme, the Bolsheviks taking advantage behind the backs of the unsuspecting Germans, was explained in short texts. Unfortunately these contained so many linguistic peculiarities they could under no circumstances be used in Germany. Immanuel had conveyed this with considerable directness, but Rickman had looked quizzical, on the grounds that Bermann Fischer's wife, Tutti, had privately told him the material was excellent. Rickman had seemed less than happy when Immanuel reiterated that the leaflets in their current state were completely unusable. Apparently they were going to be printed in large numbers somewhere in Sweden and then transported to Stockholm for onward distribution in Germany.

As luck would have it, Lucia hadn't been at home. The call from Horst was enough. He didn't know how she would cope with the idea of him being dragged into propaganda activities. He tried to calm her down.

"Horst is in touch with Kutzner at the press agency in Berlin, and we can't afford to lose that connection. It's a matter of a stable income. Small but important, you know that."

Lucia herself had typed up most of the articles that were sent to the Berliner Zeitung press agency. They involved fairly innocuous items devoid of any personal tone or political slant, news from the Baltic and Nordic states. Ever since Immanuel had been forbidden to work in the German national press, Lucia had always said there was something unsavory about this contact in Berlin to whom they sent articles with some regularity. It was she who kept track of the correspondence and the accounts, and to distinguish between the different clients, she marked the articles sent to Berlin with a B; articles for *De Telegraaf* were given an A for Amsterdam; texts for *Basler Nachrichten*, the longest and most ambitious, bore the abbreviation BA.

It was relatively easy money. Moreover, it was a near miracle that this press agency, which succeeded in placing articles in a number of German-language minority newspapers in Poland, could still operate alongside the German state-controlled press. It was obviously living on borrowed time. Immanuel had no idea what pressure Kutzner might be under, and he had no way of finding out. Was Ilse Stübe, who had been a little too Moscow-friendly for his liking, still in the office? His brother was the one who had closest contact with the agency, but where was Gerhard today? Immanuel feared the worst, and his brother kept appearing in his dreams in the most appalling scenarios.

The Berlin address had figured in his darkest dreams too. There had been talk of Ilse Stübe taking a more prominent position, but that didn't seem to have happened. Allied to this was the fact that he had never gotten to know Kutzner, who for nearly two years had played a key role in the whole thing. He had never wanted to voice his deepest concerns, but in essence Kutzner could well have been appointed by the powers that be. The intention might have been to exploit the network for purposes other than those originally shaped by himself and his friend von Scheliha, press attaché at the German embassy in Warsaw, who was certainly no friend of his superior in Berlin. Finding ways of circumventing Nazification of the press had been their single goal. Was it possible that von Scheliha had been removed as well? And if that were the case, what was the point of the agency, and why did it still exist?

But he couldn't deny that he welcomed the four hundred marks transferred every month into his account at the Gothenburg merchant bank. In truth the money was sorely needed. The rest of the time he tried not to let his thoughts dwell on the Berlin agency. But on this blustery autumn day the storm clouds within him gathered with renewed force, agitated and exceedingly dark. As the afternoon wore on he recalled Lucia's anxious question.

"What sort of a name is Horst? That's not a person's surname."

It was as if she sensed that the business with Horst would lead to problems. To comfort her he rang home from the office, something he would never normally do.

He tried to take her mind off it. There was plenty of good news to focus on today: the meeting with Tor Bonnier, delivery of the manuscript. It was a great pity the day would have to end with a meeting that was causing so much unease. Just as well to get it over with.

He walked briskly down Birger Jarlsgatan toward Nybroplan and followed the quayside out to Blasieholmen. When he entered the vestibule of the Strand Hotel, he was met by a clean-cut young man who clearly recognized him, for he rose immediately from a velvet couch and held out his hand. He introduced himself with a barely visible smile that expressed little warmth. He was as terse as he had been on the telephone.

"Horst."

"I'm sorry if I've made you wait," Immanuel said, though he wasn't in the least late. Something about this man made him nervous. "Have you reserved a table here?"

"I have no knowledge of Stockholm's restaurant life," Horst said curtly. "I arrived yesterday and I'm leaving tomorrow. Wherever you suggest."

The only place Immanuel knew was the Opera Bar. When they came out onto Arsenalsgatan, they were met by strong gusts of wind and wild swirls of leaves. It was difficult to hear one another in the gale, but Horst managed to convey that he had important matters to discuss and was grateful for the meeting. Very important matters, he stressed.

They walked through Kungsträdgården and, just as the clock struck quarter past seven, entered the foyer of the Operakällaren and climbed the short stairway to the bar. They sat down at one of the tables by the window overlooking the church. The waiter, by this stage well known to Immanuel, took their order and returned almost at once with glasses and two bottles of Ramlösa water. Horst broke the silence with civilities about how much it meant to his colleagues in Berlin that there were reliable writers outside their own country, not least in the outlying regions that had hitherto managed to stay out of the war. He drank his water, and a look of deeper gravity crossed his young face.

"Mr. Kutzner would like you to know that you can continue to count on the four hundred marks in payment every month, although the articles were withheld for a period and it has been a long time since anything could be used in the *Kattowitzer Zeitung*. The *Lodzer Freie Presse* hasn't printed anything for many weeks either, but of course you know that."

What was he trying to say? Despite his immaculate

appearance, the man had something troubled about him. He kept looking around as if he were afraid of being seen in Immanuel's company. Something was bothering him, and he could hardly have come to see Immanuel merely to inform him that the payments would continue to be made with unbroken regularity. He appeared to be deliberating before he spoke again.

"These are unusual times, and sometimes one has to be prepared to provide services one hasn't previously been accustomed to. Don't you agree? At least that's the way it looks in the reality in which I am living. You have a family, I understand? Kutzner told me you have two children."

They were alone in the Opera Bar, and the waiter who had been behind the bar counter had now disappeared from sight. The other guests had made their way to the dining room. It was completely quiet.

"Yes, I have two sons. They're living here with my wife and me."

What was Horst getting at? Was he really a person sent from the agency in Berlin? In fact, was he from the field of journalism at all? It didn't feel like that. Instead Immanuel was reminded of one of the innumerable legation assistants he had come across in various cities over the years. In his memory they merged into one polite but evasive person, always with the same faultless High German accent. He recalled the group of subordinates around von Scheliha at the German embassy. New faces constantly, and yet always inherently the same person. In his mind's eye he could no longer visualize these assistants to the press attaché. Young men who were at once both obliging, almost servile, and somewhat reserved. It was a type one only encountered in the labyrinthine world of diplomacy, so heavily regulated by statutes and protocols. Yes, Horst might well be an emissary from the German embassy rather than the representative of the newspaper world he claimed to be. State control of the German press had changed everything. And Horst was not the sort of person one could imagine among journalists.

Horst cleared his throat nervously, apparently intent on explaining himself. "As I said, sometimes one has to make an extra effort, especially in times of war. And in your case we'd like a little behind-the-scenes reporting. I'm sure you understand what I mean. When you mix with journalists from different parts of the world, voices from the so-called neutral press, you hear things. And when you run into people from the diplomatic world, sometimes you might gain knowledge of any clandestine activities afoot. What we mean quite simply is politically interesting information."

Of course. He should have known. Immanuel realized that this would be a balancing act, and he had to curb the anger that was threatening to surface. The situation required the utmost discretion. He didn't want to appear antagonistic or too dismissive. Nor did he want to inflate the whole thing into a debate about principles, even though the proposals being made by the clean-shaven young man on the other side of the table holding a glass of water in his hand basically crossed the line of acceptability. Was it even an offer, or was it a demand being placed upon him in this insidious fashion? He decided to try and wriggle out of it.

"But Mr. Horst, you must understand that I can't get involved in this sort of thing in a country I know so little about. I'm the wrong person. You're sure to find someone more suitable without any trouble. My knowledge of this city is for the most part rudimentary, and I know only a handful of people, all of whom are in the same precarious circumstances as my family and myself."

Horst was silent for a moment as he poured the last drop of Ramlösa into his glass. He looked around at the extravagantly designed art nouveau setting. Curiously, they were still alone. Yet Horst continued in an even lower voice, as if he were afraid they might be caught in the act and overheard by people unseen but nevertheless somewhere in their immediate vicinity.

"As I pointed out, we haven't placed your articles for a long time, at least not consistent with the scale agreed in the contract. Four hundred marks is a relatively good rate, especially if no work is done. We thought the lack of normal reporting could be offset by activity of a slightly different kind. As I said, a glimpse behind the scenes. I presume you'll still need the fees in future, won't you?"

"As I said, I'm not a suitable candidate. I don't know enough about this country; it's as simple as that."

Immanuel did his best to make it look as though he took the conversation lightly. He studied the man opposite him: short hair, perfectly slicked side parting, rye-blond forelock brushing a fascinating pair of rimless spectacles held in place by an extremely thin silver frame. Horst was an absolutely impeccable young man, with a calm, cultured comportment, but nevertheless radiating a harshness that emanated from his speech. He pronounced words with an articulation that left nothing he said unclear or vague. That was also true of the next sentence, enunciated with an edge that could only be described as savage, even though Horst hadn't raised his voice in the slightest.

"You have a wife who may wish to return to Germany at some time in the future, isn't that right?"

Immanuel felt a chill sweep through him. "We have already discussed this, Mr. Horst. You're repeating yourself," he said, before realizing that wasn't the case.

They hadn't spoken about an eventual return to Germany. This notion was his own. Among the many thoughts that had filled his mind in the last few moments was the realization that in the likelihood that his family were to outlive him, they would need the greatest discretion imaginable. In any event, there was no longer any ambiguity about whether what Horst had to say contained an inherent threat. It also had become increasingly clear what type of services he meant and what kind of information he hoped Immanuel would transmit.

"This doesn't concern intelligence about this country. We're not talking about Swedish relations. What I'm trying to convey is that we have a special interest in the other warring powers with a presence in the city, and we imagine that you find out about activities with some degree of regularity and are able to follow certain trails. To be frank, this is a request that Mr. Kutzner regards as fully justified, given the financial recompense you enjoy. A remuneration, let me stress, that no one will challenge in the circumstances."

What did Horst know about Immanuel's acquaintance circles? It could hardly be a secret that he was on a friendly footing with the diplomats Joen Lagerberg and Sven Grafström, both of whom had been a great help during the last few months in Warsaw. Without them the move would have been quite simply impossible. And cultivating cordial ties with a small crowd at the German embassy in the Polish capital hadn't happened behind closed doors either.

Be that as it may, the Polish connections belonged to a bygone age and were hardly of relevance to his new situation in Stockholm. No one could reasonably have known about the quite remarkable happenings of the last few weeks. A flood of half-thoughts raced through his fraught mind in less than the time it took to raise the almost empty glass to his lips for a last sip. The fact that Bermann Fischer had influential friends among British expatriates in the city and that some of those characters had appeared in Immanuel's life was not something they could know about in Germany.

Horst continued relentlessly, oblivious to what was going on inside Immanuel's head. "In short, you have nothing to lose by demonstrating a little cooperation. But you might have something to gain. And, as I would like to emphasize, this is not just about you. You have a wife, as you said, who looks in every way delightful, and you have two sons who might be grown men by the time the war comes to an end. They look handsome, the boys."

Horst was quiet for a moment but had another question to ask. It sounded more like an order. "You must have had thoughts about leaving this country if it gets crowded here. That would be understandable."

Immanuel said nothing. How could he reply? That of course they had considered the United States, had not given up hope of Great Britain? Even investigated possibilities in China and Cuba? He remained silent.

Instead Horst added, as if talking to himself, "It's not beyond the realms of possibility that the work we're after could be carried out somewhere else. Perhaps in London. By no means impossible that we could be of assistance."

Was Immanuel mistaken? Had the young man been dispatched to help him? Could the threatening tone he thought he'd heard be a figment of his imagination?

A small leather briefcase suddenly appeared on the table, and from it Horst took a pile of documents, at the top of which was a portrait of Lucia. Under it he glimpsed the boys' passport photographs, affixed to some kind of form. On another photograph, several years old, the boys were dressed smartly in new jackets. Both were holding their father's hand. Immanuel was wearing a coat and hat. His face was hidden.

Karl. Henrik. Lucia. Immanuel stared at the photographs of his family. Horst continued to make his skillfully articulated case, returning to the phrase about the pointlessness of closing any doors. "There's something I want to hand over to you," he said. "But I don't want to do it here in the restaurant." He stood up, with a gesture toward the cloakroom.

In complete silence they walked back through the cold and rain to the foyer of the Strand Hotel. Only after they sat down at a table in a room next to the reception desk did Horst begin speaking again, having retrieved something from his coat. He opened a paper bag containing two objects, which he placed on the table.

"You must be careful with this liquid. It is highly poisonous and is only to be used when you have something to communicate that can under no circumstances become public knowledge. The pen is easy to handle, and the whole thing is fairly self-evident. You can have a closer look at home."

Now they both stared at the small glass receptacle containing a greenish-yellow fluid and at the black fountain pen, a German Tintenkuli. Horst put the items back into the paper bag and pushed it across to the other side of the table.

"When you have something to communicate, simply write it down with this ink. Mr. Kutzner will have no problem revealing the text."

Immanuel remained in his seat, the paper bag in front of him. A minute or two passed before he gave Horst a guarded nod in a vague parting gesture, stood up, and walked through the revolving doors. He noticed his face reflected in the glass. The bag was in the inner pocket of his coat.

17 VILLAGATAN

Snow had been falling all night. The streets were quiet, and it was difficult for cars to get through. Clearing hadn't even begun on Villagatan. It was Madame Kollontai's decision that the German journalist, the one who wrote as Dr. B., should present himself so early. It was the only chance of fitting in one more meeting that day. Now she regretted it. Morning hours were the most productive, her time to write up the sometimes almost indecipherable notes she had made during the night. Events of the last few days had been exhausting. Constant meetings with foreign minister Väinö Tanner's emissaries, sometimes at the embassy, more often at the Grand Hotel. Now there was talk of the Finnish minister himself coming. The person who had worked behind the scenes to bring about the meeting, probably within the week, was Hella Wuolijoki. The press officer at the Finnish embassy had spoken of her as an unusually creative Communist. All she could do was agree. Apparently Wuolijoki was a friend of the German dramatist Bertolt Brecht, who had been living in the city for some time.

She couldn't help feeling slightly irritated that this mediator had played such a decisive role without any involvement on the part of the embassy. Quite how it had come about, she couldn't fathom, but she was all the more eager to regain the initiative.

They had indeed been busy days, filled with very difficult decisions and a great deal of apprehension about the future. It was not uncommon for her to be in touch with Moscow in the middle of the night, and the Swedish foreign minister kept late hours too. It was fortunate that her need for sleep had diminished in recent years. She used the quiet hours of the early morning to work on her journal.

She sat at her desk upstairs, looking out of the window at the street. There was not much light penetrating the gray clouds. The snow was still falling, snowflakes swirling in small eddies before settling on the windowsill. She leafed through the pile of papers and read out the morning's corrected draft. Her voice was so muted that had someone entered the study, where she was always alone, this rare visitor would have heard only a faint murmur. Occasionally she paused and crossed a word out or added a short phrase.

> The cipher messages often arrive late at night, and in these charged times, as we move into peace negotiations with Finland, I am ready to set off at a moment's notice for Arvfurstens Palats, where the Ministry of Foreign Affairs is located now. There is no longer anyone living there, but in my imagination the halls and corridors of the palace are peopled by shadows of the past. The founder of the Swedish royal line lived here, one of Napoleon's officers who was adopted by the Swedish king.

The last few weeks had been turbulent, among the most unsettling in her life, which certainly hadn't been lacking in drama hitherto. If it wasn't communications from Moscow, it was telephone calls from the press office, which was all the way out on Katarinavägen. Or it was questions from TASS or Intourist that for some reason had to be answered immediately, regardless of the time. The official Soviet presence in Stockholm was large, perhaps too large, and sooner or later all questions ended up on her desk. It was time-consuming.

No one thought twice about troubling her with the most basic of visa matters, and in recent weeks it had become clear that the strain on the Siberian railway had been mounting. For some refugees the long journey across the Soviet Union was their last chance to leave Europe. It was becoming increasingly apparent that they were Jewish families who had discovered this final eye of the needle. Rumors abounded. According to one, Shanghai was a place where you could settle without a visa. But more often than not it was the lure of a sea passage from Yokohama to San Francisco that drew them. Be that as it may, consular questions had become much more taxing.

The new Swedish foreign minister, Mr. Günther, was evidently something of a loner. He had nothing against receiving visitors after midnight when all his colleagues, even those who worked into the evening, had long since left the department. She had recorded these nighttime excursions in her writing.

> At night I am admitted to the old palace building, not through the parade entrance, but by a discreet side door. The night watchman escorts me through the maze of corridors and halls still furnished in the style of the Napoleonic era, to the reception room, where I wait to be called in to see Minister Günther. I am not bored as I wait for his summons. I settle into a familiar mood, pushing aside all thought of my current task and indulging in fantasies about old times.

Passages such as these made her happy that she kept a diary, not simply a diplomat's notebook but an account that one day would be read as literature. At this moment she was certain of that, and she felt a sense of satisfaction that made her forget the politics of the day.

I walk past a succession of sumptuous but now dimly lit halls and salons in the old palace and up to the reception area, where I wait to be called into Günther's office. The night watchman is tired. I am alone in these extraordinary surroundings, a palace from the eighteenth century. And I ask myself: What would the Swedish king's adoptive son, Jean Bernadotte, with his southern temperament and his naive view of the world, have said if he had come across an aging but still handsome woman wandering around in the old castle at night? Would he have taken her to be the lover of someone in his French retinue, or would he have decided she must be a conspirator, sent to spy on him—heir to the Swedish throne?

She arranged the papers in a neat sheaf. While she was happy to dictate letters, articles, and lectures, she had always chosen to write up her diaries herself. Her Excellency's personal records, which stretched back decades, required a very different role of Emy Lorentzon. Every other month she made sure the manuscripts were transferred to Triewaldsgränd, the little side street linking the squares Munkbron and Järntorget in Gamla Stan, where a friend, a woman doctor, locked them in a secret filing cabinet that they both regarded as safe.

But at the moment Miss Lorentzon had other things on her mind, for the first guest of the day, the young German journalist who had visited Madame in the villa out on the island on one of the last warm days of autumn, had already taken a seat in the salon next to the grand piano. They had recognized one another at once—Immanuel recalled her friendly welcome on the terrace and their rather odd conversation about black sunflower discs turning toward the sun. He also remembered their walk down to the water and his surprise at being taken into the secretary's confidence regarding the fair-haired young woman's plight and her rather undesirable brother, the armed boatman.

After the first excruciating meeting with Madame Kollontai, Immanuel had discounted any possibility of a second chance for a private exchange of ideas. But this time the initiative was Kollontai's, and the invitation had been brought about by mutual acquaintances in the diplomatic corps. The envoy Lagerberg, his benefactor from the embassy in Warsaw, had indicated that the Soviet emissary wished to meet him. In fact all three should have been involved, but Lagerberg had been unable to attend and now Immanuel sat on his own, waiting for her to receive him.

She handled the diplomatic game with discretion and the utmost finesse, but now, Lagerberg had said, her thoughts were directed to the increasingly German-friendly leaning of the Swedish press. He had added that Swedish allegiance to the German cause, which often went hand in hand with a knee-jerk skepticism toward everything Soviet, troubled her.

Immanuel had been surprised when a formal invitation arrived in the letterbox on Frejgatan. Now he was sitting in an upstairs salon, browsing through magazines containing articles about embassy events. The salon was decorated in a style befitting a banker or bourgeois politician with a taste for the applied arts. The rugs and wallpaper were remarkably colorful, indeed quite ornate. On the grand piano stood an array of lavish bouquets of flowers that looked bizarre, given the season.

He started reading a richly illustrated piece about Red Army Day the previous year. The embassy could celebrate in the most grandiose fashion, it seemed: it wasn't just about diplomats and attachés dressing up, there were singers, actors, and the famous revue artist Karl Gerhard, with his merry entourage. It had obviously become a tradition, and on February 23, Stockholm society had grown accustomed to being invited to Villagatan for caviar and vodka. There had been plenty of politicians at the previous year's party, but the foreign minister had stayed away. Mr. Sandler was seldom seen at functions of this sort nowadays, the author of the article noted. But his deputy, cabinet secretary Erik Boheman, usually attended. Why had he passed up this popular event? the writer wondered. Could it possibly have something to do with increasing political tensions?

How different the atmosphere must have been in the embassy then and in the diplomatic corps as a whole, indeed in the entire city, Immanuel thought. The idea that the country's foreign minister should find time for events with revue artists was almost unthinkable. Now Sandler had been replaced by a minister even less festively inclined, and the country was under threat from all quarters. The magazine's pages were teeming with photographs of bigwigs from the armed forces, perhaps present to pick up news at first hand and gain a sense of the Soviet mood. Immanuel didn't know many of them, but here and there he spotted a familiar face. Funnily enough, he could glimpse Lagerberg in one picture, wearing tails and talking to a Russian official. In the background he could make out Lagerberg's diplomat friend Sven Grafström and Grafström's wife. The writer went on to report that the German envoy, Prince Victor of Wied, was absent, perhaps on account of the Nobel Prize crisis. But on the other hand, General von Uthmann had been more visible than ever in the salon. The military attaché could be seen in several photographs, wearing a uniform adorned with a large number of medals. With him was the mustachioed Hans von Euler-Chelpin, Nobel laureate in chemistry, and the latter's handsome wife.

Immanuel had moved to a chair by the window overlooking Villagatan when, with scarcely a sound, Miss Lorentzon reappeared behind him.

"I'm so sorry, Madame is slightly delayed. Would you like a cup of tea while you wait, sir? She won't be long."

"A cup of tea would be nice, thank you." With a slight nod toward the magazine, Immanuel added, "What parties you throw in this place! Illustrious guests from all over Europe!"

"Not only Europe," Miss Lorentzon said. "Look at the bottom. No, hold on, the next page. There's Sugihara, the new vice-consul in Kaunas. And farther down we have other long-distance guests. Ambassador Wang and his friends."

She turned the page and pointed to a group of Asians being presented to a man wearing an extraordinary quantity of medals and decorations, identified as Baron Stiernstedt. Under the photograph was a quotation from the Swedish baron: "What a cultured man Mr. Wang is, so well educated! The crown prince holds Chinese culture in the highest regard and is fascinated by its art treasures. The court is planning a trip to China next year."

"Yes," said Miss Lorentzon, "there was so much more conviviality here before the outbreak of war. Now the atmosphere surrounding our embassy is distrustful, as if Madame weren't doing all within her power to secure good relations between our nations and find ways out of the crisis in Finland."

"I'm sorry, but 'crisis' might no longer be the right word,"

Immanuel said, intending to add something about the progress of war. But this wasn't the appropriate place or time for discussing politics. He changed the topic. "The minister just uses the villa on the island during the summer, I suppose? A fantastic place, but maybe not very practical in the cold and snow."

"Funny that you should ask about the Kassman villa today," the secretary said. "It was confirmed yesterday that we'll take over the whole estate as our summer residence from the beginning of May. Last summer we had the villa on trial until early autumn, and Madame was extremely pleased. But despite Mr. Kassman's financial worries, he only wanted to make the villa available one season at a time. Now it's been settled, though, and we have access to the villa for at least three years, which, as Madame says, is an eternity in these troubles times."

Miss Lorentzon took the opportunity to tidy the pile of magazines while Immanuel continued to browse through the report on Red Army Day. There were some old faces from the cultural world too, the article declared: an anti-fascist and painter by the name of Grünewald, and the opera singer Pålson-Wettergren. Another picture of Euler-Chelpin with his enormous mustache and elegant wife. And one photograph after another of Karl Gerhard, the city's redoubtable King of Revue, known for his sarcasm and his vitriolic songs about current affairs.

Immanuel wanted to be certain not to forget Gerhard's name, and was taking out his pen and notebook when Miss Lorentzon, who was obviously still thinking about the summer residence, interrupted. "Madame and I had given up hope of the villa, and we tried out a small boardinghouse on Lidingö one weekend," she said, leaning slightly over the tea table right behind him. "Modest, nice enough. Otherwise, we've often moved out to Saltsjöbaden for the summer."

Immanuel had heard about the Grand Hotel in Salts-jöbaden, owned by the wealthy Wallenberg family, but he had never been there. It hadn't been an appropriate season for that kind of trip. He understood it to be a splendid spa hotel in the European style, with countless negotiations conducted in its sa-lons or in rooms hired by representatives of various embassies in the capital, not least the Finnish and Soviet.

Immanuel's family was not truly settled in the city. That morning his wife had remarked that there was a markedly de-serted feel about it, and that compared with Warsaw, Stock-holm was a cold place. That applied to the inhabitants, and also to the city itself. The people hadn't really managed to make the buildings their own or occupy the streets, Lucia thought. It was certainly beautifully situated, and the way in which the water weaved through the city everywhere was striking, yet many of its buildings were plain and rather dreary, especially in the part of the city where they lived; utilitarian, with no regard for aesthetic qualities.

It was different in the city center, where they had admired the many buildings in the art nouveau style—the Royal Theatre, naturally, but also a post office so imposing it was a match for any banking emporium or great theater. That morning, in the snow on Villagatan, Immanuel had been particularly struck by a row of entrances decorated with intricate trailing patterns from the animal and plant world that spread across the stuc-coed facades, twirled around the windows, and reappeared in the ornamental oriels and the curves of the balcony railings. Even if the art nouveau style was in general more restrained here than in more southerly parts of Europe, these features gave the city a melodic lightness. On their strolls together through the city, Immanuel and Lucia had marveled at the arched gables and windows on Drottninggatan. They regularly passed a bath-house too, whose ornamented facade and huge windows reminded them of the serpentine moldings around the pool at the bathhouse in Breslau, a place they had often visited when they were newly engaged.

Outside, the snow was falling more heavily. Miss Lorentzon disappeared elsewhere, and Immanuel immersed himself in another of the magazines, this one containing an article about his hostess. This was no photo reportage of embassy parties but a serious discussion about emancipation of the modern woman. Two quotations were highlighted in bold type. He spelled out the first to himself and was pleased he understood the Swedish: "The pregnant woman must remember that she no longer belongs to herself, she serves the collective, she produces from her own flesh and blood a new unit of labor, a new member of the labor republic." Madame Kollontai was photographed in the embassy, indeed by the very same window at which he was now sitting. She looked rather majestic in her fur coat. The second quotation was in even bolder typeface, giving it the appearance of a heading: "Marriage is a business deal of secondary importance for women in the new society. Everything must be rationalized, even our creches."

Immanuel had finished his tea, and was starting to feel a little impatient. After standing up to stretch his legs, he took a few steps toward the small room adjacent to the salon. The wide sliding doors were open, inviting him to walk in. On a round table, under an oval gilt frame containing an oil portrait of an aristocratic lady in evening dress with deep décolletage, stood a framed photograph beside a vase of white lilies. Immanuel leaned over the picture and saw to his surprise that it was a signed photograph of the British First Lord of the Admiralty,

Winston Churchill, who was hardly known as a devotee of the Bolsheviks. In recent days his name had appeared in all the newspapers. It was declared no longer to be a secret that the instant Chamberlain was judged definitively to have lost his mandate, Churchill would take over. Immanuel had commented on the rumor himself in a short item published in *Basler Nachrichten*. What this shift in power would mean for the Nordic countries was a question Albert Oeri had put to him in a telephone call only a week earlier. It was a question to which he needed to find the answer.

Through a half-open door he caught sight of a painting of Lenin reading a newspaper. He had just seen the same painting in one of the magazines. Its position was unusually high on the wall, in one of the few spaces not occupied by bookshelves. No great painting on purely artistic grounds, Immanuel was thinking when he heard a familiar voice behind him. Once heard, never forgotten. He turned to meet the gray eyes he remembered so well from their meeting on the island. It had been only a few months before, but it felt like a memory from a previous life. Madame Kollontai held out her hand, but began speaking before Immanuel could take it in his own.

"Your editor Oeri is criticizing in increasingly pointed terms our analysis of Nazism as a capitalist society in its last convulsions. It is alleged that we see current German politics as a transitory end stage preceding the socialist revolution. I am quoting the words: 'transitory end stage.' Where on earth did he get that from?"

In the look she gave him it was clear these words of reproval were seriously meant. But was she expecting an answer? After an uncomfortable pause she added, "Will you please inform Mr. Oeri that this has all been plucked from the air? He has fabricated these quotations. For they are intended to be read as quotations, are they not? A fatal misjudgment of the Nazi threat, he writes; but who has worded this, if not Mr. Oeri himself?"

Immanuel cleared his throat, embarrassed, but couldn't find an appropriate answer. As they sat down by the photograph of Churchill, Madame Kollontai must have noticed her guest's quizzical expression as he glanced in the direction of the First Lord of the Admiralty, for she picked up the portrait and looked at it for a few moments. Then she put it back next to the vase of lilies.

"A stylist," she said in a gentler voice. "A genuinely great stylist. I particularly admire his biography of Marlborough. I devoured each volume and couldn't wait for the next. I recently expressed my admiration in the presence of the head of the British mission, and in no time at all the signed photograph arrived with the kindest handwritten greeting. A civil tone is indeed possible even when political differences seem unbridgeable."

Miss Lorentzon had entered discreetly through the sliding doors. She moved silently across the room and lit a number of candles, spreading a warm and rather soothing light.

"The real reason for our meeting is, as you know, a different one," Kollontai continued as Miss Lorentzon returned, wheeling a trolley with a samovar and teacups, which she proceeded to place on the table. She then sat down in an armchair a few meters away.

"It concerns reports in the Swedish press about incidents in Lapland being presented in an unfavorable and ultimately unacceptable way," Kollontai went on. "It's obvious that *Aftonbladet* can spread whatever untruths it likes, as long as they are packaged in German-friendly jargon. This adventurer they referred to last week . . . I've forgotten his name—"

"Pantenburg," Miss Lorentzon said from her armchair. "Vitalis Pantenburg."

"Exactly. Not a name to retain. In fact not an individual to take note of in any regard. His book is bizarre and of no consequence whatsoever. But now it's been translated into Swedish, and one has to wonder at the entirely uncritical reviews printed in the Swedish press. Listen to this nonsense, these lies dressed up as pioneering prose that *Aftonbladet's* writers deem reasonable to disseminate to their readership here in the capital. Please read out what I've underlined, Emy." She passed a torn-out page to the secretary, who stood beside the trolley and read out a long piece, apparently a quotation from the new book. Kollontai's face was expressionless as she gazed across the room and let the secretary read without interruption.

"'Lying in the remotest part of the north by the distant Arctic Ocean, far from the incendiary flames stoking world politics, is a lesser known but by no means less dangerous political storm center. Like an underground fire it flares up, now here, now there. We read of spy planes and border incidents, of secret underwater craft and vessels of unknown nationality. But let us not for a second be duped by this shroud of mystery. There can be no doubt that all this activity has been instigated by the Third International, whose leadership rests in Moscow. Propagandists and activists are regularly caught in the northernmost provinces, Muscovite emissaries, sometimes officers of the Red Army in disguise.'"

She fell silent, and Immanuel wondered if he was meant to comment on this remarkable passage, written by the German polar explorer who had been staying at the Hotell Reisen at the same time as his own family. For some reason his travelogues had become popular in the whole of northern Europe, including Sweden.

Clearly Immanuel's friend Lagerberg had suggested him as a reasonable person with whom to have this conversation, as if he could give advice to a diplomatic authority of Kollontai's stature. Perhaps Lagerberg had seen it as an opportunity to contrive an unofficial audience for himself. But then little Madeleine, his adopted two-year-old daughter, had suffered another ear infection and been awake all night. It was the third time this winter, he had explained on the telephone. He wasn't worried, he had added, but he must take her back to the doctor, and maybe they would need another bottle of the drops he must try to force into her.

Anyway, strange though it was, Immanuel was now sitting with Madame Kollontai, discussing Swedish journalism and the impending Nazification of the Swedish press. The conversation soon strayed to the German press too.

"Is the process complete?" she asked, adding in a rather reproachful tone: "I can see no indication that the *Frankfurter Zeitung* is an exception, as is sometimes claimed. How do you see the press landscape, discounting for now Mr. Oeri's liberal view?"

He gave a brief account of his own situation, mentioning *De Telegraaf*, of course, as well as *Uusi Suomi* and *Dagens Nyheter*. He stressed that Pantenburg was in no way an authoritative voice in the German press—a popular travel writer perhaps, but completely without political influence. He couldn't explain why Pantenburg had been singled out by *Aftonbladet* and given so much Swedish publicity. He also agreed that the Swedish newspapers, with a few exceptions, liked to report on minor attacks, probably pure accidents, as if they were evidence of Soviet presence in Lapland.

For a few moments it seemed that there was a consensus in the room.

"An oversensitivity has developed, and it has to be traced back to German propaganda," Kollontai said. "As soon as any sign of alarm can be recorded in the country's northern regions, the press assumes we are behind it. As if it couldn't just as easily be a question of English or German interference. Or the Swedes who created the problem themselves, which is most likely."

It wasn't clear to Immanuel where this discussion was leading. He added something he had gleaned a few weeks earlier concerning *Dagens Nyheter*, which could scarcely be accused of excessive enthusiasm for German politics. "Do you know what they're saying about Tor Bonnier, the proprietor? I've only just heard this. The Oriental with the Old Norse name, that's what his Swedish employees call Mr. Bonnier nowadays."

They were interrupted by heavy footsteps and loud Russian voices from the next room. Two gentlemen appeared in the doorway so abruptly, they must have been close at hand. One was taller than the other by a head and had a vigorous and slightly untidy beard; the smaller one was bald, and wore spectacles with uncommonly thick frames. Immanuel jumped when their headlong entrance into the room intruded into the conversation, but his hostess didn't appear in the least surprised. She turned in her armchair to receive a document from the man in spectacles. He bowed reverently, his arm stretched to its limit. It took only a couple of seconds for her to register that the matter was urgent. She stood up and hurried out of the room.

Immanuel remained seated. He had seen the spectacles somewhere before. He could hear Kollontai speaking in the adjacent salon to the men, who he assumed must be members of the embassy staff, or possibly from the news agency TASS. He couldn't decide if she was annoyed or just upset by the matter, but the tone of the conversation suggested that feelings were running high.

It suddenly dawned on Immanuel where he was, and with whom. He had been drawn into the discussion and very nearly disclosed everything about his own situation. Of course it was true that the *Frankfurter Zeitung* was fully Nazified; almost all his colleagues had been replaced. He hadn't set foot on German soil for six years. He had left Warsaw, certainly, but for the most part to visit the Baltic countries in which a number of his friends from Breslau's Social Democratic circles had settled. They were in fact the people who had made it possible for him to leave Poland. Some of them were also Swedes, but basically it was von Scheliha at the German embassy who had been at the center of it all. He was living dangerously these days. The question was whether he should carry on with his covert activity. The risks were enormous.

Immanuel had been one of the first to concur with von Scheliha's proposals. Together with his brother, Gerhard, he had assisted in the creation of a network that, with considerable vigilance, managed to maintain its reporting unfettered by the propaganda of the national press. The articles were placed in provincial newspapers only, but nevertheless provided a space to breathe freely.

But it was obvious that because of his intimacy with Moscow-friendly elements, von Scheliha was teetering on the brink of the abyss. Perhaps he had already toppled. Perhaps he had taken Immanuel's brother with him. The press agency in Berlin appeared to have survived, but what did Kutzner, the editor who still seemed to be in business, want?

It was fortunate they had been interrupted, or he might have been tempted to reveal too much. What had Lagerberg said about him? Perhaps Kollontai already knew about Ilse Stübe, the young revolutionary, and the circle of Moscow loyalists around von Scheliha?

It was quiet again in the salon facing the street, and Immanuel moved across to the windows. He looked down to see three women in dark-colored coats hurrying along. The sight seemed familiar and he had the idea he had seen a painting somewhere depicting those very women. The snow was falling so slowly that some snowflakes seemed to possess the magical power to rise up toward the white sky, instead of circling downward to the blanket of snow covering the cobblestones in the street. These small white particles, seemingly weightless, flurried around the women's shoulders and heads. They landed on their navy-blue coats and on their comical headgear. Each was wearing a flat cotton cap held in place by a black velvet ribbon that ran along the edge and separated the smooth cloth above from a pointed end, which in all three cases was resting on a chignon. It gave them an air of gravity and discipline. Perhaps the severe hairstyle was part of the nurses' uniform; in any case the three women were practically identical.

Presumably Sophiahemmet was their destination in the swirling snow. Under their navy-blue coats they would undoubtedly be wearing blue skirts with aprons and white-collared blouses, as he had witnessed on his visit to the hospital. The matron had highlighted the symbolism of the headwear and the fact that the nurses had to sew those flat caps themselves as part of their diploma. Then she had examined Lucia with a thoroughness that had exhausted her.

With a heavy heart he recalled the conversation at Sophiahemmet. It had been Lagerberg, whose father-in-law was some kind of director of the entire hospital, who managed to arrange the examination without Lucia being officially registered as a patient. It would have been too complicated and expensive, his friend had said, without going into further detail about what it all would in fact have cost them. It had begun with the severe matron asking questions, while a young nurse made notes in a large white notebook very much resembling an artist's sketchbook. There had been talk of cardiovascular problems, of inadequate circulation, of every possible vascular disorder with a Latin name. A young doctor with thick glasses had been called. He had spoken fast in a Swedish Immanuel couldn't follow, repeated the word *homeostasis* several times, but directed all his questions to the matron rather than the patient herself. Unfortunately he had also said something about excess weight, which was repeated and translated into German.

Memories flooded his mind. In Żoliborz his wife had managed a household with a cook and nursemaid. Here in Stockholm she was on her own with all the shopping and cooking. No wonder she was worn out. He stood by the window, staring out at the snow, but his thoughts were elsewhere. Lucia had suffered a series of dizzy spells since they arrived in Stockholm, and in the last few weeks it had grown worse. She was barely able to get up in the morning without fearing for her balance. It was true, she had grown a little heavier, but the word *overweight* had been an unpleasant surprise. He could recollect her very first attack on the quay. It had genuinely given him a fright.

Startled by a movement behind him, he was woken from his trance by Miss Lorentzon. Guiltily she explained that, with regret, Madame was obliged to end the meeting. Unforeseen events had required her to leave the embassy at once.

Immanuel nodded and looked around for his things.

"Madame would also like to exchange a few words about Bermann Fischer's family, who still don't seem to have managed to get away," Miss Lorentzon said.

Immanuel was reluctant to revisit this issue, but naturally he listened politely to what she had to say while he put on his hat and coat.

"You understand, it's becoming urgent. The border to Japan will be closed very soon. Madame was distressed when she read the articles about the German boat forced to return from Cuba. Barriers are being erected everywhere. Did you read about that terrible misfortune? It must have been a nightmare to be aboard that fateful ship."

What was she getting at? Immanuel didn't know how he should react to her display of thoughtfulness. Was this really Madame Kollontai's thinking, or was it Miss Lorentzon's?

"Of course the question is whether you have entertained hopes for your own part. If you had similar plans for yourself and your family, you'll have to hurry. The only person who is still issuing Japanese transit visas is the vice-consul in Lithuania. Do you know our Japanese colleague in Kaunas?"

Immanuel shook his head. No, he didn't know him.

"As I said, you need to hurry." Miss Lorentzon gave him an impenetrable look as she held the door open for him.

SNOW CRYSTALS

The sky was bright blue, the snow dazzling white. Vitalis Pantenburg was very familiar with the area, not just with the Luleå peninsula. He enjoyed being out on Lulefjärden, and liked taking solitary walks to the sound between Kallaxheden and Sandön. It was astonishing that in summer boats could pass through the narrow sound. By sinking a vessel there, it would be possible to block the channel into the harbor, as he had explained in precise detail in one of his earliest reports.

To reach the city from the south necessitated taking the ferry across the Lule River from Gäddvik or Bergnäset. The various roads into the city merged into one, which together with the railway passed between the Mjölkudden hill and the cove at Skutviken—a vulnerable position with traffic routes exposed, he wrote in his notebook, important for defense of the city and especially suitable given the view the hill provided. When the sea was frozen, it was possible to walk across the narrow sound. He had documented all this meticulously. Some of the rolls of film had already been developed. As usual he had ordered the photographs geographically rather than chronologically.

Once again he had been given his favorite room at the Stadshotell. It had a ceiling four meters high and was opulent in the extreme, as indeed was the whole building. The carved decorations on the brick facade created a metropolitan feel seldom encountered so far north, though admittedly there were some interesting properties along Storgatan, such as the amusing tower house between the white palace of the Riksbank and the cathedral. Luleå was so small a city that its atmosphere was altered by a large party of engineers and businessmen staying at the hotel at the same time. They walked in groups along Storgatan before gathering en masse to inspect the cranes in the iron-ore port and the new radio mast on Mjölkudden. People were used to foreign visitors at the ore port, especially Germans and Englishmen. There were large commercial interests at stake, and it wasn't uncommon for hotel guests to be demanding.

It had been an intense week, with a stay in Stockholm before the journey continued north. A small group would continue to Kiruna and Narvik after the conference. Nothing wrong with that, Pantenburg thought, but now he had only five days left in Sweden, and he was looking forward to focusing entirely on his work out on the ice. He was thinking about that morning's excursion during the hours of strongest sunshine, when the light on the snow had been quite breathtaking.

The late lunch at the Stadshotell had been a merry affair, with not only Pantenburg, who a few days earlier had received the Swedish-German Society's medal of honor, but also a number of young researchers who had all joined the society's field trip to Norrland. Apparently Hans von Euler-Chelpin, Nobel laureate in chemistry and a leading figure at the university college in Stockholm, had initiated the prize. It was also he who had presented the medal during the grand ceremony in the dining room of the Hotell Reisen on Skeppsbron.

Now they were here again, all the young scholars he had already come across at the Stockholm lectures. Visits to the Reisen had become a tradition for him. After he had lectured on his polar expeditions he had been back twice, and even stayed for the suppers organized after the presentations. He had made worthwhile acquaintances, particularly in the diplomatic corps. Even the head of the mission himself, the somewhat pompous Prince of Wied, would usually attend and ask some polite questions of the young researchers.

That evening's arrangements at the Stadshotell in Luleå were intended as a finale. Pantenburg's address as polar photographer was scheduled after the main course. With the coffee he would then read a few pages from the new book that had made him famous not only in the German-speaking world but in the Nordic countries too, where he had spent many years, frequently traveling, often on foot, in the mountains and across the wide expanses of snow. The fact that his wife, Liselotte, often accompanied him and had a not insignificant role in his photographic work had made his stays in the Arctic Circle more than tolerable. But she wasn't with him on this trip. It involved political assignments in the service of their country that she wasn't party to, didn't even know about. And in this case the politics was associated with a purely commercial undertaking that, according to the professionals, needed the right man. There was no doubt that his already large readership looked up to him. A hero of our time—those were the words used in the very first meeting at the IG Farben headquarters in Frankfurt am Main, on the second floor of Hans Poelzig's elegant building. He had been astounded by the directors' enthusiasm and had immediately accepted their invitation to become the German camera industry's new poster child. There was the promise of a camera named after him, and the possibility of a smaller one called Liselotte.

But before the evening's festivities at the Stadshotell could begin, Pantenburg had a long-planned visit to make in the port. He had walked down to the water straight after the protracted lunch and was now looking at the barracks-like building from a distance. The warm rays of the afternoon sun shone on the yellow facade. Waiting on the upper floor was the young gentleman he had arranged to meet, perhaps already a little impatient. The door on the end of the barracks wasn't locked—it wasn't necessary in this city—so he simply entered and took the stairs up to the Iron Ore Line's technical office.

After knocking briskly on the gray door at the top of the staircase, he stepped into a large, bright room where a smartly dressed man was leaning over some maps.

"Come in," the man said, not very invitingly. "I've put together some material for you." In front of him were nine maps, all highly detailed. "They're from *Sweden's State Railways: Upper Norrland*. The book is twenty years old but not much has changed, even though the unloading facilities in both ports have obviously been modernized. I mean Luleå and Narvik."

He must have cut the nine pages out of the book with a scalpel. They lay in a neat row on a long desk under the window. There was a view out over the water past the last piece of track on the Iron Ore Line, extending down to the quay. Light streamed in through the large windowpanes. The man now straightening up the maps was the Iron Ore Line's most senior engineer, a youthful Swede with whom Pantenburg had made a nodding acquaintance at the German embassy on Hovslagargatan in

Stockholm. It was the head of mission, the Prince of Wied himself, who had introduced him as a thoroughly dependable Swedish National Socialist. Obliging and loyal, the prince had said.

The engineer had prepared an exhaustive presentation and began to speak in a way that reminded Pantenburg of a lecturer whose introductory courses in electronics he had followed in Hanover. The Swede indeed seemed to be addressing an audience in an auditorium.

"The Iron Ore Line came into existence, as everyone knows, for the transport of iron ore from the mines. It was therefore obvious that opportunities had to be created for unloading onto ships. The English located their iron-ore port here on Svartön. The wagons were equipped with hatches on the bottom for emptying into the ship's cargo hold from an elevated position via chutes. You can imagine what the sound was like. There was a constant roar, like thunder. But since that time electronics have helped us modernize the process."

He pointed to a ruler on one of the maps. "The border point was located on the Swedish side. Katterjåkk is the name of the power station that supplied the energy for all the drilling required to make way for the marshaling yard. It has six tracks and a train shed almost a hundred meters long. A lot of rock had to be bored out to create a turntable that would withstand the harsh climate. It's dark and grim here in December, as I'm sure you're aware. It's already getting lighter now. The heavy steam engines rolling from the mines were the largest in Europe and required a large number of maintenance staff. The roundhouse in Riksgränsen held ten engines from the start. But now, of course, we have electric locomotives."

He suddenly looked slightly embarrassed. "But perhaps this

isn't of much interest to you? You spoke in your letter about delicate issues. I presume you mean places that are particularly sensitive that enemy craft would concentrate on in an attack."

Pantenburg didn't even manage to clear his throat before the port engineer picked up the ruler and struck it forcefully against the map on the far right. "The tunnels. You must have questions about the tunnels?"

"Pardon? I don't know anything about any tunnels," Pantenburg said. "Should I be interested in them?"

"Everybody asks about the tunnels. They're obviously weak points in the rail connection. Extremely weak. Everybody ought to ask about the tunnels."

Pantenburg wondered who the engineer considered "everybody" to be, but had no time to ask before he continued.

"Rickman was obsessed with the tunnels. Wanted to inspect every single one. He even tried to persuade some of our drivers to come to a stop inside the Nordals tunnel, which is half a kilometer long. On the Norwegian side there are more than twenty tunnels and passages through the ice. We call them snow galleries. Rickman wanted to investigate all this minutely, especially the Katterat tunnel. That's the longest. It's supplied with electricity from the power station down at the river in Hundalen."

"Rickman?"

"Yes, Rickman. Alfred Rickman."

Pantenburg clearly looked so quizzical that the engineer felt obliged to interrupt his presentation. "You don't know Rickman?"

"No, sorry. Should I?"

The engineer disappeared for a second behind a tall bookcase concealing a row of desks piled high with books. Pantenburg heard one of the piles fall over and some of the books clatter to the floor. The engineer swore, but instantly appeared with one book in his outstretched hand.

"It is truly regrettable that an Englishman gained access to all this material. My predecessor was a capable engineer, but unfortunately politically blind. I'm sorry to have to say this, but he must have been instrumental in Rickman's reconnaissance of rail access and the port's capacity. You're following in his footsteps, Mr. Pantenburg. In many respects he is the mirror image of you, or a twin. Your doppelgänger, one might say."

He handed him a linen-bound book. The author was Alfred Frederick Rickman, whose name was printed on the cover in smaller letters than the title. Pantenburg took the book, opened it, and flipped through at random. At first glance it appeared to be an ambitious piece of research, with chapters on the most important mines, railway connections, and port facilities. The report was amply illustrated with photographs of places Pantenburg immediately recognized. He placed the opened book on one of the tables by the window overlooking the port. It was the same view as the picture. The photograph must have been taken from the building they were in now. Perhaps Rickman had taken it from the very same office in which they were now holding this conversation.

The Swedish engineer's face was serious as he looked at the book. He sighed deeply. "Yes, my predecessor must have let Mr. Rickman enter our premises. I'm ashamed to think about it. It's unforgivable."

He was silent for a second or two and then said in a shrill voice "Heil Hitler!" and disappeared behind the bookcase. Returning a few moments later, he seemed to have decided, with forced equanimity, to cut to the chase. He said Rickman's book was basically sound and worth reading. He emphasized that he had never met the Englishman himself, just seen him from a distance in the dining room at the Stadshotell a few times, more than a year before. At that time he had held a more junior position in the office, but even then he found it lamentable that English visitors were received in such an unduly expansive way. He shook his head. The only consolation, he said, was that Rickman's book might be of some help. There were also quite a number of new facilities that were not mentioned in the Englishman's book. He pointed down at the rails running along the quay and explained what could be seen to the left of the stationary wagons on the track.

"In order to defrost the wagons, we've had a steam generator built in the upper marshaling yard. If you look more closely, you'll see the long pipes with outlets for hoses that are laid out along the track. Normal thawing time is three and a half hours for one train. Inside the steam generator there are large blowtorches driven by kerosene. They are deployed to heat the parts around the hatches. Then the sides of the wagons can be tapped clean. Lightly frozen ore can be shaken loose. The machines make a terrible din." He rolled the maps up and placed them in a cardboard tube that he handed to Pantenburg, along with Rickman's book.

It was time to return to the hotel. With a firm handshake Pantenburg thanked the engineer for their fruitful discussion and set off into the failing light, the cardboard tube under his arm.

Pantenburg's most important performance was ahead of him. His task during the meal was to sum up the week's events. No one was talking about it, but everyone knew that a serious conflict had arisen concerning attitudes to the Nobel Prize, which in recent years had sadly been used for distasteful shows of political chicanery. In consequence, three national prizes had been established in Berlin for art and science and found worthy recipients. The whole thing was in many ways unfortunate, and impeded the attempts by Euler-Chelpin and the Swedish-German Society to foster closer exchanges between the nations. There was no satisfaction in the prize having been awarded to three German scientists the previous autumn. Indeed it was seen by many as a provocation, and the Prince of Wied had been recalled to Berlin for talks. It was a sorry state of affairs. And it was all the fault of Carl von Ossietsky, the little traitor, who had retrospectively received the Nobel Peace Prize and thereby utterly destroyed the award's reputation in his homeland.

Should he make any comment on this situation in his speech? Pantenburg valued the Swedish-German circle. He was conscious that his own research was no match for that of the physicists, chemists, and biologists on the trip. His strength lay somewhere else entirely. And it was by no means trivial. It was quite clear that his presence at these gatherings aroused just as much enthusiasm as the scientists'. Yes, he could claim with some satisfaction that he was the one most of the dignitaries were drawn to on more festive occasions when the real socializing took place.

Walking briskly back to the Stadshotell in the increasing cold, he wondered how he could best allude to his respect for the other prizewinners. In their lectures at the Reisen most people had paid tribute to older scientists they regarded as a source of inspiration. The anatomist Gustaf Retzius was one of those whose name came up repeatedly. His article about the female mathematician Sonja Kovalevsky's superficially quite normal brain, weighing 1.385 kilograms, was illustrated with photographs showing the organ from different angles. These were projected as slides during a lecture on female intelligence, delivered by a young anatomist. His talk had caused much merriment among the men present.

"How is it possible that these 1.3 kilograms contained within a totally normal female cranium could produce a work as groundbreaking as *On the Motion of a Rigid Body about a Fixed Point*? I must confess that, as a scientific discipline, anatomy faces a challenge it has not yet mastered. Thank goodness our colleagues at the Karolinska Institute preserved this miracle, floating in alcohol in a glass jar. I propose that at our next meeting here in Stockholm we ask to inspect this female mystery!"

The applause had made it hard to hear what one of the young men in the front row wanted to add. "Maybe they've preserved other parts of this astounding woman's body?"

The mirth had known no bounds, and the audience had difficulty in focusing on the tribute to Helge von Koch that followed, despite the speaker, a young mathematician, projecting von Koch's famous snowflake onto a screen in the dining room. Just like the Russian Kovalevsky, von Koch was to be viewed as a disciple of Gösta Mittag-Leffler, president of the university college in Stockholm and a man perceived in these circles as the driving force in aligning Swedish and German seats of learning.

By the time Pantenburg reached the hotel, darkness had fallen. He entered the foyer, which was ablaze with lights, and sat down in one of the armchairs. Even if he hadn't followed the mathematical reasoning he was now trying to recall, he had tried to memorize the definition of the Koch curve, because he was intending to speak about snow himself and wanted to introduce a bit of mathematics into an otherwise rather prosaic presentation. He picked up his notebook and in a low whisper read out what he had written. He envisaged inserting this line as if en passant into one of his stories about snow.

"Take a line. Divide the line into three equal segments. Make a copy of the middle segment. Place both copies at an angle to each other such that the overall length of the line remains the same. Repeat from step two for all the new lines generated in each successive operation. And voilà, ladies and gentlemen, a snowflake!"

It had sounded so simple when the young mathematician was pointing at the screen in the hotel dining room in Stockholm, but now he could make little sense of his notes. He would like to have found an ingenious way of referring to Kovalevsky's brain, but couldn't come up with anything unforced and, above all, witty. All the more necessary to reference Professor Mittag-Leffler and the mathematical snowflake in his dinner speech, as a way of demonstrating that he belonged in the scientists' world.

Three Swedes in heavy woolen suits had sat down in the armchairs behind him for a conversation about something clearly preoccupying them. It concerned articles in the Communist newspaper *Norrskensflamman*, as far as he understood. His Swedish wasn't good enough to follow the loud debate. But it was clear they would soon be putting a stop to whatever was bothering them, a prospect that seemed to invigorate them even more.

He opted to continue his preparations in his own room, where he put away the tube of maps, placed Rickman's book on the shelf above the bed, and gathered his thoughts. He was, as the gentlemen of IG Farben liked to point out, the great connoisseur of never-ending snowfields and glacial arctic cold. And, most important of all, as they emphasized with force: he was the greatest patriot, ready to step forward when his country needed him.

He looked at himself in the mirror, tidied his hair, and strode resolutely out into the corridor with his script in an elegant case under his arm.

From the dining room on the lower floor he could hear a murmur of voices that grew louder as he descended the wide staircase. When he reached the ground floor and joined the throng of people, it was already time for them to take their places at the extravagantly laid tables. He found his name on a card at the top table, on the platform from which everyone was now being welcomed to the gala dinner. One of the young men from Agfacolor Neu, the same man who had spoken a few days earlier at the Reisen, was the first to speak. After a few humorous remarks about the modest days when the Corporation for Aniline Production from little Rummelsburg was trying to establish itself in the market, he moved on to a flattering summary of IG Farben's significance for the advance of photographic technology.

As expected, Pantenburg was surrounded by dignitaries from the IG Farben board. Everyone was now seated, and his gaze traveled freely across the large room. It was full of men in suits or uniforms. But his eye fixed on the ceiling roses. The stucco in the function room was magnificent, quite spectacular for these latitudes. The hexagonal rosettes reminded him of the snow crystals he had studied exhaustively and of his attempts to photograph them through a new magnifying lens.

He found it difficult to concentrate on the long-winded courtesies, but was looking forward to presenting his own thoughts, which would undoubtedly impress the audience, especially the delegation from Agfa. He wanted to get it over with. He had nothing against a good dinner with fellow countrymen and could by all means enjoy the odd glass in the stylish bar. But when all was said and done, this was about creating interest in the new camera. The directors of the Agfa division developing the little camera were here in force, with not only the whole team from Lichtenburg but also that from the new factory in Munich.

"The ore port is the city's main attraction. The ice in winter naturally stops all the shipping, but the ore trains carry on, the ore being stored on Svartön."

Someone else was speaking now, clearly the German consul in Luleå. It was evidently his task to introduce Pantenburg, since he was launching into the subject of the evening and quoting long paragraphs from the latter's latest travelogues. It was only just possible to catch his polite words about the chemical industry's achievements in Germany amid the inattention in the room. There was hubbub from tables nearer the reception area, and a group of officers drank a noisy toast just as Pantenburg was introduced and approached the rostrum.

He looked out at the assembled group, put his script in order, and pushed his long forelock back in the characteristic way familiar to all from portraits in the newspapers.

"Let us begin with the basics," he said in a forceful voice to engage attention.

When the noise didn't abate, he cleared his throat loudly, and two gentlemen on the same table helped by tapping their wineglasses with the small silver knives they would be using for the cheese.

"The basics, then. I'll begin with a question. Why is snow white and not transparent?"

It was still not quiet in the dining room. Some of the

gentlemen from Agfa had already consumed several glasses of wine and were involved in conversations they seemed unwilling to interrupt. Eventually, however, Pantenburg gained the attention he was accustomed to when speaking in public. He took a breath, allowed the silence to settle, and then began.

"Snowflakes form when the temperature in a cloud goes down sufficiently far below zero. That you know. The condensing water vapor in the cloud freezes, and small ice crystals are created. Because of the composition of water molecules, the crystals form hexagonal prisms. What we call snowflakes are created by the crystals being repeated successively in clusters of increasingly complex formation. The final appearance of the snowflake depends largely on the temperature of the air and the degree of humidity. The snowflakes' unique shapes mean that, in contrast to water droplets and ice, they reflect almost all the light."

Pantenburg fell silent and picked up the glass of water the waiter had discreetly placed in front of him, raising it slowly to his lips. He let the ensuing hush descend before taking a sip and holding the glass up to the stuccoed ceiling, as if this were the very water of which he had been speaking.

"That is why, gentlemen, snowflakes appear to be white and not transparent. Well, that was it. Shall we return to this splendid meal?"

The somewhat inebriated engineers and their colleagues from Zeiss laughed loudly. A spontaneous toast was proposed. But soon interested silence descended again, and Pantenburg could continue. He combined impressions from the barren wastes with remarks of a more technical nature, in particular his attempt to capture photographically the ice mass and all the luminous phenomena he had previously described meticulously in articles for the Nordic Society and the Norwegian publication *Ragnarok*.

No one could be totally sure whether it was Pantenburg's connections with the political elite that had conferred his status, or whether it was his reportage that had generated the grandees' enthusiasm. But the fact that Wilhelm Canaris himself, chief of the German military intelligence service, had attended the supper in Stockholm with his wirehaired dachshund and his extensive entourage had not escaped those in the know. The strength of the diplomatic and military presence on this excursion to the north was also a clear indication that great hopes were placed in this towering and in every way impressive explorer. That even a group from Zeiss Ikon had accepted the somewhat unusual invitation to participate in a conference organized by a main competitor was yet another sign of the speaker's standing.

The new book carried obvious political force. It was a huge success, its author admired not just for his physical aura but also for the heroic language that made his lectures and articles unmistakable. It was clear that Pantenburg himself and everything he touched held a luster from which the camera industry as a whole might benefit. Zeiss Ikon had decided to exploit the opportunity, and an enthusiastic man in a polka-dot bow tie distributed the popular Baldur box camera, named after the youth leader Baldur von Schirach, as a gift to all the conference participants. A Baldur had now been placed next to every water glass.

After brief assessments of the various optics companies' new lenses and shutters, Pantenburg moved on to a short period for questions, all of which concerned snow crystals and the crystallization process itself. Many people joined in the discussion, and the clamor of voices made it impossible for the audience farther back to follow the arguments, which led to a degree of frustration.

After applause and some grandiloquent thanks, the by now red-faced German consul took the floor and proceeded to more topical issues. He was concerned about the number of Moscow-friendly collaborators who were regularly being caught, not least in Luleå, where the editorial staff of *Norrskensflamman* unfortunately attracted dubious followers. But as luck would have it, there was also a reliable newspaper in the city with a trustworthy team of editors who were taking a hard look at these Bolshevik interlopers.

The consul turned to a group of Swedish gentlemen sitting at the table at which his own place had been vacated, and where a stylish woman in a hat, by all accounts his wife, enthusiastically proposed a round of applause for the gentlemen in question. Pantenburg recognized them. They were the men in the foyer who had been complaining about *Norrskensflamman*.

"It's a disgrace," the consul said, "a disgrace that Bolshevism can flourish in this way in an otherwise civilized community of hardworking people."

He raised his glass to the whole gathering, turning this way and that, and burst into a toast for German-Swedish friendship, which could find no more brilliant representative than their speaker that evening. The noise in the room had reached such a level that barely anyone could hear what was being said. People started moving between the tables, and a number of eager individuals pushed forward toward Pantenburg. One man brazenly attempted to drown out the others with his question:

"What do you have to say about the bombs that fell on Kallaxön in January? It was an Ilyushin DB-3 plane flying into Piteå. It was said to be heading for Boden, but when it was over the Lule River, by the village of Avan, it changed course. What do you say, Mr. Pantenburg—is it reasonable to believe the change was caused by the severe snowstorm?"

Pantenburg knew about the incident and about the controversy it had sparked, but before he could gather his thoughts, two of the loyal editors from *Norrbottens-Kuriren*, the ones who had been sitting at the consul's table and enjoying the applause, elbowed their way to the front to deliver a special invitation to a small get-together after the meal at the home of the consul, a great friend of German culture, and of engineering and the technology industry especially.

Questions came from all directions. Two women came forward with copies of Pantenburg's book they wanted signed, something he managed to do despite being pushed from the side by another man somewhat the worse for wear.

With a broad smile he turned to the eager editors, shook their outstretched hands warmly, and promised to come to the consul's. "Of course I can't refuse a little *nachspiel* with those of like minds." He climbed onto the podium from which he had given his speech, tapped his water glass, and cleared his throat loudly. The din subsided.

"Gentlemen, friends, I wish I could answer all of your highly pertinent questions, so important in this time of unrest and pressure from the east. I hope that my closing remarks can shed some light not only on the event about which you have asked, the Russian bombs in January, but also on all the baffling patterns now occurring in the magnetic fields we move in here in the north."

In conclusion he was going to read selected paragraphs from *Russia's Grip on the North*, his most political book, which had generated a great deal of interest in Sweden too, not least for the dramatic photographs.

He held a slender volume in his left hand. Placing it in front of him with a theatrical gesture, and once again pushing his long forelock back, he opened the book and read in a slightly louder voice than during the lecture. True to form, he began with the book's grand finale about iron and granite. It always worked particularly well on official occasions.

"'The unifying chain of steel and granite has not yet been forged into a common defense front between Sweden and Finland through Åland. A vigilant sentry, Finland keeps lone watch. Sparse lines of patrol aircraft fly incessantly across the proud, wide northland, where so much virgin territory still awaits colonization. From behind their polished barrels, on granite rocks rising out of the Baltic Sea, keen-eyed artillerymen watch the gathering storm clouds in the east; deep in the dark forests and brown bogs of Finnish Karelia and in the barren arctic wastes, the trained eye of the watchful border guard penetrates the dense thickets on the other side of the blue-and-white posts that mark the sharp divide between two irreconcilable worlds. That their vigilance be not in vain, this cannot be a matter for Finland or the Nordic countries alone. It must concern all of us who, from the bottom of our hearts, believe in upholding Western cultural values.'"

He paused for dramatic effect, and spontaneous applause filled the room. He looked at the audience, who seemed to have decided on a display of unqualified enthusiasm. He continued with a passage about the militants and activists regularly being caught in the most northerly regions—Muscovite emissaries, sometimes officers of the Red Army in disguise, he read, and was interrupted by another passionate round of applause. Muscovite activists were what the gentlemen from the conservative newspaper wanted to hear about, that was clear. They nodded in approval. Now it was the delegates from Agfa who were demanding silence. Instead of reading from the book, Pantenburg elaborated upon the central idea that Russia "wanted to expand into the far north of Europe," a phrase he kept repeating.

When the book was published in its German original, he said, pushing his hair back again in another dramatic gesture, this effort to reach the North Atlantic had not escalated into war. At that time, little more than a year ago, it was still a matter of warning signs. Now, after the explosions at Mainila and all that followed, it was almost impossible not to accept the book's fundamental hypothesis. He carried on reading in a quieter voice.

"'If one thinks about the law that says that force lines radiating from a source of energy intensify where they meet the least resistance, then a superficial examination of the geopolitical force field in the far north leads to the conclusion that Russian foreign policy aiming for supremacy over the ocean must first be established here. The warning signs already emanating from this force field would appear to confirm my view.'" He added in a resounding, almost triumphant voice: "Yes, as I said, this is no longer a matter of warning signs, but of actual aggression. Of war."

Loud boos could be heard from the far end of the room. Some kind of altercation had broken out in the back rows, and a group of men were yelling at one another as they manhandled a man and a young woman out into a foyer situated behind the large doors, through which the entire company had entered a short while earlier. Violent shouting was heard, even though the doors had been closed immediately.

It was obviously a small group of troublemakers from the radical left-wing circles around the *Norrskensflamman* newspaper.

In the back rows, ten or more people had been drawn into the scuffle. The whole of that end of the function room was on the move, and hardly anyone noticed the consul's attempt to thank Pantenburg for his brilliant lecture. Instead everyone surged out into the foyer and to the bar facing the other wing of the hotel.

Pantenburg put his papers in order and placed them in his leather case. He was intending to make a short detour to his room, but in the foyer he was stopped again by a group of devoted ladies who surrounded him, wanting his autograph. His popularity among women had spread to Sweden too, as had been apparent in Stockholm. He managed to escape their grasp but found himself instead at the consul's mercy. The consul shepherded him to the side, saying in a thick voice that his true admirers were waiting in the bar.

Pantenburg had very little choice but to be dragged along and to force his way into the crammed bar. Next to the high windows were a number of marble tables in a row. The *Norbottens-Kuriren* editors were sitting here with some of the Swedish scientists. A slim waiter in a white jacket with a double row of gold buttons was energetically attending to them.

The consul, visibly proud to be able to deliver the evening's main attraction, pushed Pantenburg ahead of him. They were met with words of unadulterated praise and hearty backslapping. But a heated debate was going on at the tables. A dispute had arisen over an editorial in that day's newspaper and was about to degenerate into a row.

"He expresses himself far too cautiously on the Jews. Listen to this." It was the third of the gentlemen from the foyer, who was waving a newspaper in the air, which he quoted in a loud voice and with exaggerated deliberation: "'It is certainly correct that outward character can influence a nation's temperament, but at the same time we know that it is primarily other factors that constitute what we call a people. The stuff of genetics, race.'" A young man in a tuxedo, his countenance confident, replied, "But that's right, isn't it? It's a good thing it's so clearly stated."

"Well, I think it can be stated much more clearly. And I believe it's all the more important to say what we all know. What we all feel," the man with the newspaper said.

The noise in the bar didn't die down entirely, but the buzz of voices and the clinking of bottles and glasses subsided appreciably, as if everyone suddenly realized important matters were being discussed. After a moment's silence the man in the tuxedo exclaimed, "Jews stink. Their body odor makes you feel sick. Just thinking about it makes me retch."

A murmur of glee permeated the bar. Some of the men over by the elegantly curved counter proposed a toast. Amused laughter came from the back.

"They stink! Aha! Finally someone tells it like it is. Have you smelled Professor Katz, for example? His breath induces a gag reflex in those fine students who reluctantly sit in the front row of the lecture hall."

The laughter swelled.

"That's right. I totally agree."

It was a short man with gold-rimmed spectacles who had spoken. He wiped the beads of perspiration from his shiny brow with a white handkerchief and waved around a small pamphlet disputing the appointment of the psychologist Katz as a professor at the university college in Stockholm.

"Our arsenal of scientific concepts can certainly help us to unravel complex issues. But sometimes we have to speak plainly. The stink of Jews is what I smell. In politics and in universities.

The fact is, in some of the country's editorial offices it's no longer possible to breathe. We also have to consider that from the world of these Jew-friendly gentlemen, the step to total Jewish dominion is not a large one."

No one noticed Pantenburg slip out into the foyer. He mounted the wide staircase and returned to his room, where the book was waiting for him. His English wasn't perfect, but he had soon made his way through the first chapter.

LETTER TO GERMANY

The black flowers were contorting in his dream. He jolted awake and looked anxiously around the room. Needless to say, there lay his wife, her face turned toward him. She had suffered a series of attacks in the last few days, but now she was in a deep sleep, breathing peacefully. He was relieved she was on the mend. Nothing gave him such a sense of calm as the sight of her gentle features in the dark.

Lucia's collapse had happened on the quay only an hour after they had arrived in Stockholm. The boys had raced up to Gamla Stan to explore the lanes that led to Skeppsbron and, thank goodness, didn't see it happen. The family's suitcases were already waiting for them in the foyer of the Hotell Reisen. But a large sack containing some of their bulkier possessions had been transported across the Baltic Sea in a hold two levels below the passenger deck. A crane lifted out one packing crate after another, turning back and forth in a way the boys found funny. They swung in the air for a moment before landing almost soundlessly on the quayside. It had to be the turn of their sack soon.

It was a sunny morning. The gulls noisily circled the ship's funnels, and Skeppsbron was full of life in the glow of autumn sunshine. The boys were tired of waiting and had disappeared, but Immanuel and Lucia were still standing by the water when their heavy sack eventually appeared. It was lifted high in the sky, swayed to and fro when the crane swiveled to the quay, and was lowered slowly toward the ground. But before it was half-way down, calamity struck. For some reason the sack came off the hook. It fell several meters and landed on the cobblestones with a dull thud. A thick cloud of dust rose as it hit the ground. Before he had time to register that his typewriter and various other vital possessions were now probably in pieces, Immanuel had worse things to think about. At his side his wife lay unconscious on the cobblestones. Gently and without a sound, she had collapsed. He fell to his knees beside her. For a brief second he believed she had stopped breathing.

A few hours later she was lying in bed in the hotel room with a cup of tea on the bedside table and a woolen blanket over her legs. The color had slowly returned to her cheeks.

Since that time much had been sorted out. They lived a quiet life. There continued to be things of concern, of course. But where did these mad dreams come from, night after night, making him feel as though the end of the world was nigh? Darkness shrouded his thoughts for hours after he woke. If truth be told, they never properly lost their hold over him, and as soon as he fell asleep they reappeared with images full of foreboding. Like a portent, the black discs atop the lofty sunflowers, twisting as if in agony next to Madame Kollontai's terrace, had obtruded into his mind and brought such unease that, barely awake, he sat up in bed. After resting his bare feet on the cold parquet floor, he stood up. As he passed the half-open door he felt a draft from the kitchen. The boys were asleep in their room, the door ajar. It was just before six in the morning, and there was no hint of daylight.

Immanuel went into the study and sat down in the shabby armchair. He leaned toward the bureau, in the top compartment of which he had hidden the fountain pen and the glass bottle of pale greenish-yellow fluid. On the label someone had written the letter *T* by hand, very clearly. Was it Horst who had inscribed this single letter to remind himself what the bottle contained, or was it Kutzner, the editor in Berlin? The pen, which had provided the boys with a great deal of fun, was right at the back of the drawer where it couldn't be seen.

But Immanuel's fingers soon found it in the dark, and now it lay on the table in front of him. He switched on the lamp, whose oval shade created a sharp cone-shaped beam, despite the bulb's dimness, and examined the pen in the subdued light. The top and the bottom parts were shiny and black, but they were separated by a gold band featuring the trade name Rotring and the specific logo of this modern writing implement, which could be filled with ink of different colors. When the pen was unscrewed, a transparent inner barrel was exposed that held the liquid. Immanuel lifted the transparent part up to the light, and the shadow that fell on the desk revealed that the pen was as good as empty. Gripping it gently, he emptied the reservoir. A thin trickle of water disappeared into the darkness, the last vestige of the boys' riotous game.

They hadn't touched the glass bottle with the greenish-yellow substance, for Immanuel had stowed it away as soon as he witnessed the boys' interest in the fountain pen's many delights. The fun had ended abruptly when his wife, who instinctively viewed the pen and glass bottle with misgiving, intervened. She tidied it all away with a comment about gladly throwing them out with the rubbish. She would prefer to forget the day they had entered the house, she said. Perhaps by now she had stopped worrying; it was two months since they had been consigned to the depths of the pigeonhole from which Immanuel's tentative hand had retrieved them this early morning. He unscrewed the lid and recalled Horst's words. Secret intelligence. An effective method of hiding the real contents of a letter from third parties. For a person in Immanuel's circumstances, it could have beneficial consequences. This he had stressed with an ingratiating smile. By performing painless services now, Immanuel could avoid unfortunate situations in the future. It certainly could do no harm at all to appear useful, and it would probably open doors that would otherwise be shut.

Immanuel had remained tight-lipped, but he knew well enough what was at stake. If he was deported from Sweden, he and his family had nowhere to go. A return to Germany was equivalent to a death sentence. He hadn't been granted a visa to England. No one knew what the future held, Horst had repeated several times, as if to fill the uncomfortable silence. It sounded as much a threat as a promise.

Immanuel examined the slender tube through which the pen was filled. He opened the glass bottle and lowered the ingenious device into the colored liquid, which was instantly drawn up. It was a pale, toxic green. The weight of the pen was different now, and it had a more balanced feel in his hand. To make space on the desk, he moved to one side the typewriter his wife used for typing up his articles. He lifted it a couple of centimeters above the surface of the desk and was amazed by its weight. He put it down with a thud. It was a Rheinmetall brand and belonged to the Weil family, who had been helpful enough to lend them two machines for which they no longer had a use. The second was a Mercedes Selecta and was on the top shelf of the bookcase. Lucia preferred the Rheinmetall machine, the same model she had used for many years in Breslau and then in Warsaw. How many articles had she typed up on that German machine? Hundreds. Maybe thousands. Unfortunately, the Weils' machine had a different keyboard, which led to a number of unforced errors.

He tried the pale ink on one of the white sheets of paper his wife used. Almost immediately the writing was invisible. When it dries, Horst had said, you don't see a thing. He stood up, still barefoot on the cold wooden floor. He took a few steps and carefully closed the door to the hall, even though his sons and wife were certain to be deeply asleep and unaware of anything happening in the study. He sat down again by the lamp and wrote his first lines with the green liquid. The words evaporated in an instant.

> After much effort, I have managed to identify local Secret Service representation. I came into contact with a Mr. Rickman, who has conducted a study of Swedish iron and written a book about it.

He paused for a second to check that there was no sign of dawn outside. The street was dimly lit by a streetlamp standing at the corner of Frejgatan and Norrtullsgatan. The windows opposite were all still pitch-black. He held the sheet of paper up to the table lamp. The liquid had evaporated and the writing had disappeared, as if by magic. He added a few more lines about Rickman, whom he intended to call Uncle Richard in future, and what he knew of his activity. Despite the moment's gravity, he felt a sense of satisfaction when he placed a full stop after the valediction: "Sincerely yours, Kant." What other choice of alias could there be for a man named Immanuel, born into the world in the city of Königsberg? Was it too obvious? No, no one who wasn't already aware of the information in Kutzner's possession would understand it. No one knew who the letter writer was. Staring out into the darkness, he allowed the letter to dry for a few more minutes.

He felt a strange apathy. The first signs of life could be seen on the other side of the street. Suddenly there were lights in a number of windows, even though it was Sunday and most people had the chance to sleep in. He took his usual fountain pen out of the desk drawer and wrote a short, innocuous message over the invisible text. Would it have been better to write this official letter first? Let it dry properly and last of all add the invisible lines? Perhaps the normal ink made the invisible writing difficult to read? How was he, of all people, supposed to know? He read through the letter. His hand. His words.

Dear Mr. Kutzner,

I am very happy with the "Tintenkuli" you sent with Horst. I am using it for the first time and hope that you will be pleased with its performance. Relations with my Uncle Richard, of whom you have heard reports, have not been very helpful to me so far, but it looks promising for the future. He is a very mistrustful man, and he has little gain to expect from any connection with me, but I hope to come into closer contact with his family and thereby win his trust. Although he does not yet have a command of the Swedish language, he has made himself quite at home here, and it is always interesting to observe such a man exercising his profession. He works in the commercial sector, as I understand it, and not with the official authorities, only private individuals, but he has had some beginner's luck. Of course the war is causing serious disruption.

Materially, I am not doing as well as I was at the beginning, and I have to waste a great deal of time on sidelines, only to get anywhere close to the right sources. Of course we suffer to some extent from the poor postal services; as well as disruption occasioned by the war, there are delays caused by the ice, etc. It will be interesting to see if this letter reaches you, for instance. What do you say about my possible transfer plans?

Sincerely yours,

Kant.

Immanuel folded the letter and put it into one of the light-gray envelopes he found in the desk drawer. He addressed it to Mr. E. Kutzner, PO Box 23, Berlin NW 40, Germany. For a second he wondered whether he ought to write "Kant" as sender on the back of the envelope, but decided not to. He had only one stamp left in the drawer, but that was all he needed that morning. The sweet taste of the adhesive stayed on his tongue. The letter was stamped and ready on the desk, and outside it was now light.

He put away the fountain pen and the glass bottle of green liquid. "To dare is to lose one's footing momentarily," he said under his breath as he slipped on his jacket. He donned his overcoat and hat and opened the front door. The smell of sour milk hit him as he entered the stairwell with the letter in his inner pocket. *Not to dare is to lose oneself.* He couldn't recall where he had read these lines recently, but by now he was on his way down the stairs.

Perhaps it was Kierkegaard? He went out through the main entrance and noted that Norrtullsgatan was already bustling.

He turned right and strode briskly in the direction of Odenplan, where the nearest postbox was. That was where he had
sent off all his articles over the last few months, to Amsterdam
and Basel and one or two to the press agency in Berlin, the ones
his wife was so concerned about.

Yes, it was definitely Kierkegaard, and the passage continued, if he remembered correctly, along the lines of reaching a
point, sooner or later, where the only solution was to choose—
and then one made the right choice. An article by Albert Oeri
in *Basler Nachrichten* had been introduced with the quotation.
He remembered it now.

The kiosk on Odenplan was already a hive of activity. A tram
stopped and set down a group of passengers. The stream of people seemed never-ending. When he crossed the track himself
to reach the other side of the square, it was a struggle for him
to avoid colliding with the throng of people on their way to the
church, where a morning service was due to start imminently.
The bells had started to ring as he entered the square.

He thought he glimpsed a familiar face, but the tram had
started moving and obscured his view. He was standing by the
postbox when he heard someone shout, and indeed, he had not
been mistaken; it was the earnest figure of Professor Katz approaching. He had his son, Theodor, with him, who looked
grown-up in his overcoat and dark hat. Immanuel was aware that
Professor Katz was being subjected to anti-Semitic attacks by
students as well as the press. He had already heard repeated stories about the torchlit procession and the hateful pamphlet that
claimed to be about Jews destroying Swedish culture, but which
was primarily an attack on Katz himself and his appointment
as professor at the university college in Stockholm. Immanuel's
sons had told him about conversations at school, in which some

of their classmates had laughed at their name and talked about Jews and all the outlandish things they were allegedly involved with. The words "Jewish bastard" had been used, something a number of the boys must have learned at home. At first Karl and Henrik had pretended they hadn't heard. Then they tried to laugh the whole thing off.

The Katz boy had attended the same school as Karl and Henrik, but was a few years older and had recently matriculated. It was clear that things weren't easy for him, with the persecution of his father and the burden of all the slander. Now they were standing in front of him, father and son. What were they doing out in the city so early in the morning? Immanuel didn't have a chance to ask them, for the professor addressed him immediately, handing him a small brochure he had taken out of his inner pocket. "This was what I referred to," he said tersely.

Immanuel inspected the slender publication and read the Swedish title: *The Scandalous Katz Appointment*. It was, according to the subtitle, a contribution to history of Swedish culture's Judaization.

"I hadn't read it myself when we last spoke, hadn't even seen it when all the articles started appearing. It's been cited favorably in *Aftonbladet*, and my colleagues sometimes mention it in a tone I don't know what to make of. Apparently Professor von Euler-Chelpin has read it." He fell silent, and his body rocked back and forth in a compulsive way. His eyes darted from side to side and then seemed to fix on a faraway point, as if all the time he was trying to read the clock on the other side of the square. "Of course you understand what this means. We can't stay in this country. That should be beyond doubt by now."

It was as if Professor Katz had totally forgotten that he had already related all this and had in fact written down his impressions in a chain letter of sorts that he had sent to his friends and acquaintances, including Immanuel and his wife. The attacks had begun two years previously, he wrote, but instead of petering out they had intensified, and young National Socialists could storm in at any time and disrupt his lectures. The worst attack, which was some time ago, he had described repeatedly. But the threat had not lessened.

Now Immanuel was regaled with the entire account in the letter again, more or less word for word. On the ill-fated afternoon it all came to a head, he had thought at first he would lock himself in his office on the third floor, Katz said, but instead he elected to escape from the university building. The angry yelling and jackboot-stamping eventually made it impossible for him to make himself understood, and all he could do was break off the lecture. He closed the book in front of him and hurried out of the lecture hall. Along a corridor on the ground floor he found a back door that opened onto Observatorielunden, the pretty little park lying behind the building, where there was a hill with a view of the city. He stepped out into the cold autumn air. He had left his books and notes on a table next to the lectern, and, dressed only in a jacket, he dashed up the leaf-covered footpath leading to the top. He kept turning to see if anyone was following him, but he had left the building so quickly, no one realized where he had gone. Only a few weeks earlier a bronze sculpture had been placed at the top of the hill, representing a powerful centaur rampant, ready to leap. The mythical creature's body was so taut, it appeared to be part of the bow arching between its outstretched hands.

Katz had often seen the bronze figure from below on Odengatan, and had marveled at its dramatic strength outlined against the sky. Now he stood on the terrace, its stone walls encircling the statue, and cautiously touched the cold metal.

Immanuel didn't want to interrupt, even though he knew exactly what was coming. He watched the professor's agonized face and gray temples, and he looked with some compassion at Theodor, standing patiently by his father's side, listening.

Katz carried on in an almost manic voice, and clearly, inwardly, he was still up on the hill. From there one had a view of the entire city, he said. He heard the sound of a brass band, and when he looked down over the municipal library, he was amazed to see that a procession had appeared on Odengatan. People were marching with torches and banners, and whenever the band paused, the crowd chanted slogans he couldn't catch. There were hundreds of young people, maybe up to a thousand, moving along toward Odenplan. There they stopped, brandishing their banners, soon filling the whole square. He didn't immediately realize that this torchlit procession was a protest against him personally, and against his appointment as a professor. But when it did dawn on him, he knew then that his days at this seat of learning were numbered.

But where could he and his family go?

Theodor kept twisting his head to look around, and gestured toward an approaching tram. It was obvious he couldn't listen to any more of this and wanted to move on. Perhaps they were on their way to friends, or had simply been out for an early walk and now were on their way back home to Karlaplan. The son pulled at his father's coat like a small boy.

"Where can we go?" Katz repeated in a serious voice that was neither despairing nor reproachful, but simply asking a sincere question. As if he really did want an answer. As if he wanted to find out if there was an alternative he hadn't yet thought of.

When he looked at Immanuel, his expression was pragmatic rather than melancholy. Then they had gone, without saying goodbye, swallowed up by a new stream of passengers descending from the tram, whose doors opened exactly at the spot where they had been standing.

Immanuel was left standing beside the postbox. The gray envelope remained inside his inner pocket. Under his coat he was still wearing his pajama jacket. Would he get home before the family stirred? Without posting the letter, he crossed the square.

THE SPANIARDS INN

L aurence Grand started speaking before he had even sat down at the large wooden table upstairs at the pub.

"We're not exactly the only ones to have located the Achilles' heel. Fritz Thyssen, the steel magnate who lives in exile, was abundantly clear in his advice to the French recently. It was more than just a hint. Block the transport of iron, and you'll force Hitler to capitulate. That was the big topic of conversation in Paris in the autumn. *Couper la route du fer*, he's reported to have said, in French. Funny that we should get tips from a man like him, but he's fallen out of favor. Cut off the supply of iron, gentlemen. Easier said than done, and that's why we're sitting here for the third time. Now we want to hear how it could possibly have gone so wrong so many times."

It was indeed the third time they had met, their second time at the Spaniards Inn, and Rickman could feel recriminations in the air. He had sensed it before he even entered the pub, on the steps outside, where he had met one of the two people in charge. And yet Grand was the more charitable of the pair. That chap Morton was worse. They had met upstairs on the last occasion too, to avoid any disturbance from the rowdy regulars drinking their cider in the conviviality of the bar on the ground floor.

Up here they were alone, with no one to bother them. It was here, almost six months previously, on this sizable wooden table, that Rickman had opened out the large map of Oxelösund. With a red pen he had marked all the relevant routes, both sea and land, and on a small side table he had placed photographs of all the significant mechanical equipment and buildings situated by the quay. There were pictures of the port's own icebreaker, the *Simson*, and the huge wagon tippler. All the surrounding tracks and the associated transporter wagons were well documented. A series of pictures showed the new crane with its transporter wagons, photographed from all angles, unfortunately out of focus. He had given a lengthy apology for the quality of the pictures, but soon moved on to a description of how the loaded trolley discharged its contents straight into the electrically driven wagon. It had been important for him to show exactly how this crane and the related transporter wagons could move the newly arrived ore to the yard or directly onto the boat, or from the yard to the boat. Laurence Grand had listened attentively and nodded approvingly.

That goodwill was now dashed, as Rickman could clearly sense when he sat down at the rustic table with his fiancée. It was the second time Elsa had been to this kind of meeting. Grand paid her scant attention but came straight to the point.

"So you set off on skis, you said? Had you parked the car in Nyköping?"

Grand sounded slightly impatient, as no sooner had the conversation started than it was immediately interrupted. A barmaid had come upstairs with drinks and managed to spill one of them onto the documents on the table when she was putting the first mug down. They had ordered three different ciders.

"A Porter's Perfection, a Morgan Sweet, and a Tremlett's Bitter."

The girl with the tray looked around, unsure where to put the other two, which were full to the brim. Before she could ask, Grand had taken the tray out of her hands and placed it farther down the table.

"Thank you. Thank you. This will do," he said crossly.

It didn't really matter that a little cider had spilled on the table, but it was yet another source of irritation for Grand, who wanted to shed some light on the whole mess before his superior arrived. It was obvious that, time after time, these amateurs were making mistakes that couldn't simply be explained away as bad luck.

Attack is the best form of defense, Rickman evidently thought, returning to the question of whether they had chosen the right kind of explosive. This complaint had been discussed exhaustively at each meeting, and Grand was well and truly sick of it, especially as Morton, who made the final decisions but still hadn't arrived, was utterly convinced that the debacle had nothing to do with explosives but was down to fundamental incompetence. Rickman picked up the thread again, however, and Grand let him carry on.

"Certain forms of dynamite perform badly in the cold, as we know. Nitroglycerin 'sweats' from the cardboard tube, so the stick of dynamite gets clammy. Confounded little crystals form, and they're slippery and make you lose your grip. Nitroglycerin on its own differs from all the stuff that's absorbent—ammonium nitrate, sawdust, and whatnot. If dynamite freezes and then thaws, it gets dangerous. It can go very wrong if you don't take it damned slowly."

While Rickman was speaking, Grand looked out the window at the trees on the heath, their bare branches outlined against the sky as if they were sketched in charcoal on a sheet of gray paper. He felt tired. It was already growing dark, and soon all that would be discernible from up here would be the lampposts illuminating the narrow thoroughfare between the pub and the old tollgate. Rickman continued his litany of explosives options, though he had utilized none. The operation had been aborted several times before it went that far. But he was concerned, because one chilly morning the other week the dynamite had frozen in the wooden box, even though it was insulated. It had been a cold winter, and the longer hours of spring light had brought no warmth. They had carried the box out of the warehouse on Näckströmsgatan and cautiously moved it to the warm cellar on Grevgatan to thaw. But this was dangerous, he wanted to point out, coming back to the matters they had already talked through many times.

"As you know, English dynamite is sold packed in round cylinders of paraffin paper of the same diameter as the boreholes they're normally used in. Every stick of dynamite weighs a hundred and twenty-five grams. That gets very heavy when you're talking large volumes. Then when the dynamite starts to sweat..."

Grand could listen to this no longer. He made a show of turning toward the window when Rickman started to repeat his mantra.

"Nitroglycerin sweats. The whole stick of dynamite gets clammy and difficult to handle because of the slippery crystals.

Thawed dynamite is rubbish. I say it again, we need TNT. Rods of TNT."

Rickman caught his breath. No, the mood was patently not the same.

They had seen each other twice before. Once in London, once in Stockholm. Rickman and his fiancée, Elsa Johansson, had nothing against a meeting in London, as they planned to settle somewhere in the north of the city after the wedding and needed to look around. And now they were back at the Spaniards Inn by Hampstead Heath. The pub was situated right next to the heath and only a short distance from the park surrounding Kenwood House. It was Grand from Section D who had suggested meeting here; quite why, no one knew. He always appeared from behind the building, as if he had walked through the wood at the north end of the heath from Jack Straw's Castle, the other popular pub in the Hampstead area. It wasn't difficult to travel out to Highgate and then walk along the northern boundary of the heath, through the park, and out of the large gate on Hampstead Lane. All the same, it was surprising that he hadn't chosen a more central meeting place. On the bend beside the pub the road was too narrow for cars to pass in both directions, and they had to slow down to avoid collision. From the secluded table on the first floor, one could look down on the cars meeting in the gap between the tollgate house and the pub, as if threading their way through the eye of a needle.

Last time, Major Desmond Morton had arrived later than the others, in an official car with a chauffeur, and this time appeared to be no different. They had already been speaking for almost an hour when a car stopped just beyond the tollgate to let out a man who then hurried across the street.

Sure enough, it was Morton.

As soon as Morton entered, it was clear that Sutton-Pratt, the military attaché in Stockholm, the one who had originally suggested Rickman for the job and who was obviously now sick and tired of all the shenanigans and excuses, had apprised the major of the group's latest fiasco. Morton's irritation was palpable. In short, they had tried to go as far as they could by car. But to be able to get out onto the ice, it was essential that everyone had the right equipment. In the morning, therefore, they had stopped in the small town of Nyköping to buy an extra pair of skis as well as boots and poles and other paraphernalia. There was a sports shop adjacent to the large hotel, and that was where they had selected the skis. Elsa Johansson, the only one who could converse with the young man in the shop, had become embroiled in a needlessly deep discussion over which ski wax was required for the ice. Was it not indiscreet to purchase this equipment so close to the site where the whole operation was going to take place, and to actually reveal that they were going out on the ice? Must that not be considered rather ill-advised? Yes, Rickman agreed, but he had laughed it off. And the episode with the skis was nothing compared to the disastrous excursion a few weeks previously, when they had driven into a ditch and had to call out a breakdown truck from Nyköping.

Mishaps, setbacks, sheer ineptitude, or, as Grand had expressed it in his first report to Morton, idiocy, pure and simple. This gang, whom Sutton-Pratt had engaged and to whom Grand himself on several occasions had lent his support, despite accounts indicating that they were clumsy and downright incompetent, would cast him in a very poor light if all the circumstances were put on paper. Even so, the height of stupidity had to be the affair with Biggs, the adman, who had been persuaded to join them on a few trips even though he had enough difficulty climbing only a couple of stairs with his wooden leg. The first time this was recounted, Grand couldn't believe his ears. He had laughed, thinking it was a joke, and that the adman moved *as if* he had a wooden leg. That he might have been stiff, or particularly ungainly.

That wasn't the case, however. They had taken along this lame chap, a British advertising manager with the Paul Urban Engström store, on a night excursion to the port in Oxelösund. "He hopped along on his wooden leg faster than the rest of us," Miss Johansson had said with a laugh.

The whole thing was a farce that must not get out; on that they were all agreed. These reports must not reach the higher echelons. But how should they proceed now? Was it best, once and for all, to declare Rickman and his group ill-suited? The fact that they had failed on their very first reconnaissance had emerged at the previous meeting. The atmosphere then had been quite different, and they had joked about how hilarious it was to end up in a ditch with all that camera equipment and all that plastic explosive. The breakdown people hadn't opened the boot containing the explosives, thank goodness, and Rickman had pretended to be alone in the car. Miss Johansson had hidden in the wood, with the rucksacks containing the maps and rolls of film. She had brought provisions for the road, so they didn't starve, despite the length of time it took for the tow truck to arrive.

Morton sat down at the table, in the same position as last time. On that occasion Rickman had just published his book about Swedish iron ore with Faber & Faber and could comment with authority on anything concerning transport distances, volumes, and port facilities at Narvik, Luleå, and Oxelösund. Eventually the conversation had focused on Oxelösund, the increasingly important port lying seventy-odd miles south of Stockholm, which had been transformed from a minor pilot station to a community of over three thousand inhabitants, all as a result of the traffic so central to German-Swedish relations. Rickman had wearied his taskmasters with an in-depth description of how a three-thousand-ton vessel could be fully loaded in eight hours, and that with a workforce of only seven men. Thanks to modern loading and unloading equipment, the labor force in the port had been reduced from six hundred to just over one hundred, he had explained, and he had even gone into the intricacies of how the mechanics of the cranes were designed. They had learned that the equipment, the largest of its kind in Europe, had been supplied by the Brown Hoisting Machinery Company and had already been in service for twenty years.

Rickman had located and documented the most vulnerable sites. Confident of success, he had guaranteed complete collapse if the explosive charges were placed in the precise positions he had identified and circled in red. They had drunk to it in cider and had in fact emptied so many mugs that their subsequent descent of the steep staircase felt a trifle unsteady.

But since then, one debacle had followed another. Rickman shifted the blame. It was bad luck, of course, and some of his colleagues had caused him trouble. In addition he was dissatisfied with the explosives he had collected from Sutton-Pratt.

At the Spaniards Inn Rickman was onto his third cider. Morton and Grand exchanged a knowing glance of resignation. They plainly had no alternative but to allow him one more chance, and for the last few days impatient questions had been coming from the very top. Besides, they had invested too much in this businessman. Had Rickman actually realized that his initial task, to map out all the important ore mines and port facilities in the country, was only the first step in the bigger plan now entrusted to him? Did he seriously believe that the Faber & Faber editors were really interested in his exposition and had intended to publish these tedious reports about port capacity and crane installations to delight their sophisticated readers? The same readers who had come to know the new publisher through the selected poems of W. H. Auden and T. S. Eliot and translations from French.

What Rickman had in fact considered to be his own role remained unclear. But what he thought was basically irrelevant. If there had been any other possibilities, they would most certainly have terminated his assignment. But no such options existed. Now, instead, Grand repeated the question about how the actual sabotage would happen. He preferred the technical questions; he left the politics to Morton.

"How will it happen, you're asking. Yes, how will it happen?"

Rickman might have been slightly drunk, or maybe he was just impatient and couldn't hide his excitement as he now unrolled a large sheet of paper. It came from a tube he must have concealed under the wooden bench fixed to the wall next to the window. He began with the mechanical details, which he reeled off at speed. He dashed back and forth around the table, pushing Miss Johansson out of the way at one point to find the right item on the drawing.

"Right. Listen to this. I'm talking about TNT rods. They'll cause maximum damage if we manage to fix them on the inside of the cranes' legs, preferably on the two legs that are resting on the quayside right next to the water. The whole structure will collapse and hopefully fall into the sea. The rods are activated by detonators. They must detonate at the same time, of course, otherwise there's a risk that the charge going off first will prevent the others ever being triggered. Do you follow me?"

He glanced briefly at Grand and Morton, but as neither of them reacted, he continued with his elaborate speech, which, given that it flowed like running water, he must have rehearsed in front of his fiancée.

"There is a solution! I can solve it with a pentyl fuse, a fuse wire that's actually a very elongated charge. The thing is, the whole wire catches fire and detonates instantly. Bang!"

Gesticulating more and more energetically, he didn't stop to ask the gentlemen from the Secret Service if they had any questions, but kept up his frenzied monologue.

"Now we get to the exciting part. We connect these clever little wires to all the detonators, thus creating a circle. As the last step in priming, we attach a powder fuse to one of the detonators. When it detonates and the heat spreads to the pentyl fuse, the whole damn thing explodes into a sea of fire. Everything in one go. Boom!"

The room was quiet. The sound of voices and clinking from downstairs could be heard, but Grand and Morton remained silent. Eventually Grand leaned forward over the drawing and asked: "And where will you be when this sea of fire makes the crane collapse?"

Rickman was relieved that the oppressive silence had been broken and saw the chance to rebuild some trust by dwelling further on the technical side.

"The powder fuse can have a burning time of ten minutes or more, but of course we'll be working with electric detonators and timers. They're called signal relays, and we'll set them for forty minutes, let's say. Or for twenty-four hours. When the cranes fall, we won't be in Nyköping any longer. We'll be in the office in Stockholm."

After a moment's silence that was broken only by Grand lighting one of his slim cigarettes and Rickman taking large gulps of cider to hide his nerves, Morton stood up, took a few steps toward the staircase, and leaned on the wooden banister.

"Good. That's what we'll do then. You'll receive the go-ahead via Sutton-Pratt within the next ten days."

Morton had never shown any interest in technical details and addressed only matters of principle when he did speak. The fact was, whatever he said almost always developed into some kind of political exposé that required a number of listeners. It was odd in more ways than one, Rickman thought. The level of noise in the Spaniards Inn had risen in a crescendo and smoke from the bar on the ground floor was so thick that even the air upstairs resembled a bank of fog like the one shrouding the trees on the heath outside. Morton spoke as if he had a large audience.

"The Germans produce just over twenty percent of their iron ore themselves; the rest is imported. French and Spanish ore is declining, as is ore from Canada and North Africa, for different but related reasons. Now have a closer look at the production from Grängesberg, recorded so meticulously in your report, Mr. Rickman. In recent years the Germans have bought nearly seventy percent, which actually corresponds to eight percent of the entire country's export of goods. Naturally we too have imported iron from Grängesberg, but that's a question of a modest ten percent. You understand where this is leading. If anyone asks what the Germans' Achilles' heel is, it's very easy to identify. Yes, gentlemen, Swedish iron. And that is what we're now going to bring to a stop."

The barmaid, who had reached the point on the stairs where her friendly face could be seen between the banister spindles, asked if the gentlemen would like another round of ciders, which Rickman affirmed with a nod. But Morton didn't seem to notice anything going on around him.

"The French talk about a *drôle de guerre*, a fake war, and I've heard the Poles too are amazed that real acts of war haven't spread. The phony war, they call it—I can't pronounce the Polish words. At their last meeting the entire British cabinet was discussing how the Swedes can be forced to nail their colors to the mast. Everyone's now agreed on the importance of the mining areas and the need to block transport not just from Narvik but from Luleå too. And when the port in Luleå freezes over, from Oxelösund as well."

Grand was leaning against the window frame, apparently deep in thought. Rickman and his wife-to-be did their utmost to follow the argument and were anxious to demonstrate that they were on top of it all, which was only partly true. It had been the same at their previous meetings. Morton's pontifications seemed to go on for an eternity.

"It's been clear to everyone, even to Foreign Minister Sandler and definitely to his successor, Mr. Günther, that we can put more pressure on the Swedes than the Germans can. Let's forget the transport of iron for the moment and look at the whole picture. For the last few years Swedish exports to England have constituted thirty-three percent. Compared with around fifteen percent to Germany and Austria combined. Nota bene: only fifteen percent combined! Then think about transatlantic trade, and how dependent on us the Swedes are for shipping crossing the Atlantic!"

Why Morton felt the need to analyze the world situation in

front of this little gathering remained unclear, but while his colleague from Section D calmly smoked his cigar, Rickman and
Elsa Johansson emptied their mugs of cider, and the racket from
downstairs persisted at the same deafening level, his survey of
the tensions in the north continued. Elsa Johansson, who was
passionate about the battle against the Nazis and could speak
at length about the fight for freedom, made one or two attempts
to chip in, but Morton would not be stopped.

"The traffic from Narvik can be halted, of course it can be
halted. But at what cost? You know about Operation Wilfred,
a very simple little thing our dear First Lord of the Admiralty
has planned. One single ship being sunk in the channel leading directly to the port. And in Luleå as well. But to boost
the effect, the ship's full of concrete. More or less impossible to recover. Not a bad idea of our good Churchill's, who
would personally prefer more heavyweight maneuvers. He
would have liked to widen the war to include Norway as well
as Sweden. The Swedes have to be forced in. They must be
compelled to join our side."

"I'm sorry, but can we be completely sure that the Swedes
won't choose the German side, if it comes to light that the sabotage is a British initiative?" Elsa Johansson had finally managed
to get a word in.

Morton carried on as if he hadn't heard her. Some words
about Sweden's new foreign minister and another quote from
the First Lord of the Admiralty.

"As I said, he doesn't give much for their so-called neutrality,
he's seen through that. When Oxelösund blows up, the Germans will give in."

Rickman and his fiancée had heard similar speeches from

Morton, and from Sutton-Pratt in Stockholm. And they read the newspapers, both the British and the Swedish. But Morton's endless elucidation was soon too convoluted and specific for them. It wasn't easy to figure out all the controversies that split the Supreme War Council into factions. The same was true of the differences of political opinion that tended to render these cabinet meetings so turbulent. Perhaps Morton believed himself to be an educator, but neither Rickman nor Elsa Johansson could distinguish properly between the various committees, and they couldn't remember the decision-makers' official titles. They were both aware of the rumors that Chamberlain was about to resign, but quite what that meant for their plans, they had no idea. Nor did they know where Lord Halifax stood on these matters. Of course they realized that Sandler, of whom there had been much talk at their first meetings, had been replaced as Sweden's foreign minister by a taciturn maverick by the name of Günther. Elsa Johansson in particular followed the developments in Swedish politics, but she had no chance of grasping Morton's European exposés, especially since they were interrupted periodically by patrons who peered inquiringly from the stairs to see if there was room up there, and by the good-natured barmaid.

"A Tremlett's Bitter, a Porter's Perfection, and a Morgan Sweet. Or did you say two Tremlett's Bitters? I forgot there were four of you up here."

"They're not in the least disagreeable, the foreign minister and Boheman, his right-hand man," Morton continued, as if nothing had happened. "The banker he associates with, he isn't unpleasant either. I mean Mr. Wallenberg."

"Two Tremlett's, then. I'll be back in a minute."

"All this is being talked about now, but Churchill had decided as far back as October. Operation Catherine won't be enough. The sabotage of Narvik won't be enough."

Some things had now been repeated so many times, Rickman and his fiancée could hardly avoid picking up the most important. Churchill, First Lord of the Admiralty, was the one most passionate about blocking the transport of iron. It was essential, using methods that were neither diplomatic nor military, the minister repeatedly stressed. The highest priority was to stop maritime traffic from Oxelösund, and, true to his impatient character, he insisted on the earliest possible action. He had emphasized the importance of Oxelösund back in October. And if they understood correctly, they had now been given the green light. That was all they needed to know.

"A Porter's Perfection, a Morgan Sweet, and a Tremlett's Bitter. No, actually, two Morgan Sweets. Did I get it wrong after all that?"

Four more mugs of cider were placed rather clumsily on the table while Morton reported on various meetings with Swedish representatives, one Björn Prytz, Sweden's minister in London, and state secretary Erik Boheman.

Rickman attempted to gather his thoughts. There were a number of things he had never understood, and now it was too late to ask. Was Morton working for a central body or directly for Section D, like Laurence Grand? It was evident that Grand, the engineer, led the work of the section. Yet Morton behaved like the superior, and Grand accepted it, nodding in agreement, sometimes being quiet and thoughtful, never objecting. Rickman recalled the previous meeting at the pub, when the mood had been relaxed and they had tasted and compared different kinds of cider. Tremlett's Bitter from Somerset had been the favorite. It was copper-colored and smooth as velvet.

Now a full mug of this same classic stood on the table before them, untouched. It was clear Grand was about to break up the party. No one wanted any more to drink, no one wanted to listen to any more arguments. Rickman mustered the strength to underline the importance of the correct explosive one last time.

"Nitroglycerin sweats through the cardboard sleeve. The sticks of dynamite get clammy and slippery," he said doggedly.

This was his overriding message, and a prerequisite for the success of the sabotage. It was absolutely crucial to fix the TNT rods to the cranes' legs. And large quantities of pentyl fuses were needed.

But he couldn't get another word in edgewise. Morton made one final grand pronouncement involving something Lord Halifax had recently stated. Grand slapped Rickman on the back with a little too much gusto, gave Miss Johansson a quick kiss on both cheeks, and disappeared down the stairs.

WAGNER EVENING

When Immanuel entered the lobby to the Bermann Fischer family's apartment in Gärdet, the entertainment had already begun. Loud piano music was pouring out of the sitting room. Resounding chords met him in the hall, where there was a throng of people around the door to the drawing room. An elderly woman took his heavy winter overcoat, crammed it into an already full cloakroom, and kindly told him, if he would like a drink, just to help himself. She pointed down a corridor that led to the softly lit kitchen.

Before he had gone more than a few steps, he caught sight of Tor Bonnier's cheerful face. Mr. Bonnier was wearing a jacket of a brighter material than his gray trousers, and his trademark bow tie with blue spots on a green background. He had a youthful, relaxed demeanor, despite the rather heavy eyelids, his age hard to determine, maybe over fifty. To his surprise he could see the publisher, who was Bermann Fischer's benefactor and co-owner of the publishing house on Stureplan, hurrying toward him. For a moment Immanuel thought there must be a misunderstanding.

With his right hand outstretched and in a tone that was quite effusive, Mr. Bonnier said, "Wonderful! I was just inquiring after you. I hoped you'd come this evening. I was asking our hosts a moment ago, and they promised you'd be here. Do you mind if we sit down in the kitchen for a while? It's too crowded in the drawing room anyway, and I have a few questions it occurred to me you might be able to answer."

He took Immanuel's arm in a companiable but firm way and ushered him along the narrow passage to the kitchen. There were some children playing on the floor in the semidarkness, and in a small side room he could glimpse teenagers perched in a window facing the street. He remembered Bermann Fischer saying that the whole family was welcome. Perhaps he should have brought Lucia and the two boys after all. But there were reasons for not doing that tonight, for this particular evening held other plans. Next time he would definitely bring them. At least they would be able to speak their own language.

As a young man, Mr. Bonnier had worked for Karl Franz Koehler, the bookseller in Leipzig, and his German was so faultless, only those who knew his extraction could hear a faint Scandinavian accent that could equally have been a touch of North German, or a personal idiosyncrasy. Whatever the reason, he spoke quickly and effortlessly about all manner of things. About the publishing house and the winter darkness that could easily make one pretty gloomy. What did his family think of their adopted city? Had they already settled in, his wife and sons? Perhaps they might enjoy spending time with the older Bonnier boys? They were a bit too old, of course, but Lukas hadn't taken the school-leaving exam yet, so there wasn't much difference. Anyway, he said, they should all be introduced to one another. It would be nice.

"And now I have a question relating to my wife, Tora. You haven't met Tora yet, regrettably. You'd get along. The thing is, she's managed to break into the world of film. And her new novel—*Mrs. Emma Smith's Diamond*, it's going to be called—is a tremendously exciting story that might work for an American readership, and why not for a film audience?"

It was difficult to know where he was leading, this publisher who had not only made Bermann Fischer's life in a new country possible but had also created the conditions for an entire exile culture, small but full of life, and with connections to writers spread the world over. Immanuel had been hoping to shake hands and at most perhaps exchange a few courtesies. Instead he found himself listening to these personal, maybe even private, reflections. Bonnier carried on talking about the boys in his new marriage, his sons Simon and Karl-Adam, the latter not yet of school age, and, with a troubled look, said he was asking himself how they would manage a journey of the kind he was now planning. How would this huge step affect such young people, who had scarcely been out of Sweden?

"Whether it's feasible to risk this massive leap in these increasingly dark times, that's what I want to talk to you about. Tora and the boys, they'd survive, of course. I heard about your efforts on behalf of our dear hosts. In some ways I regret their decision to leave us for America, to take the jump that Thomas Mann was so belligerent about in Dalarö last autumn. Mann took the plunge himself two years ago. But I understand, I completely understand. And now I think that maybe we ought to follow suit. It's not at all simple, not at all, but it's becoming imperative. Everyone can see it, and the pressure on me to sell the newspaper is getting harder to deal with."

It began to make sense. Gradually it dawned on Immanuel

what the conversation was about. Bermann Fischer, who had never expressed any gratitude for the relatively daring feat of the Soviet stamps in his passport, must have told him about the escapade. Perhaps in a way that exaggerated the extent of his contribution. It was possible Tor Bonnier believed that the German publisher family's planned emigration to North America was something Immanuel had arranged and facilitated. Perhaps he was living in the hope that Immanuel, who was himself essentially trapped in this, for him, foreign city, held a secret trump card.

Immanuel could now see Bermann Fischer approaching in the passage from the hall. He was gently pushing an elderly lady in front of him. Mr. Bonnier was standing with his back to them amid the rowdiness of the kitchen and carried on in a slightly overwrought voice.

"Good Lord! To my ear it sounds a bit like Jules Verne. From Bromma to Velikiye Luki. Then Moscow, Vladivostok, Yokohama. In heaven's name! A miracle that all the stamps and papers are in order. I'm told you even convinced our capricious madame at the Soviet embassy. If I may confide in you, I also have some support from the top—maybe you know that Günther is a friend of the family. He was a colleague on *Dagens Nyheter* for a long time, and will gladly help me, he says. He spelled it out: he'll help me with the bank transaction."

He was interrupted by Bermann Fischer, who squeezed in between them, eager to introduce his stately mother-in-law. Hedwig Fischer had recently joined the family in Stockholm. And this was the first time she had taken part in one of the musical evenings the family loved to arrange. Her late husband, Samuel Fischer, had started all the music-making and kept it alive for years in the villa on Erdener Strasse in Grunewald. Many a great pianist had performed there before an animated audience of mostly literati and artists, week after week, year after year.

Mrs. Fischer was no spring chicken, but she made an almost majestic impression in her full-length black dress, her hair up. She had finally managed to sell the villa but had lost virtually everything she owned. Paintings by Corinth, Liebermann, and the French Impressionists, the entire library, it had all gone. The only things she managed to save were a few pieces of furniture and the Bechstein grand piano. Thank heavens. It was the one now standing in the Stockholm drawing room and was used on evenings such as this. Happily, she had also brought all her personal correspondence with writers, family, and friends.

Unfortunately what she had left behind in Berlin, said her son-in-law only half in jest, was her previously excellent memory and her ability to recognize faces. It might therefore have been to avoid embarrassment that Bermann Fischer was herding his mother-in-law around among the guests himself and making sure unnecessary misunderstandings were averted.

"Where's Brecht?" she asked her son-in-law in an imperious voice. "If he really is in Stockholm, he should make himself known," she added, before Bermann Fischer had time to say that Brecht had sent his apologies.

Brecht, who lived only a short taxi ride away, had been very sorry he couldn't attend. He would have loved to listen to Fritz Busch, the conductor who had resigned in protest from his post as musical director in Dresden, and was to work at the opera in Stockholm for a season. With his son, a young director who had already been hired for Glyndebourne, Busch was now going to perform *Così fan tutti*. Busch was the guest of honor this evening and would also answer questions and talk about the musical program for the spring.

"You're not Mr. Brecht, by any chance?"

Hedwig had turned to Immanuel. With an apologetic glance in his direction, Bermann Fischer tried to set things straight. In a voice that betrayed no reproach but some degree of frustration, he explained once more to his mother-in-law that Brecht had sent his regrets, but there were lots of other interesting people he was eager to introduce her to, not least colleagues in the firm.

"Here we have Dr. B., the new editor I was telling you about earlier today, an excellent writer we all read in *Basler Nach-richten*, who'll most certainly be an outstanding replacement for our friend Zuckerkandl. He's only just started his new job, but already he's a highly esteemed colleague. And what's more, he has his family with him here in Stockholm, his very wise and beautiful wife, and his clever lads whom Gaby, Gisi, and An-nette already know. What are they called again, the boys?"

"Karl and Henrik."

"Of course, now I remember. Karl and Henrik. Clever boys, so smart in their new coats last time I saw them. They've learned Swedish in a few months, I heard from my girls."

Immanuel nodded and prepared to make polite conversa-tion with Mrs. Fischer. He was about to ask how the move from Berlin had gone, but the grand lady had already spotted other guests farther down the kitchen and marched toward them, in-tent on finding out if they happened to know where Mr. Brecht was. Neither Bermann Fischer nor his wife could understand what had awakened her new interest in this man of the theater, Brecht. It had begun at breakfast, he explained, when Brecht's name was mentioned for the first time. The dramatist and his wife, Helene Weigel, had left Denmark some time ago and were now living in a large wooden villa on Lidingö with their two teenage children.

Bermann Fischer hadn't published any of Brecht's plays, but he had made his acquaintance many years previously, through his colleague Peter Suhrkamp. He had recently invited him up to the office on Stureplan. It had been a warmhearted reunion, and despite the seriousness of the situation and the darkness of the Swedish winter outside, a lively conversation had ensued in the half-light of the office. Brecht had already decided to go to America. It was the only conceivable salvation, he said. If one wanted to survive and perhaps even continue writing, at any rate. He was still living in the hope that it would be possible to leave Europe by boat from Lisbon. Or maybe from Gothenburg direct to New York. He had looked askance when Bermann Fischer had revealed his by then advanced plans to escape Europe with his entire family by going east. That anyone would choose the rot of Moscow, Vladivostok, Yokohama, hadn't even crossed his mind.

Bermann Fischer laughed when he mentioned Brecht's skepticism.

"Are you serious?" Brecht had asked. He was stunned into silence lasting what must have seemed an eternity, staring out over the people hurrying across Stureplan in the cold. After a moment or two of staunchly holding his tongue, he burst out laughing and proceeded to utter the word Vladivostok at speed, in a pronunciation that was presumably supposed to sound Russian, but mainly sounded comical. This was followed by a torrent of puns and onomatopoeic constructions he obviously kept in reserve for any occasion that might demand the invention of something about traveling by train.

"Vladi, Vladi, Vostok, Vostok, Vostok. Aha! Such a pleasure to travel on a train that sounds like that, all the way across

Siberia. My little Stefan will love it. He's always adored railways, large and small, even the miniature variety."

Bermann Fischer had brightened up with this conversation and at that moment decided to get to know Brecht properly. For various reasons, that had never happened. Their similar situations might smooth the way to what had seemed impossible in Berlin. So it was a pity Brecht couldn't come. The only consolation, he told Immanuel, was that there were sure to be subjects that interested him more than the topic of the discussion here tonight. Which would be Fritz Busch's reluctance, never spoken but well known in inner circles, to perform Wagner's opera in Stockholm.

The music in the drawing room had come to an end, and to follow, after a brief interval, there would be a discussion interspersed with short musical intermezzos. A number of guests took this opportunity to stretch their legs. Some made their way to the kitchen in search of refreshments. Immanuel, who had given up the thought of a meaningful conversation with the hostess's mother, seized the chance to find a space in the drawing room, which wasn't very large. The ceiling was comparatively low in this modern building, and there was only room for a dozen chairs around the huge grand piano. Some of the audience had been standing behind the black instrument, leaning against the wall, and at once he saw Josephson, the librarian, who was politely listening to one of Zuckerkandl's expositions. These had a tendency to be lengthy. This one concerned the music critic Eduard Hanslick's significance as an arbiter of taste, and his waning relationship with Franz Liszt and Richard Wagner, whom he had hitherto much admired, which had culminated in a critical review of the first performance of *Lohengrin* in Vienna. The fact that Hanslick was later to emerge as a caricature of the small-minded Jew incapable of understanding German art was clearly something that interested Zuckerkandl so greatly, he could talk about it for hours. Josephson, who had a passionate but less intellectual affinity with the composers he happily revisited, listened patiently to the monologue, which had now reached Wagner's revenge.

"He certainly meant to retaliate in any way he could. You're familiar with Beckmesser, the fop in *Die Meistersinger*, the one who sings like a cantor in the synagogue. Wagner talks about a gurgling, yodeling, gabbling racket. It's the Jew's musical contortions he's talking about. It's as clear as day it's a portrait of Hanslick. Hans Lick he was called in the first draft, then Veit Hanslich, so there's no doubt who Wagner modeled his caricature on. All this is sure to come up as an example in our discussion this evening. There aren't any earlier examples of Jew-hating in music, as long as we stick to a certain level of music, at least. I'm eager to hear what our German colleague from the opera has to say about the matter. Everyone knows Busch is opposed to staging Wagner."

Immanuel had made his entrance to the drawing room without Zuckerkandl seeing him, but as he approached, Josephson caught his eye and looked decidedly relieved at the prospect of a welcome interruption to the harangue. He held out his hand and said in his usual affable way, "How nice to see you! I didn't see you arrive. Weren't they wonderful pieces they performed? And what volume!—almost deafening if you're standing here right next to it."

He was leaning against the gleaming grand piano, stroking it tenderly, as if it were a large, motionless animal.

Zuckerkandl, who fortunately had broken off and didn't seem inclined to continue his thread, turned enthusiastically to Immanuel, slapped him on the shoulder, and said, "But above all, this evening is about your father's achievement! About how Jewishness sounds."

Immanuel didn't know what to say.

"Sorry, what do you mean?" Josephson said.

"Exactly what I say. How does Jewishness sound, in the temple, in the ghetto? In the markets from Kiev and Warsaw to Paris? How do these notes resound within Christianity? And conversely, how do the strains of Haydn and Bach enter the great synagogues and Jewish homes all over Germany? In a nutshell, Germans and Jews in music. Their acoustic lives. This subject has long fascinated me, but I'm an amateur. No one knew more about it than Immanuel's father." Zuckerkandl laid a reverent hand on his colleague's shoulder. "Do you know about this, Josephson? This young man's father succeeded Zvi Hirsch Weintraub as the main cantor in the synagogue in Königsberg. He was the greatest expert on Jewish music after Salomon Sulzer, maybe greater. Both as historian and compiler. Just imagine if he'd been here this evening."

"Unfortunately my father's dead," Immanuel said tersely, feeling rather embarrassed about being thus drawn into a discussion on something he knew so little about, and which basically had never interested him. That his father's musical archive was now in a university on the other side of the Atlantic was not something that preoccupied him. But Zuckerkandl had brought it up on numerous occasions, and he ought to perhaps feel happiness and pride rather than the mild discomfort that beset him whenever he was expected to say something about his father's work. This time, however, he got away with it, as their hostess was tapping a wineglass and in a few kind words asked everyone to take their seats again.

Without warning, and before the murmur of voices had subsided, a powerful, glorious music burst from the grand piano, which seemed to be playing itself. Someone must have been sitting hidden behind the music stand all the time. Or this diminutive person had managed to hoist himself onto the stool behind the magnificent instrument without Immanuel noticing. Whatever the case, someone was now playing with a vigor so intense that the music filled the room, laying siege to the listeners' thoughts and minds.

As abruptly as it had begun, the music ended. The imposing figure of Fritz Busch was now sitting in front of the piano. Although Immanuel had never had the pleasure of meeting him, he knew of his import for continental music. But it was a different, younger man in a checked jacket and bow tie who spoke first.

"The Jew speaks the language of the place where he has lived from generation to generation, but he speaks it as a foreigner. Let me explain what this can mean for the musical situation today, and why it is in no way a pejorative characteristic, as everyone seems to think."

The well-groomed young man, obviously Swedish but with excellent German, was perched on a high stool next to the piano, his legs crossed. There was an open book on a music stand in front of him, and he was flicking impatiently through a bundle of papers on his knee. He spoke rapidly with barely a pause. It wasn't clear whether he was speaking freely from the heart, or possibly paraphrasing what was in the manuscripts he kept glancing at nervously.

"Virtuoso figures. A kaleidoscope. An ever-changing play of colors. But is Mendelssohn essentially void? Do his compositions lack deep intrinsic value? He is so interesting, always interesting, but does he go beyond the skilled entertainer's tricks and devices? Does his music ever touch soul and heart? Let us now hear a piece by this equilibrist. And I will return to the concept of soul and heart and what they can mean in a time of division."

He gave a signal to the invisible pianist. Josephson was sitting right at the front, next to the grand piano, and his eyes lit up. Immanuel now recalled that the librarian had spoken about concerts organized by the family in Gamla Stan. Of course, it must be Josephson's son who was sitting hidden behind the keyboard, producing these swelling notes. It was quite uncanny to experience a concert like this, without the pianist himself being visible. The boy must be uncommonly short, he thought. No one else in the drawing room appeared to find it strange, so Immanuel assumed the little musician had been introduced earlier, before he had climbed onto the piano stool in his hiding place.

It seemed the young man in the bow tie had prepared a kind of musical essay, with short illustrations performed by the musical wonder child. After one or two observations, the lecture was broken by a few minutes' piano playing, before the man anxiously cleared his throat and carried on.

"The Jewish musician reverses the styles and forms of all eras and all past masters, in favor of the most perplexing ragbag of chaos. Let us illustrate that now with a few passages from Meyerbeer's *Le prophète*, which according to Wagner displays all the weaknesses we're speaking of, and which in this case demonstrates that the composer is conscious of the deception. I quote: 'This composer has made it his life's work to maintain this deception.' And finally, the view that exemplifies the author's critical finesse and insight: 'In truth, Jews are far too astute not to know what has been happening with their music.' "

A wave of protest broke out in the drawing room, and for some time it was impossible to distinguish what anyone was saying.

"Finesse? Incredible!" shouted an elderly gentleman from the back. And other voices joined in a chorus of loud disapproval.

"Ladies and gentlemen, dear friends, we will all have the opportunity to discuss what has been raised here. Please be so kind as to calm yourselves. This is a musical lecture which is more deliberate than some of you might suppose."

Fritz Busch's rich voice was heard above all the others in the room and did indeed have a calming effect on the gathering. He, the great conductor, had the principal role this evening, not the young music critic, who seemed intent upon provoking the audience. The context to this evening was Busch's reluctance to perform pieces by Wagner at the opera house, where his plan for the season was to present a program consisting of Hindemith, Berg, and some local composers, notably Berwald, alongside *Così van tutti*. The Concert Society's committee had recently expressed a special wish to have some of the German guest's famed interpretations of Wagner as part of the new season's repertoire, if only some of the most loved overtures? But up to now this had led nowhere, giving rise to a certain irritation that was growing and had even reached the press.

Busch had only performed in Bayreuth once. That was many years ago, but his version of *Die Meistersinger* had made such an impression on this most particular of audiences that he was instantly regarded as worthy of note. Obviously during Busch's time in Dresden, Wagner had frequently formed part of the repertoire; his *Tannhäuser* was legendary. Entirely different, but still in the same class as William Furtwängler and Bruno Walter, everyone said. Considerably better than the young Austrian Herbert von Karajan. But here in Stockholm they were being denied all that. There was great disappointment, and people demanded an explanation. Was it a political stand?

"*Steigerung* is the excellent German word to best describe my way of reading Wagner." The young debater in the bright jacket had started speaking again. He was a pupil of Wilhelm Peterson-Berger, who was very influential in Stockholm, he worked for the Concert Society, and he was chairman of the committee of a new friends' association that was organizing conversations and lectures on the art of opera. Clearly he knew about the great German conductor's relationship to the composer and interpreted it as a reaction to Wagner's currently oft-cited anti-Semitism. Now it seemed he had decided to take the bull by the horns and resolve the issue from the inside. His tactic appeared to be to construe Wagner's most controversial statements such that they were turned into something positive. Not by dialectics, he stressed again and again, but by reinforcing and enhancing the concepts. Only by intensifying the arguments and by forcing Wagner out of himself, as it were, could his ideas about sensory catastrophes and stimuli be transformed into what must be perceived as positive attributes for a new era, an era that was most definitely not Wagner's and whose music he could not have imagined.

It was obvious from the first moment that his reasoning didn't convince the present small company, who had made up their minds to show even greater appreciation for the pianist's intermezzo. Applause filled the room after each interlude, even though the little pianist remained hidden behind his well-polished instrument. On the other hand, the audience showed an increasingly marked hostility toward the debater, who assiduously continued to develop his convoluted argument.

"Music that doesn't unsettle, that doesn't stimulate the senses, can no longer be viewed as relevant in an age when our senses are permanently overstimulated. And the music that succeeds best at stimulating is Jewish music. Wagner makes this oh so clear."

An angry murmur rippled through the drawing room. Somewhere at the back an elderly man was shaking his head vigorously and muttering something inaudible. Bermann Fischer looked quizzically at Fritz Busch, who had remained quiet so far. Would there be any reaction to this peculiar address? Immanuel could see Zuckerkandl, who basically loved any kind of polemic, preparing to launch himself into the discussion. He had some phrases scribbled down on a piece of paper in readiness. Now he stood up and waved the piece of paper in the air.

At that moment Immanuel felt someone gently nudge his left arm, which was resting on the back of the chair. When he turned, he discovered that Tor Bonnier had been sitting right behind him the entire time.

The publisher leaned toward him and whispered, "This isn't going to lead anywhere, I'm afraid. Why don't we have another drink in the kitchen while they sort this out? It was a very fruitful conversation we were having just now, I thought. Before we were interrupted by our host and his somewhat one-track-minded mother-in-law."

Immanuel nodded, but at the same time tried to imply that he would like to wait for a suitable moment to leave the drawing room without calling attention to himself. He was actually quite curious to see how the stern Fritz Busch would react to these tirades about Jewishness in music. They sounded horrendous to Immanuel, but the young critic clearly saw them as somehow useful in making sense of modern-day progressive music. If Immanuel stood up and left the room, it might be taken as some kind of signal.

The atmosphere in the room was tense. Would Busch enter into the argument, or would he choose a more conciliatory path and say that he simply preferred different composers now, and there were others more suitable than he to impart the enchanting light of *Das Rheingold* to these latitudes? It was something in that vein Busch had hinted when he presented the season's repertoire. Immanuel recalled Zuckerkandl explaining this, when he had indicated in the office what this evening's conversation would revolve around.

"A question. I have a question." There was no mistaking the voice. Only one person here spoke with such a strong Viennese accent. It was Zuckerkandl, of course, who couldn't stop himself and didn't intend to wait for what Busch had to say. He had taken a step forward toward the speaker, and with one hand on the grand piano and the other motioning wildly with the piece of paper, he began speaking in a way that suggested a lengthy comment was to be expected.

"I can guess where you're going with this. Let me quote from the text that forms the basis of your observations. Might one in fact see certain changes in direction concerning artistic catastrophes and sensory stimulus as positive characteristics of the music of our age, even though they were originally framed to be pejorative? It's possible, it's possible. But consider the discussion of pathology, of how, basically, the Jew harms music. I paraphrase."

Zuckerkandl was gaining momentum. He clearly intended to present what he had to say as if he were on a stage. Everyone acquainted with him in the drawing room knew the risk was high that his speech would be weighty in all respects. Bermann Fischer looked around anxiously, but all faces were turned expectantly to the young Austrian, who after all was known as a powerful speaker. His unruly hair had a life of its own, though he tried to keep the wildest curls in check by pushing them behind his ears. He cast a quick glance at the piece of paper in his left hand.

"As I said, I paraphrase, but I stay close to the wording in the medical metaphor that I believe more profoundly defines Wagner's ideas. He asks: How did the Jew become a musician at all? His answer is: through decay. Yes, decay."

Zuckerkandl paused for dramatic effect, and for a moment the drawing room was silent. Immanuel heard someone breathing heavily behind him and cautiously turned to look. It was the elderly gentleman sitting next to Tor Bonnier, who only a few minutes earlier had objected so loudly and who had now fallen asleep. The publisher's seat, however, was empty, and Immanuel saw him in the hall, gesturing insistently and repeatedly that they should carry on their conversation. He pointed in the direction of the kitchen and disappeared from view. Immanuel took the plunge, endeavoring not to make a sound as he carefully rose to his feet and made his way out into the hall. Behind him he heard Zuckerkandl resume, his dialect giving an impression of both playfulness and sarcasm.

"Let us listen to Wagner's diagnosis. Listen to this! Only when a body's inner death is manifest do outside elements take possession of it, but merely to destroy it. Then the flesh dissolves into a teeming diversity. At this point can anyone believe the body is still alive?"

Immanuel found Tor Bonnier in the kitchen with a cup of tea in his hand. He was standing by himself beside one of the windows, staring out into the darkness. When he heard Immanuel come in, he turned to him with a friendly gesture and suggested they sit down on a little bench behind the table, where all the drinks and snacks had been laid out. They were alone now; the staff had withdrawn and the children were playing quietly in a small room between the kitchen and the hall. There were so many children in the house, they couldn't possibly all belong to the host family. Now and then some of them looked out into the corridor, and it was as if Bonnier could read Immanuel's thoughts.

"Yes, isn't it lovely with all the children? We all help to take them in. There's been a steady flow of them arriving in Sweden since last summer. Without their parents, poor little things. My brothers and sisters and I join forces. We can't house an endless number ourselves. But thank heavens there are families with close ties to the Jewish community who are prepared to help. The Bermann Fischers have little Fritz Cohn, the girls' cousin, living here. He was the one with the tie and the horn-rimmed spectacles who was doing such a good job helping with the cloakroom. Did you see him? His parents haven't been given an entry permit. Who knows if Fritz will ever have his family here. Bermann Fischer had the sense to have the girls baptized by Pastor Niemöller in Wilmersdorf. That way they avoided the J-stamps. The pastor has made life easier for several Jewish children we know."

Immanuel hadn't noticed little Fritz in the cloakroom, but that was no doubt because he had arrived when the music program was in full flow. On the other hand, he did know a great deal about stamps and visas and entry permits. If he wasn't mistaken, this was the very subject into which the affable grand publisher wanted to delve more deeply. In the drawing room, thoughts had whirled through his already slightly addled brain. Had he heard correctly—were they intending to move the entire Albert Bonniers Förlag to the United States—or was it only Tor Bonnier who was wondering about moving with his immediate family to a part of the world where they could live at a safe distance from the German demand for Aryanization? Was he thinking of selling *Dagens Nyheter*?

Sure enough, Bonnier promptly came back to his main focus, the question of itineraries and the necessary consular preparations. Evidently Bermann Fischer had recently informed him of his precise travel plans, as yet undisclosed to anyone in the office on Stureplan. At the end of the month, or in April at the latest, the couple and their three daughters would be on their way eastward. First by plane, then train, and finally ship. A journey lasting three weeks. His mother-in-law and other members of the extended family would join them later, all being well by summer. But the publishing house in Stockholm would not be dissolved; the activity would continue. There were no plans to stay in California, where Thomas Mann had settled. New York was the destination.

Apparently Tor Bonnier was toying with the same thought. Perhaps it was his wife's fascination for the film world and her success as a screenwriter that had sown the seed. Anyway, their travel plans were solid enough for repeated pressure from the government to sell off *Dagens Nyheter* to strike home. Selling the newspaper was an opportunity, a possible avenue.

"You understand these aren't easy decisions," he said, with a serious expression that was at odds with the lighthearted amusement that had marked their conversation up to now, but was more consistent with his tired eyes. "You must keep this to yourself. I know Bermann Fischer has the utmost confidence in you and has already entrusted you with important matters. What I'm telling you now cannot be mentioned outside our little circle, but Günther has guaranteed ways to transfer the capital that will be freed up by the sale. To be honest, he's started to insist, and he brings it up every time he has a chance. Seemingly pressure has increased from the German side—we read statements like this every day."

He took a folded newspaper page from his inside pocket, opened it, pointed to one passage, and asked Immanuel to read the final sentence. Immanuel went through the Swedish word by word: "It is important to note that Jewish people are not desirable, whether it be as branch managers, commission agents, or directors of our German subsidiaries." Before Immanuel could grasp the context or even what newspaper it was from, the publisher folded the article up again and quickly slipped it back into his jacket pocket.

"We're going to experience blockades by the Germans. And not just with respect to companies owned by Jews. Any Jewish element in the staff will be enough. This is already in full swing. Günther keeps saying he wishes me and my family well. He's an old friend to us and wrote some fine reviews when he counted himself a writer. And you have to understand the challenge he faces. Our family is a thorn in the Germans' side, no doubt about it."

Only now did it dawn on Immanuel who Tor Bonnier was talking about. The Günther referred to wasn't a business acquaintance or a colleague in the publishing house, but Christian Günther, for several months now the foreign minister. This was remarkable. Shocking, in fact. Was the country's leading publisher, personal friend of the foreign minister and surely other members of the government, turning to Immanuel and asking for help? Help from him, an immigrant who was grateful for having just been given the most lowly employment and who was in a state of deep uncertainty about his own family's prospects? Bermann Fischer must have massively exaggerated his contribution; that was the only explanation he could think of. Or Tor Bonnier had got it all wrong and confused him with someone else entirely, someone who could broker diplomatic contacts not even Günther could offer. Christian Günther, the foreign minister with the characteristic rimless spectacles. This taciturn and, according to the press, reclusive Günther, who wanted to help should Tor Bonnier feel compelled to move the family's presumably significant fortune out of the country.

Clearly the new minister saw no opportunity to observe the same distance from the Germans as his predecessor had done. Immanuel had himself quoted the speech that Rickard Sandler had given to the students' union in Gothenburg. Günther would never make a speech like that; he was more cautious, many would say more tactical, in his moves. The directives from Berlin, often delivered by the German chamber of commerce, had also become harsher in tone. Immanuel had followed all this with interest, and he had already attempted to describe the altered mood in politics in a short article for *Basler Nachrichten*.

Old Mrs. Fischer appeared in the kitchen again, and she had Zuckerkandl's wife, Mimi, with her. Mrs. Fischer wished to be driven home to the villa in Grunewald. She wasn't always in this state of confusion; she had days of absolute lucidity too. But this evening she had taken it into her head that they were in the publishing house offices on Bülowstrasse in Schöneberg. The fact that she had left Berlin almost five months previously and now had her own home very close to the young family's apartment on Asrikegatan was neither here nor there. Mimi Zuckerkandl, who had translated the book about Marie Curie and was a close friend of the family, listened patiently, despite having good reason not to be in the best humor herself. She and her husband should have left for New York several weeks before, but everything was delayed and now they were nervous about their visas. Nevertheless, she chatted amiably with the elderly lady, who spent a long time expounding the villa's virtues. It had been architecturally designed by a friend of her husband's.

"An objective art nouveau style, no unnecessary flourishes or artistic trappings. In a word, no frivolity, but a considered and in some ways low-key form in which the people who occupy the rooms can express themselves."

Mimi Zuckerkandl remembered the villa in Grunewald well. It was a much publicized work by the architect Muthesius. She had visited it herself many years ago and recalled its charm. It wasn't at all strange that Mrs. Fischer dreamed of being back there. But of course the fact that she now wanted a taxi to take her home to the villa at once made the situation difficult to handle. Mrs. Zuckerkandl was hoping for rescue, preferably by the son-in-law.

"A taxi will be arriving very shortly," she said, to keep Mrs. Fischer happy. Mrs. Fischer was actually in excellent spirits and was recalling her friend Henry van de Velde's accolade after his first visit to the villa. The architect, he declared, had succeeded in embodying his hostess's hairstyle in the very conception of the house. It was a funny idea that appealed to her, and now she really did want to go home.

It had become crowded in the kitchen, and Tor Bonnier was now involved in another conversation. Immanuel seized the chance to slip out into the hall. He found his coat in the cloak-room and decided to sneak away before the evening ended and everyone said their farewells at the same time. The powerful music was still flowing from the drawing room when he opened the front door and stepped outside into the cold.

GRAND MAL

People had no reason to leave the comfort of their apartments for the darkness outside. Nighttime here was silent and deserted, as if the wide boulevard was uninhabited. Relatively little snow had fallen over the last few weeks, but there was frost on the ground. The earth under the leafless trees was frozen, and crunched beneath Immanuel's slippery soles. There were lights in some of the windows even though it was approaching midnight, so there must be people behind the grand facades. Farther down the road Immanuel saw an elderly gentleman in a hat walking his dog, but he soon disappeared. The peace was broken only by the occasional passing of a car. The headlights illuminated the trees when they turned the corner from Sturegatan and dazzled him. As the lights swept past, he could see the mist of his breath in the cold.

It was pitch-black on the other side of the avenue, where Stockholm's Olympic stadium was eerily dark, like an ancient fortress surrounded by forest. Even in daylight the brown brick construction spread an air of gloom.

He was searching for an address in one of the imposing

properties just ahead of him, diagonally opposite the somber arena. It was noticeable how much activity there was at this particular spot in the street; cars stopping, people getting out and hurrying through the door. He was so close he could see a chauffeur in uniform in an especially impressive official car drop off two men, who rushed across the pavement, their coats flapping. The car was stationary long enough for him to make out the oval sticker that all embassy vehicles carried. He tried in vain to distinguish the combination of letters.

Immanuel wasn't dressed for this type of nocturnal escapade. He had left the Bermann Fischers' musical evening without a plan, still not certain whether he should visit the address Rickman had given him. It was altogether absurd to follow the whims of a man he hardly knew. But now his family's future was at stake. Why Rickman had insisted on such a late meeting had been unclear from the start, and at the time it seemed more than a little strange. But he had been persistent, and kept repeating that it would pay to meet Mr. Fraser. It was evidently the same Mr. Fraser who had arranged for the whole Bermann Fischer family to obtain their visas for Great Britain in a matter of a few days. Now they wouldn't have any use for them, of course, but Immanuel had seen the passports and the stamps himself, when Miss Stern from the office collected them. Amid all the gravity, they had joked about there being no room for any more stamps and it was lucky they'd already got rid of the J-stamps, just on the grounds of space. Miss Stern's passport did have a red J-stamp, and she made a joke about trying to scratch it off.

Was it Fraser he had been introduced to that day at the Opera Bar, when he was offered his position at the publishing house and the Englishmen suddenly appeared? They had been a very merry lot, and Rickman had made toasts and speeches.

Immanuel could no longer recall what the man looked like, but it wasn't impossible that it was this same Fraser, a gentleman who could allegedly provide assistance when it really mattered.

The sky was black, and it was cold. Immanuel hadn't been capable of gathering his thoughts during the musical evening, but out here in the cold he could at least articulate the purpose of his late-night walk. It was, precisely as Horst had phrased it, in order to keep all doors open. Why close a door that was still ajar? His conversation with Professor Katz had touched on the wildest of escape plans, rather than actual possibilities. The boys must have heard of these plans, perhaps had spoken to the youngest Katz boy, for they were asking questions about Cuba and Shanghai as if they were already preparing for new adventures.

Shanghai? What an unlikely idea! The whole thing had begun as a vague rumor about a place to which anyone could go, where no one needed a visa. The city still had open borders. His colleagues in the office were talking about it, and the rumor spread like wildfire.

Now Immanuel was leaning against the cold facade in a way that made him almost invisible. Soon new cars appeared, sometimes picking up men in their thick winter coats and sometimes dropping them off. Sometimes they came alone, sometimes in groups. He was close enough to make out their faces.

Then the traffic came to a stop. Not a single car to be seen. A few isolated snowflakes floated weightlessly in the soft light around the lamppost on the pavement. He approached the steps cautiously and noted that the door was half open. Could he simply go in, or was there someone watching the entrance from the shadows of the vestibule? Just as he was summoning the courage to go inside, parts of the ground floor suddenly lit up. Now there was no return.

He walked up the few steps to the door, opened it, and found himself in a spacious foyer with more steps leading to a set of glass doors that swayed slowly backward and forward in the draft. He could hear the clatter of footsteps from the staircase, and two women in fur coats came toward him. They were engaged in animated conversation and passed without paying him the least attention. One pushed open the swing doors with a gesture that reminded him of a singer's flamboyant entrance onto a stage. A few brisk steps later and they opened the main door and went out into the street, where a car was waiting with its lights off. Immanuel hadn't heard it arrive. The door closed behind them, and all was quiet.

But he could hear the murmur of voices somewhere, maybe from an apartment upstairs. Soon it seemed as though the noise was filling the whole stairwell. He paused on the first floor, and the elevator passed him on its way down. There was a whiff of tobacco in the air. At first it was just a hint, but the higher he went, the stronger the smell became, as if he were nearing some kind of establishment or club. Perhaps a restaurant? They were to meet on the fifth floor, Rickman had said, and added that Immanuel didn't need to ask for him, because he would look out for him all evening and couldn't possibly miss him.

It now felt slightly alarming that Rickman had suggested they meet just before midnight in an apartment whose owner wasn't known to him. He sensed quite clearly that it would have been wiser to return to his sleeping family at home on Frejgatan after the evening at Bermann Fischer's, instead of setting off on a nocturnal sortie. The boys were sure to be asleep in their room facing the courtyard, and Lucia had probably gone to bed early. Her dizziness had been causing more problems lately. There was no doubt she needed to see a doctor, and they ought to take

Lagerberg's offer of another, more exhaustive examination at Sophiahemmet very seriously. The private hospital wasn't far from here, somewhere out there in the darkness near the stadium. He should have been devoting all his time to these crucial things, instead of wandering around at night.

Nonetheless, he now stepped resolutely over the threshold to the apartment on the fifth floor, where the door stood wide open and from which a welter of voices clamored.

He pulled a heavy curtain to one side. A naked woman with her hair down was sitting in a dark-blue velvet armchair, immersed in lively conversation with two young officers. They had both removed their jackets, but, judging by the stripe on their trousers, it was obvious that they were in uniform. With wide gestures the woman was expounding on something that appeared to be of moderate interest to the young men. Were they officers, or more likely chauffeurs? Their jerky movements and clumsy handling of glasses and cigarettes indicated that they were extremely drunk. The woman's long hair swung to and fro, and she kept leaning so far back the armchair tilted dangerously. Her hair brushed against Immanuel's left arm, in which he was holding the coat he had taken off on the stairs, a coat that was not nearly warm enough for the weather.

No one appeared to notice his presence. He moved around the apartment and noticed groups of men accompanied by women in varying modes of undress, sitting in sofas or armchairs, in rooms separated from each other only by velvet curtains that largely concealed what was happening inside. The smoke in the first of these individual little salons was so dense, it was like staring into a cloud. He rubbed his eyes and made his way deeper into the large apartment. Through the gap between two sliding doors he thought he could see a different room, and when he entered, he discovered a surprisingly spacious atelier. From a high window he saw the lampposts on Vallhallagatan.

The sky was as inky as the woodland surrounding the Olympic stadium on the opposite side of the boulevard. It was impossible to discern a dividing line, as if the wood and the sky were merged into one single state of blackness. It was quite possible this airy studio had once been a workplace for a sculptor or artist, but now it held a circular bar, from which gentle gramophone music was playing. A young man in a white shirt was serving behind the counter, and a number of gentlemen in pairs or small groups were deep in discussion. There were no women to be seen.

Immanuel leaned with his back against the bar. He really wasn't interested in having a drink. Should he take his leave of this dubious den as quickly as possible? At his side two gentlemen were speaking loudly in German.

"Pajala is the latest, and a few weeks before that, Kallaxheden. And just excuses. Luleå doesn't have any special significance, strategically, she says. A typical northern Swedish port for the export of sawn timber, the minister claims. Timber! Permit me to smile."

"Yes, who the dickens does she think she's fooling? But it might have been the airfield building at Kallaxheden that was the target, not necessarily the port."

Immanuel was close enough to hear every word. He soon realized the conversation was about the Soviet bombs that had recently fallen on locations in northern Sweden. Madame Kollontai had played the whole thing down in the press. Her press counselor had talked about a navigational error. Immanuel didn't want to appear nosy, but he remained where he was. The two respectably dressed Germans continued to exchange thoughts about current political events in irate tones. Were they journalists or possibly officials of some kind, perhaps at the German embassy?

A much younger man was standing farther round the bar, his back to Immanuel. As he was taking off his jacket, he turned, revealing his face for a second. Immanuel gave a start and was swept by a sense of unease, for he recognized the joyless features at once. It was the boatman who had ferried him out to the island. He didn't know why he found the young man's presence ominous, but he did.

The discussion at Immanuel's side moved on to other events in Norrland, and with some difficulty one of the Germans translated passages from a Swedish newspaper that he had opened on the counter. "'The deafening detonation occurred at about quarter past three. The effect was devastating. Occupants of the adjoining property were woken, rushed to their windows and could confirm that *Flamman*'s editorial office was ablaze. But even people several kilometers away attest to the ear-shattering explosion. Several neighbors say there was a smell of petrol. The severity of the blast was evidenced by broken glass found a long distance from the building.'"

It was referring to the attack on the Communist newspaper *Norrskensflamman*.

"What a hell of a bang that must have been."

"Yes, they got a louder wake-up call than expected."

The event had been condemned on the radio by the Swedish prime minister and keenly discussed in the press in the last few days. According to the article, the explosive charges had been primed in the basement where the rotary press was located. The editorial office on the ground floor was empty when the explosion occurred, but the five people on the floor above died instantly. Postmortems revealed so much soot in their lungs, it was clear they must have been killed by the fire itself.

The press had focused on the potential legal consequences when the guilty were caught. It was obviously a case of arson. There was no doubt it was politically motivated, and it wasn't surprising it had been picked up in the foreign press too.

"Amazing that the people on the top floor survived," the man with the newspaper said, holding it up to show a photograph of the blazing offices. He folded the newspaper and continued translating. "'Smoke and flames were billowing toward them, but they managed to get out even though all the fire escapes had been destroyed. Unbelievably, only one of them suffered light burns when the sheets they lowered themselves down on caught fire.'"

It was quiet for a moment, and both men lit cigarettes with a lighter handed to them by the obliging bartender. He glanced in Immanuel's direction, under the assumption he might like to order. The German who had been doing most of the listening pointed to the photograph.

"At least it's taught the Swedish Muscovites a proper lesson, as they deserve. They're disseminating rubbish to the public, all sheer allegation and deplorable scaremongering. That's what Wied says every time I see him. There's been talk of us needing to crack down, but now, thankfully, our Swedish friends appear to be taking care of the problem themselves."

"On the subject of the envoy, I wonder if it'll be Wied who greets the guests this evening. Maybe we'll see them all. I've seen Pantenburg before. There's a rumor Walter Schellenberg from the SS will show up. Some of his girls are working tonight. Obviously he'll lure a few of them back with him to Berlin."

Immanuel had also read about the attack against *Flamman*.

All those who had lost their lives were linked to the newspaper's editorial staff, apart from the two children, of course. But their mother had worked periodically as a proofreader. Speculation over who was behind the operation had naturally gathered pace. One trail pointed to Swedish National Socialists, another to *Flamman*'s competitor, *Norrbottens-Kiruren*. One of the conservative newspaper's editors had been taken in for questioning.

The two Germans carried on entertaining one another while they waited for someone to join them. Immanuel had moved slightly farther away, to avoid giving the impression he was interested in their conversation. He looked around the large room, feeling increasingly desperate. Why had Rickman arranged to meet in a bar like this, and full of Germans to boot?

Soft music was still coming from the gramophone, and he thought it might be sensible to order a drink after all, so that he didn't stand out from the other guests clustered in groups in the bar. A few meters away the bartender was speaking to the blond boatman, whose gloves were on the counter in front of him and who was leaning forward to say something Immanuel couldn't catch. On top of his shirt he was wearing a wide harness that formed a cross in the middle of his back, together with a holster only partly concealing a compact handgun. Immanuel had seen it once before, in the sunshine that morning out on the quay.

"It's a Walther P38, the nifty new pistol that was developed for the German Wehrmacht and is about to totally replace the Luger P08 as a service weapon."

The voice behind Immanuel was familiar. He hadn't seen anyone approach, but there was no need to turn around; he knew with complete certainty who had arrived. What was Ascher doing here at this hour of the night, in a smoky atelier full of people he had no wish to get to know better? Somehow it seemed pre-ordained that his rival should turn up.

"There are a lot of people here tonight. A grand visit is due," the journalist said, with no further explanation for his presence, as he took his place at the bar between Immanuel and the two men with the newspaper. He wasn't the type to ask if he was disturbing anyone, still less if his company was welcome. "A German scientific expedition has arranged its end-of-trip party in Stockholm. They have some political bigwigs as patrons, so it's hardly surprising we find the occasional armed guard here this evening." He nodded toward the young man with the pistol.

Ascher remained by Immanuel's side, evidently waiting for his colleague to comment. Immanuel chose to say nothing. He might have felt embarrassed to be found in a place like this in the middle of the night, a place no family man had any reasonable grounds to linger. But when it came to Ascher, it didn't matter.

Why had Immanuel always felt so suspicious of his colleague? He recalled articles about the Curia and about the political circles around the Holy See. It was no surprise that Ascher had exceptional contacts in the Vatican; he had been posted in Rome for several years and cultivated friendships. He had made the most of his time there and converted to Roman Catholicism, but to no avail: he still had a J-stamp in his German passport.

Without prompting, Ascher returned to a previous discussion concerning flight response in animals and man as a creature of escape. "Can one escape from oneself, you're wondering now, or in other words, evade the person life has made one? Run away from what one had learned to accept? When all means of escape are closed and every door confronted is impossible to open, then nothing remains but to flee within."

"Pardon?" Immanuel wasn't just tired of the conversation, he was now totally confused as well. It was time to withdraw. Clearly Rickman didn't intend to make an appearance with his obliging friend from the embassy. And Ascher was not someone he aimed to waste any more time on. He could no longer concentrate sufficiently to grasp what the man was angling for.

But Asher would not be deterred.

"The line of escape runs in two directions, one might say. But it isn't enough to be left at the starting point. No, here it's all about being inventive and finding another permutation, a way out into a different freedom. Do you recall the dialogue with Rosencrantz?"

Immanuel's expression was blank. "Rosencrantz?"

"Yes, Rosencrantz."

"I'm sorry, that doesn't mean anything to me."

Ascher fell silent, but only for a moment. It was as if he were getting ready to pounce, poised to drive his argument to its logical conclusion.

"That's the course the prince of Denmark prescribed. The way of sickness. Of the simpleminded. He who cannot extricate himself and flee can find a way into a different kind of free zone. All that's needed are some medical certificates and corroborating behavior."

"You mean someone declares you sick?"

Ascher nodded. He gazed across the increasingly busy bar. Some women were sitting by the tall atelier window, smoking.

"It's the ultimate way out. There's a doctor at Beckomberga who's prepared to help me. It won't cost more than a month's rent. Grand mal, two hundred crowns. Dementia praecox, same price."

That was when Immanuel caught sight of her: the fair-haired

woman from the island. She was leaning against an armchair, scantily clad like the other women. His eye followed her through the thick smoke as she left the room.

Ascher prattled on about escape routes and medical certificates. If Immanuel understood him correctly, he was intending to have himself declared sick to avoid deportation. Was that possible? Whatever the case, Immanuel wasn't going to listen to any more of his nonsense. Nor was he going to wait for some benevolent Englishmen who had no intention of turning up.

He put on his coat. Instinctively, he felt for his inner pocket. The letter was still there. He had carried it around with him for several days, sometimes forgetting it was there, next to his chest.

He recalled Lucia's skeptical questions about Horst and the bottle of green ink. *What does he want from you? Why on earth did you get yourself into this?*

It was as if she had sensed all along that the meeting with Horst would lead to some kind of trouble. Immanuel had tried to pacify her, but she hadn't stopped weeping until it was time for bed, and then more from exhaustion than any diminishment of her fears.

All this flashed through his mind as he felt the letter in his inner pocket. It could easily have fallen out when his coat was folded over his arm.

It was high time he left. Got out of this smoky atmosphere and into the fresh air and headed for home. As he pushed aside the heavy curtain separating one of the small recesses from the very first room, the one opening onto the stairwell, he saw Karin being led away by her brother. She was no longer half naked like the other women dispersed around the room on velvet sofas and chaise longues, but wearing a dark coat. Her brother held her arm in a firm grip, as though pushing her along.

Immanuel saw them enter the elevator. He took the stairs. When he came out onto the street, they had already disappeared. He turned left onto Villagatan and soon reached Humlegården. There he took one of the footpaths and walked briskly down toward the National Library. The park sloped gently in that direction, and he strode down with ease, his tiredness overcome. The cloud had broken up and above him the sky was starry. He kept looking up to see the starlight through the mesh of leafless branches.

He could breathe freely again. A sense that in that moment something had been settled overwhelmed him.

On Birger Jarlsgatan he followed his usual route home from the office. West on Birger Jarlsgatan to Roslagsgatan, then left onto Odengatan. Every day he passed the address his friend Lagerberg had pointed out as the house Hermann Göring stayed in during his years in Stockholm. Now the city was quiet and dark, the only light cast from a streetlamp onto the pavement here and there; the facades were black, people's homes in darkness.

He could make out the centaur with its arched bow on the hill behind the library, a single streetlamp giving luster to the metal. The half human, half horse looked as though it would take a leap out into the night at any moment. Only the occasional car passed on Sveavägen. When Immanuel arrived at the postbox on Odenplan, he took out the envelope to make sure it wasn't unduly crumpled. Without stopping, he pushed it through the slot and gave it a little shove. It fell to the bottom of the box without a sound.

32 FREJGATAN

It was soon after eight when the doorbell rang. The boys had just left, reluctantly. The interrogation went on in the kitchen for barely half an hour. A younger colleague made notes on a pad while a slim gentleman in a suit asked questions in remarkable German. They had asked Lucia to wait in the sitting room, but she heard every word.

"And so you were given the ink by this man Horst? Are you sure that was his real name, Wolfgang Horst?"

After a few minutes they closed the kitchen door. She could hear the conversation continuing inside. It had been made clear at the start that the men were from the police, but that was all. Suddenly the kitchen door opened, and she could see her husband's white face in the doorway.

He disappeared into the bedroom to put on a different shirt and a jacket that matched his trousers. The men from the police stood in the hall, saying nothing.

"They say I have to go with them. If I'm not back this afternoon, you'll have to explain to the boys. Don't worry."

He put on his coat and, accompanied by the two

expressionless men, went out into the stairwell, where the sour smell was stronger than usual. The outer door closed behind them. Neither of the Swedes had said goodbye to Lucia. She was left standing alone in the hallway until her legs gave way beneath her.

Later she wouldn't be able to explain what happened next. Instead of telephoning Mrs. Lagerberg or the Grafström family, she simply sat on the rug in the hall. She tried to reach for the little telephone book, but the table was too far away. She leaned against the kitchen door, stared at the dark-blue wallpaper, and lost herself in its pattern. How long she sat like that, she didn't know.

She was no longer in the hall, alone in the second-floor apartment belonging to a family she scarcely knew. The fact that her husband had just been taken away by the police wasn't on her mind now. The light surrounding her was soft and warm.

She was floating in the cool water of the Lielupe River, which flowed out into the Bay of Riga. It had been an unusually warm August. The boys had bathed from dawn to dusk, while she sat on the sand, reading. As the afternoon drew to its close, she and Immanuel would walk along the shore, and when the sun touched the horizon, she too took a swim. They had chosen a shallow cove, and by the end of the day the water had warmed up perfectly. A few meters out, the bottom was no longer sand but covered with smooth stones, black and even. She picked some up and let them dry on the beach. The black color they had in the water vanished, and they turned gray when they dried on her towel.

She liked swimming underwater, as she had since childhood, when she used to bathe in a lake outside Częstochowa. She could disappear under the water for so long, sometimes the boys were alarmed. Or they may have said they were, just to make it more exciting. The cove they had chosen was so shallow, they could still touch the bottom several hundred meters out to sea.

Someone knocked on the outside door. Then the bell rang, so briefly it could have been her imagination. Lucia barely roused, even though she was still lying in the hall. In her dream she was still underwater. She rolled over on the rug, thinking Immanuel was sure to be awake and would see what was going on.

Perhaps it was Henrik coming home early from school again. Both he and Karl had been teased about their clothes. They were old-fashioned and not like the clothes the boys at school wore. Outdated and wrong, as they had discovered on the very first day. Lucia soon realized it would be essential to find something new. Yet the woolen suits had been purchased in Warsaw only the year before, and were of the finest quality. Karl had gritted his teeth and pretended not to take any notice, but twice Henrik had left school when the tormenters were up to their tricks again, arriving home in tears. He had tugged at the front door, which was open, and thrown himself into her arms, sobbing and inconsolable. Although he would soon be fourteen, he behaved like the little boy he had been when he was bullied by hoodlums at the carnival many years earlier. He had promised his mother that he would never leave Żoliborz, where no such things would ever happen. The things that did happen were just as nasty as she had feared, and large rips appeared in his jacket. Yet she hadn't been capable of scolding him on that occasion either. She never had been, and Immanuel was probably right, she did mollycoddle the boys. But what choice did she have, when Henrik was weeping in her arms again?

There was another ring. The sound was muffled and more

reminiscent of a drill than a bell. Oddly, it sounded as though
the noise was coming from somewhere faraway, maybe from the
cellar. Lucia knew there was someone on the stairs, someone
who had something important to say.

She had managed somehow to get herself to the bedroom.
How, she couldn't remember. It was as if what had happened
had faded into a mist of unreality. Was it still morning?

As she sat on the edge of the bed, the memory of the morning's visitors and the unnerving conversation resurfaced. She
put on her dressing gown and looked at the alarm clock on the
bedside table. It was midday. She had slept for hours, a deep
and eventually dreamless sleep. As soon as she stood up, she
was attacked by the dizziness that at times in the last few weeks
had been serious enough to keep her in bed. She sat down again.
The floor beneath her feet was rocking. When she shut her
eyes, it felt as though sparks were spinning around inside her.
This was the vertigo that Joen Lagerberg and his wife, Valborg,
thought needed closer investigation.

It was a good thing the Lagerbergs were in the city. Both
spoke excellent German, which was a relief. Valborg was always
as accommodating and well dressed as her husband, if less for-
mally. Lagerberg had been well known in Warsaw for his taste.
At the embassy he wore tails as standard dress. The most dash-
ing in the entire diplomatic corps, her husband had said.

Perhaps it was Valborg who had rung the bell. She had done
that the previous week, with young Madeleine, their adopted
daughter, at her side. It had been a very welcome social call. For
once the two women could have a conversation. When the men
were present, they were used to having little scope for talking to
each other.

Yes, she hoped it was Valborg. It would be nice if she came.

Lucia mustn't let her wait any longer, in case she gave up. With her left hand she could just reach the handle of the half-open bedroom door. Holding on to it, she slowly stood up. That was good, she could be upright without losing her balance. Treading very cautiously, she went out into the hall. Could she open the front door like this, in her dressing gown and slippers in the middle of the day? It might be one of the Weil brothers. Maybe it was about the typewriters.

She reached the door and opened it warily. As a gust of chilly air blew in through the crack, the door was wrenched open with a force that frightened her. The two men from the police were back. Without any form of greeting, they entered the hall and proceeded to the kitchen. Their gestures made it clear she was to follow them. The tall thin one, who was obviously the superior, started asking questions without sitting down.

"Your husband's typewriter, where is it? He says he borrowed it from the Weil family, but that's not true. Young Mr. Weil says he doesn't own a typewriter."

He marched impatiently back and forth between the kitchen and the hall, speaking fast and slurring slightly. His German was really very good. There was no problem understanding the towheaded commissioner now walking around inspecting everything he came across. After opening doors at random in the kitchen, he resumed his questioning.

"The invisible ink must still be in the study. Do you know where the fountain pen has been hidden? If you show us, it will save us turning the whole place upside down."

Lucia had sat down at the table. The dizziness had fortunately subsided, but the tiredness she felt must have been plain to see. Her breathing was labored, and before she could get a word in edgewise, the young assistant interposed with further thoughts about the typewriter, which was clearly what currently preoccupied them.

"It's a Rheinmetall brand, we could see that immediately. If it doesn't belong to Mr. Weil, it might have been loaned by another neighbor. Or you managed to acquire one of your own."

He was speaking as though Lucia wasn't in the room. Since his comments were in Swedish now, she didn't understand a word.

The assistant came out of the sitting room bearing the Rheinmetall machine and dropped it on the kitchen table with a crash.

There was a sheet of white paper in the machine; the commissioner wound the sheet down a little before starting to tap with unnecessary pressure on every key. He shouted each letter out aloud as the print appeared on the paper.

```
A-s-d-f-g-h.
```

He paused between the letters in time with each sharp strike of the keys.

"Yes, it's a German keyboard, as far as I can see. Some of the letters are missing."

He kept on hammering, following his own dictation despite the unfamiliar position of the keys. In a loud voice he shouted out his observations, which he simultaneously typed onto the paper.

```
T-h-i-s m-a-c-h-i-n-e i-s q-u-i-t-e d-i-s-t-i-n-c-t-i-
v-e
i-n t-h-a-t, i-n-t-e-r a-l-i-a, i-t l-a-c-k-s t-h-e
```

l-e-t-t-e-r A w-i-t-h a r-i-n-g o-n t-o-p.

He stopped and rolled the sheet of paper down to check what he had typed so aggressively. He nodded and continued his report.

I-t i-s r-e-a-s-o-n-a-b-l-e t-o a-s-s-u-m-e t-h-a-t t-h-e p-e-r-s-o-n i-n c-u-s-t-o-d-y u-s-e-d s-u-c-h a m-a-c-h-i-n-e, s-i-n-c-e I h-a-v-e n-o-t-e-d t-h-a-t i-n c-e-r-t-a-i-n c-o-r-r-e-s-p-o-n-d-e-n-c-e h-e a-d-d-e-d r-i-n-g-s a-b-o-v-e t-h-e l-e-t-t-e-r-s b-y h-a-n-d, i-n-c-l-u-d-i-n-g i-n s-o-m-e c-a-s-e-s o-n t-h-e w-r-o-n-g l-e-t-t-e-r-s.

Periodically he interrupted his own dictation with a muttered curse when he hit the wrong key.

"Damn, it's not easy. Oh, well."

O-f c-o-u-r-s-e t-h-e J-e-w-i-s-h f-a-m-i-l-y W-e-i-l s-a-y t-h-e-y d-i-d n-o-t l-e-n-d a-n-y-o-n-e t-h-e-i-r m-a-c-h-i-n-e-s, b-u-t t-h-a-t i-n-f-o-r-m-a-t-i-o-n c-a-n-n-o-t b-e t-r-u-s-t-e-d. I-n a-d-d-i-t-i-o-n i-t w-o-u-l-d b-e u-s-e-f-u-l i-f i-t p-r-o-v-e-d t-o b-e t-h-e m-a-c-h-i-n-e o-n w-h-i-c-h t-h-e l-e-t-t-e-r-s w-e-r-e t-y-p-e-d, f-o-r t-h-e-n w-e c-o-u-l-d h-a-v-e a c-r-a-c-k a-t t-h-e W-e-i-l-s a-s w-e-l-l.

He looked up and saw Lucia slumped on her chair in the corner of the kitchen.

"You're Polish, we understand?"

"Pardon?"

She wasn't sure he meant her, even though they were alone in the kitchen.

"You're Polish?"

"Not at all. I'm German, like my husband."

"But he stated you were born in Częstochowa. When you were young you wanted to study medicine, but couldn't finance your studies. Is that correct?"

What was this about? Had Immanuel wanted to exaggerate her qualifications for some reason? It wouldn't be the first time, and not just with regard to her but the whole family, even his brother, who hadn't completed any kind of education. She knew her husband never regretted his own decision not to finish his doctorate but to choose journalism instead. His Dr. B. byline was a joke everyone in the Basel office was aware of. But for some reason he was keen to stress Lucia's academic career, which had never even begun.

She answered dutifully.

"I studied at a school of commerce and have worked as a secretary for nearly twenty years. I type up my husband's articles. I'm German, but my father left Berlin to run his business in Poland."

Normally conversations about her birthplace would sooner or later turn to Jasna Góra, a place of pilgrimage for people from all over the world to venerate the Black Madonna. But the Swedish policemen weren't interested in that, she was sure.

"Częstochowa. Is that how you pronounce it?"

The commissioner had started speaking again, enlivened by the situation, and continued the questioning.

"So you're German. But your husband claims he's a Jew. Isn't that right? Of course, we wonder why there's no J-stamp in his passport. Has he managed to rub it out somehow?"

The assistant gave a short laugh. He obviously thought it was funny, the idea that a Jew of his own accord would erase the proof of his true origins.

"So you were the one who typed up the articles? There were a number of articles for the office in Berlin, weren't there?"

Lucia explained about the various abbreviations that distinguished between articles for *Basler Nachrichten* and those sent to Amsterdam or other cities. The number of articles to Basel was large, but the short items were often telephoned in. Her husband dealt with those in the morning. More often than not lying in bed with a cup of coffee on the bedside table, but she didn't mention that. She couldn't say how many articles had been sent to Kutzner, the editor in Berlin, but they had been fewer and fewer.

"But you didn't write the letter with the invisible ink, did you?"

"Pardon?"

"It's written by hand," the assistant added. "So that's easy to establish."

Lucia knew about the fountain pen and the bottle of green liquid. In fact she had helped her husband fill it the first time. It had spiked the boys' interest, and they had joined in too. They wanted to play with the poisonous liquid. She knew Immanuel had hidden it, presumably somewhere in the study. She hadn't seen the stuff since. It was news to her that Immanuel had actually used it.

She explained this earnestly, but the commissioner didn't seem convinced. Quite the opposite, he laughed and turned to the assistant, pulling a wry face.

"So she's never seen him using the pen, she says. But that's a lie, of course."

He stood and paced up and down in the kitchen.

"So you've been in regular contact with this press agency in Berlin. How would you like to describe its operation?"

Lucia was silent for too long. The commissioner rapped his knuckles impatiently on the table and gave her a searching look. Hadn't she understood the question, or did she need time to consider, to avoid saying anything rash?

He repeated the question. "This press agency run by Mr. Kutzner, how does it work?"

The truth was, she wasn't clear about how the agency functioned, and in fact had always thought there was something undesirable about sending articles to Berlin. It was five years since her husband had been banned from contributing to the German press. Secretly sending unsigned pieces to an agency in the capital was perilous. Her husband had always maintained that the articles were harmless and the little extra income could hardly hurt.

"You type up the articles, but your husband is the real correspondent? Have I understood correctly?"

"Yes, that's right. My husband can't manage a typewriter."

"Have you typed up all the articles?"

"Yes, in the old days my husband's brother worked at our home. He could use a typewriter. But Gerhard didn't come to Sweden with us."

"Is he still in Warsaw then?"

"We don't know. We don't know where he's gone. It troubles my husband greatly. So much so, he can't sleep at night."

Lucia knew she was being too personal. Too emotional. There was absolutely no reason to confide in them like this. These men weren't in the least interested in what had happened to Immanuel's brother, that was obvious.

"He's not the person we want to know about. We want to know about Wolfgang Horst, the one who encouraged your husband to gather information. What can you tell us about this man Horst?"

Lucia wasn't sure if she had understood what the commissioner said, and anyway she had no desire to know anything about the demands Horst had made of her husband. So she just shook her head. They wouldn't believe her if she told them the truth anyway, that she knew nothing at all about this man. That she wasn't even convinced he existed. She remembered the telephone call, naturally. She remembered the voice. And of course she recalled the puzzling conversations she had with her husband about the meeting. She had felt despondent, but didn't know why. Had her husband met Horst before, in Latvia maybe? Was he one of the men in the band of journalists who sometimes appeared at the hotel in the seaside resort of Majori? She was no longer certain of anything. She remained silent, which understandably annoyed the commissioner. He rapped on the table with his knuckles again and raised his voice.

"I'll tell you what . . ." He faltered and cast a quick glance at the assistant, who was absorbed in his notebook and wasn't aware of his superior's hesitancy.

"Let's put it this way, then . . ." He broke off again. He took a deep breath, looked out of the kitchen window, and continued at a slower pace.

"We've looked into all the guests who stayed at the Grand during the period he's supposed to have been in Stockholm, and no Mr. Horst checked in. Now we're thinking that a Mr. Horst might not exist. What do you have to say about all of this? Who came to see your husband, and who gave him the German fountain pen and the invisible ink?"

He stopped speaking and fixed his harsh gaze on Lucia, who realized that he really did require an answer.

"I don't know who this man Horst is," she said gravely.

The commissioner snorted.

"Let me ask you this: What kind of people work in this office, the ones who supply articles to German-language newspapers? In Poland, if I've understood correctly. Do they form some sort of network?"

Lucia wasn't sure what she should say. Of course she knew that the bureau had originally been established with the aim of circumventing the hard-line policies of the German press. And she also knew that some of the correspondents could no longer work in Germany and therefore lived in cities such as Kaunas and Riga. She had never met Kutzner, but of course she knew about him. Had her husband mentioned von Scheliha from the embassy, the sympathetic German diplomat who was one of Lagerberg's and Grafström's circle of friends in Warsaw, and who had helped to set up the agency?

She was about to speak, but stopped. She could feel the seriousness of the situation in her body, now heavy and sluggish. Under no circumstances would she name names unless she had to. Which people had her husband already spoken to the police about? If she knew that, it would be easier. Clearly Rudolf von Scheliha. He must have mentioned him, surely? Then there was a woman. What was her name again, the one whose head had been turned by Moscow? Ilse Stübe, or as her husband rather mockingly called her, Comrade Stübe.

The truth was, she was the one with the greatest misgivings about all this secrecy. She had always had the feeling it would come back to haunt them, that there would turn out to be something wrong about the whole setup. And now she had been proved right.

"Your husband has admitted that he assisted the British Secret Service with propaganda material," the commissioner went on, as if he had casually decided to forget the Berlin office and change tack. "Would you say your husband is well versed in that area?"

"I'm sorry, what area do you mean?"

"Propaganda. Political agitation. You understand well enough. Do you consider your husband well versed in these spheres?"

She could feel the vertigo return. But without meeting her eye, the commissioner went on to ask a series of questions, and she did her best to answer. It was as if he were reciting a list of names in order to determine if she would react to any of them. It started with Miss Stern, the ever-helpful girl in the office. Lucia was happy to speak warmly about her. She would rather not comment on Bermann Fischer; she hardly knew him, still less his family.

"What do you have to say about Rickman and his fiancée, Elsa Johansson?"

Lucia had no idea who he was talking about. She said nothing.

"Biggs, the advertising man Biggs? He must have been in and out of this house, one suspects. Wasn't he the one who paid for the British propaganda? My colleague here has an example, of course."

Without changing his expression, the young assistant who had been engrossed in his notebook leaned across the table. From his inner pocket he took out a slender cardboard tube. He swore as he endeavored to extract the contents, but eventually unrolled a flyer and placed it on the table in front of them. It was a cartoon of Stalin, who held a large saw and was in the process of cutting off the tree branch on which the German führer was sitting.

Lucia had never seen the picture before and didn't know how she was supposed to respond. She knew both policemen were hoping for some kind of comment from her side, but she couldn't pretend. She barely had the strength to sit upright. She would rather have lain down on the mat in the kitchen and closed her eyes.

"Above all we want answers to questions about Rickman, and about your husband's working relationship with him. We expect assistance from you to clear this up."

His voice, which was dry and matter-of-fact, had hardened. It was obvious the commissioner meant business.

"As I'm sure you know, Rickman had an office on Näck-strömsgatan."

Lucia knew nothing about an office, and, as far as she could recall, hadn't even heard Rickman's name. Could he be one of the new colleagues at the publishing house on Sturegatan? The only name she remembered was Miss Stern.

But now, suddenly, the men were on their feet. Were they going to leave? She could hear the assistant trampling about in the apartment. The commissioner was standing in the hall, when a shout could be heard from the study.

"Commissioner Danielsson! Here it is!" With a beam of satisfaction on his face, the young man came out brandishing the fountain pen and ink bottle. He handed them to the commissioner, who put them into his coat pocket. The commissioner had been wearing his coat the whole time, and now he wrenched the front door open.

The assistant evidently realized he had forgotten something, for he turned on his heel and went back into the kitchen. He returned to the hall bearing the heavy typewriter in his arms.

Lucia was leaning against the kitchen doorframe. All she could utter was a question. "When can I expect my husband to come home?"

They were already out in the stairwell. The air pouring into the apartment was ice-cold. Without turning, Commissioner Danielsson pushed the front door shut behind him. Before it closed completely, he spoke to his colleague.

"Did you hear that? She seems to think her husband's going to come home."

Both policemen laughed and began to descend the stairs. The door closed with a gentle thud, and Lucia was alone once more. Her slippers were still under the kitchen table, and she was standing on the rug in the hall. The draft from the stairwell had gone.

She dragged herself into the bedroom.

Her chest felt as though it was filled with a silt that was thick and black and dense, as sometimes happened after an attack of vertigo. But by the time the boys came home from school in the afternoon, she had always pulled herself together. She forced herself out of bed, and before evening she would be sitting in front of the machine, typing up the day's articles. She had managed to do that every time.

There was a photograph on the bureau by the bed, where she had placed it on the very first day. When the dawn light came through the window, she could see her husband's head bending toward her shoulder.

It was late afternoon, and the sunlight reflecting in the windowpanes on the other side of the street fell directly onto the picture. She liked the photograph. Both because she herself looked so relaxed and confident, and because Immanuel had that dreamy look she remembered from those days. The picture was taken just after their wedding. She remembered the occasion, the photographer's fussiness over the various lamps, and new suggestions, constantly, about how they should sit on the rather uncomfortable bench he offered them. She was wearing a new hat and a dress with a long row of silver buttons she had bought in a shop on Salzplaz in Breslau. It had been expensive, but she wore it at parties for years afterward. Her features were soft, but her body slender.

In those days Immanuel read poetry to her and sometimes wrote his own. He was still a young editor, and she an even younger secretary. They had moved in together a few months before.

The window in the bedroom wasn't completely shut, and noises from the courtyard floated in through the narrow gap. A neighbor was beating rugs down below.

She lay perfectly still, gazing at the picture, wide awake now. Something had made her stir. Perhaps it was the carpet beater. But now she heard something else. Was that someone at the door?

How she contrived to sit up on the edge of the bed was a mystery. It was even more remarkable that she managed to rise and shuffle out into the study in her slippers. Still in her dressing gown, she sat down at the desk and laid her hands on the typewriter keys. She heard the boys' steps in the hall. The door closed with a bang. They slammed down their shoes and schoolbags, chattering happily as they went into the kitchen. One of them shouted something about a sandwich. They were in a good mood.

That wasn't always the case. Karl usually looked impassive and serious. He was the elder by just one year, but already as responsible as an adult. Henrik, on the other hand, was never far from tears when he recounted his classmates' snidest comments of the day. He often ended up sitting on Lucia's knee and weeping, or lying by her side. Later in the afternoon they would drink hot chocolate, and when Immanuel returned from the office, the worst of the tears was generally over. By the time they gathered at the dinner table, the atmosphere was usually better, and afterward they all joined forces on the boys' homework. Only when this was done could dessert be eaten.

From today everything would be different. How was she to explain what had happened? She wasn't entirely sure herself what had taken place, nor what lay ahead.

But one thing she did know. A new era had begun. That much was clear. From now on, everything depended on her.

Lucia refused to give in to the dizziness and the ensuing nausea the second she moved. She didn't know where the strength came from, but she found it. She pressed a few keys with all the force she could muster, so that the boys would think she was working. *Clickety-clack.* This was the time she would usually turn her attention to the daily transcriptions. Today she was typing because life had to go on. Letters that didn't form words. She kept tapping on the machine and managed a lighthearted shout in response to the boys' exuberance in the kitchen. They were squabbling and carrying on, especially noisy and full of life. That was all that mattered now.

RHEINMETALL

lick-clack, clickety-clack. The sound of an interrogation report being hammered out on a typewriter of the Rheinmetall brand could be heard all over Kronoberg Park when the windows were left open in the spring air. One exceptionally warm afternoon the sharp tapping came from at least two machines, hour after hour, in one of the offices of the public prosecutor. The entrance to Kronoberg Prison was on the ground floor of the same wing. Two clerks were on the third floor, one a northerner, the other from the capital. It was their job to type up all interrogation reports.

"Damn, it's sweltering. Where were we again? Right, it was Rickman. First trip to Oxelösund. Notes for investigation reports. That's as far as I've got. I'm sorry, we'll have to start again from the beginning. Dossiers fifty to fifty-three."

"Have you seen the pictures of Miss Johansson at Belfrage's guesthouse on Blasieholmstorg? Not bad, not half bad. Rickman knows what he's doing, you have to give him that."

The one with the Norrland dialect pushed a photograph of Elsa Johansson, dressed in a black hat and white blouse, across the desk. "Apparently she got paid by Rickman, fiancée and secretary. Not bad at all!"

They were meticulous about taking turns in deciphering the notes and reading out what had been typed. But nothing was going their way. Repetitions and errors crept in, and time after time they had to yank the piece of paper out of the typewriter, crumple it up, and throw it into the already full wastepaper bin, only to start again from the beginning.

The northerner read aloud with exaggerated deliberation, in order that his colleague shouldn't miss a syllable and could hammer out sentence after sentence on the large and exceedingly noisy typewriter standing on the desk nearest to the open window. Anyone passing under the trees in the park outside could hear the jaunty *ping* at the end of a line and the clatter of the carriage return. *Click-clack, clickety-clack,* then the little bell, and then the rattling whir.

"'On Friday the 19 April 1940 at 19.15 and 19.40 respectively, Alfred Frederick Rickman, British citizen and company director, and his fiancée, Elsa Nanna Johansson, clerk, were arrested at the offices of Dental Materials, no. 1 Näckströmsgatan.'"

Being required to sit in this dusty and, as it happened, scorching hot office was no one's dream scenario on a Friday afternoon such as this, the first really warm day of the year. But it was a matter of saving one's own neck, or saving face at least, and they tried to keep their spirits up. It was best to do the job thoroughly.

Everything had been photographed, as usual, every box and every item, anything that could be described and given a name. But now that the report had to be typed up, it was the notes, rather than the photographs, that served as prompts. The first attempt to make a complete list of everything seized in connection with Rickman's arrest had failed. Now they had to pull it together. Commissioner Otto Danielsson of the General Security Service was not at all pleased. He came back time after time to collect the transcriptions and was furious when he found they weren't ready. So now the challenge was to have everything completed. All the reports concerning Rickman, Miss Johansson, Ernest Biggs, and the other Englishmen. And then there was the German journalist and the other Jews connected with the Bermann Fischer publishing house. It all had to be consistent. Danielsson was not one to turn a blind eye if things didn't add up.

"At the place where they lived, the following was found . . ."

"No, hang on, I have all that already. That page is done. It's the list of all the stuff in the basement area that's a complete mess."

The Norrland clerk sighed and started again. He read aloud in a monotone, spelling the unusual words.

"'6 suitcases, each containing 4 wooden boxes,
dimensions 25 x 11.5 x 14.5 cm, which contained in all
53.6 kilos of g–e–l–i–g–n–i–t–e,

2 electric timers with 2 clocks in each,

1 v–o–l–t–m–e–t–e–r,

11 electric detonators,

2 chisels,

1 box of nails and screws,

1 attaché case containing 28,285 Swedish crowns
in notes, 1,750 Norwegian crowns in notes, and 35
Danish crowns in notes, all arranged in decreasing
denominations,

3 modern pistols with a number of bullets,

1 drawing of Oxelösund with 3 corresponding postcards,

3 Swedish passport forms printed in 1938 with the
numbers 6981, 8509, and 9234 entered in pencil and 2
money stamps on each for a total of 7 crowns, cancelled
as normal,

1 stamp with the text "Office of the Governor of
Stockholm for Police Business" and the city coat of arms,

1 specification and description of explosives and s–a–b–
o–t–a–g–e equipment,

miscellaneous correspondence concerning explosives,
sabotage, and propaganda, and

1 small black notebook with various codes, to be covered
in Rickman's account further ahead.'"

They fell silent and could hear the church bells ringing. Was
it six o'clock already?

Naturally a variety of people had written interim reports
when the raids were made, and the investigation involved
people from several departments. But now it had come to the

transcription, and it was the two clerks who carried the responsibility. Danielsson had made that point in no uncertain terms. He, who always seemed so controlled, had come in for the last time after lunch and barked something about the public prosecutor himself wanting to see it typed up on Monday morning, because he had to deal with daily questions from the press.

It was as if, in this unexpected heat, everything was going wrong. The transcripts were insidiously connected, like a complicated chain in which each link must fit with not just the next link, but in some infernal way with all the other links. The slightest ambiguity would come back to bite them in the next report.

For example, if they wrote that Rickman's fiancée lived at Belfrage's guesthouse on Blasieholmen, but then, in the interrogation of the lady in question, she stated that she lived with Rickman at 1 Smedsbacksgatan, then the only thing they could do was tear up the previous report and add that to all the rest in the wastepaper bin standing next to the door to the corridor. It all had to be redone. And that was happening not just with Rickman and his fiancée, but with numerous details in the interrogation of Biggs, the adman from PUB, the second Englishman, Fraser, on Odengatan, and the whole odd crew connected with the German publishing house on Stureplan.

"I need a cigarette. I don't usually smoke until after dinner, but this will have to be an exception."

"Good idea. I've nothing against exceptions."

They stood by the window and pushed it wide open, letting the evening air pour in. The new leaves on the trees in the park were so delicate that the fading light filtering through them into the large office seemed imbued with green. The office could accommodate twenty people, but as they were the only ones left, now they could spread out as much as they wished.

Two newspapers were lying open on the windowsill. *Stockholms-Tidningen* reported on the seizure. A reporter from *Aftonbladet* had already ferreted out the details of the sabotage in Oxelösund. One of the editors speculated on the possible consequences had the attackers succeeded. At the point when transport of iron was seriously interrupted, he suggested, a German invasion of Sweden couldn't be ruled out, and he went on to raise the question of the coalition government's response to this provocation from the British. There was no doubt about the initiative's source. Nor the intention. Apparently the head of the legation had made himself unavailable, and his press office referred to a woolly statement from the military attaché Reginald Sutton-Pratt.

They read on with growing interest. It wasn't often their transcriptions made it into the press like this. But the whole Oxelösund drama was receiving a great deal of attention in the press as well as on the radio. Needless to say, readers were fascinated by the secret letter that put the police on the scent of the ring. The code name "Uncle Richard" had been used for Alfred Rickman.

Aftonbladet quoted Danielsson's words on doubts surrounding the deciphering of the invisible ink, since the hidden script had blurred with the visible lettering.

"That's just what we were writing about the other week!"

The Stockholmer sat down by the window with the newspaper open on his knee and read: "'It has gradually emerged that a German journalist residing in Stockholm was in contact with Berlin Correspondence Bureau NW 40. The journalist did not use his own name, but it could be assumed he is the letter writer mentioned in appendix 1 of the police report.'"

"That's our man!"

Danielsson had rushed in and out of the office that day like a yo-yo. When they had asked what all the fuss was about, he had muttered something about a dilettante. A bungler who through sheer clumsiness had managed to put a stop to a national disaster. And a gang of amateurs with beginners' luck who might have succeeded with their insanely ambitious plan. Danielsson was convinced. It was about dragging Sweden into the war.

Aftonbladet seemed to have come to a similar conclusion.

"Listen to this. If blowing up the port had succeeded, the Germans would have felt compelled to enter Sweden. According to the police, given the quantity of explosives they had at their disposal, that could have been accomplished."

They carried on smoking quietly, exhaling into the balmy air. The heat had abated, and the spring-evening birdsong could still be heard. A bell tolled in a church lower down Kungsholmen.

The man from Norrland shook his head. "I can't really make sense of it."

"I don't think anyone expects you to make sense of it, you know. Our job is to make sure that the interrogation transcriptions are accurate and readable, so that Danielsson is satisfied and doesn't start grumbling again when he's back on Monday."

"Forgive my speculation. But you have to admit, it's quite remarkable that the whole gang got caught just because that journalist's letter was held up in a check."

"Tough luck. Or sheer bloody ham-handedness. Or he wanted to set them up."

"But, damn it, he can't have been a deliberate informer for the Germans? He was a Jew, wasn't he? Yes, it says so here."

From a dossier the northerner read aloud in a voice that was supposed to sound like Danielsson's: "'The detainee is regarded in Germany as *als Jude geltend*. Those with Jewish blood are classified as follows: 1. *Jude* = 100% Jewish blood; 2. *Als Jude geltend* = more than 50% Jewish blood; *Mischling I* = between 25 and 50% Jewish blood; *Mischling II* = 25% Jewish blood and under.'"

The Stockholmer shrugged. "Bloody hell, it still makes no sense. Now we have to go flat out, or we'll be here all night."

Fatigue was beginning to set in, and they had difficulty distinguishing their own transcriptions from the newspapers' extensive reporting. After endless hours and constantly recurring names in transcription after transcription, the figures in the tangled skein surrounding Rickman had become like old friends. Especially when there were photographs of the individuals.

On the table lay pictures of the one-legged adman at the Gumaelius advertising agency, whose main client was Paul U. Bergström. Ernest Biggs, always smartly dressed and fashionable in all respects. A qualified copywriter, whatever that might entail. Principally responsible for advertising brochures for PUB, but previously worked in London, at the London Press Exchange Ltd., then at his own advertising agency. One trip after another, all over Scandinavia, year in, year out.

The northerner raised his eyebrow. "Poor devil, always so elegant in his bow tie and checked jacket, despite his wooden leg. But he doesn't make a bad living at Gumaelius, twenty-four thousand crowns a year."

"For that money I wouldn't mind hopping around on one leg either."

Apparently, Biggs's left leg had been amputated after he had been sent to the front in France in World War I. He had been a private in the British infantry but was seriously injured and repatriated. As a war invalid, he obviously hadn't been called up this time, even though he had registered his special skills in response to a questionnaire to all British citizens in Sweden sent out by Brigadier Sutton-Pratt immediately upon his appointment as military attaché in Stockholm, early in the spring of 1939. He had requested information about any expatriates' previous work and specialist training if applicable. That wasn't unusual; similar initiatives were taken by military attachés all over Europe. But Biggs had listed expertise in propaganda.

The Stockholmer snorted. "Ha-ha, I'll bet the military attaché made contact with him, I would have done too! But I'll be damned if that isn't spot-on, propaganda is exactly what PUB is doing when it tries to sell us its expensive clothes."

"But why haven't they nailed Sutton-Pratt?"

"I don't think they just send out some commissioner to arrest folk at the embassies."

"Maybe not. But what about Grand?"

"He seems to have been the man in the wings. And someone called Morton. But that bit is easy to understand. They wanted to put obstacles in the Germans' way. All the transport goes from Oxelösund in winter. A little plastic explosive on the right cranes in the port, and the job's done."

"Now I need another smoke before we tackle the Englishman."

They continued their breather over the newspaper reports. *Aftonbladet* devoted three 2-page spreads to Oxelösund.

The newspapers told the same story. Departure from the city occurred around four p.m. The young Englishmen were picked up by Rickman's Plymouth from different addresses. One was picked up at Stockholm East Station, one by the clock on Centralplan, a third on the corner of Sveavägen and Kungsgatan. By the time they arrived, it was already dark, so they couldn't see the cranes. They decided to turn back toward Nyköping, but when they reached the road that goes straight down to the port, Rickman tried to take the car down anyway. He drove into a ditch, and they were obliged to requisition a breakdown vehicle.

The clerk tossed his cigarette out of the window. "What an idiot!"

By this time they were clear about the course of events. On the second attempt Rickman parked the car at the Oxelösund railway station. The party made their way on their newly acquired skis to a headland opposite the ore quay. The distance between the observation place and the ore quay amounted to less than two hundred meters.

The explosions were planned to take place when work on the quay had shut down. There were two cranes on the quay. They were supposed to collapse when the legs broke. Each crane required two bags of explosive, which were connected to a fuse. A timer would be placed in one of the bags. White powder was sprinkled over the bag. A cigarette-shaped cylinder was placed on top of the powder. Once it was carefully broken, the liquid would eat through the casing to the powder, which would immediately catch fire.

The report in *Aftonbladet* was illustrated with drawings to make the technical details easier to grasp. In addition, there were portraits of the protagonists. Particular attention was paid to the young Swede, Elsa Johansson, deputy at Dental Materials Ltd. According to *Aftonbladet*, Miss Johansson had no objections to the plan being carried out, after learning that no lives would be lost. Ideally, Germany would be forced to make peace if Swedish iron could be blocked.

How many times had they pounded out her name? Every

now and then they would cast an admiring glance at her photograph. This woman, Elsa, was really good-looking. Born on November 27, 1906, in Karlshamn, daughter of Johan Johansson, senior engineer. In recent years employed by Karl Belfrage at his guesthouse, 9 Blasieholmstorg, where she worked in reception.

That was where she met Alfred Rickman, who stayed at the guesthouse in the summer of 1939. In June of that year Miss Johansson began to socialize with Rickman. They gradually became good friends, and in the end, she said under questioning, their friendship developed into a love affair. On September 16 Miss Johansson left her position at Belfrage's guesthouse and was immediately employed by Rickman as his secretary on a salary of 325 crowns per month.

The incompetent Brits would be jailed, and the young Swede's treason punished. It was the only thing that leaked out when Commissioner Danielsson appeared in the office, spreading tension. It was incomprehensible that a young Swedish woman could do the Englishman's bidding like this, and it undermined Sweden's credibility. It was important to record not only her actions but also her motives. After the outbreak of war Miss Johansson had become increasingly interested in political questions and what she called the concept of freedom. Clearly, she and Rickman had lively discussions about this.

The green evening light was still filtering into the office when the northerner folded up the newspaper.

"Who wouldn't want to be a free person? We have the jail directly underneath us, but this office is a confounded prison as well. It's nearly seven o'clock, and we're not even halfway through."

"Our elegant dove of peace is probably still here, if she hasn't already been moved. Maybe the rest of them are as well. And the German. But we don't give a damn how the whole thing's connected. Read out the search of premises now, slowly."

In an overly deliberate voice the northerner read aloud from the notes once again: "'Findings in the office included four wooden boxes of the same dimensions and type as mentioned above, but these boxes contained only a piece of felt and a crumpled sheet of paper. There was also a collection of propaganda material and a printing block for a flyer.' Are you keeping up?"

Click-clack, clickety-clack.

"'The following day a search was carried out in a cellar of the house at the back of 4 Grevgatan. The cellar in question is rented to the Windsor Tea Company Ltd., which in turn rented half the space to Rickman. Rickman's part of the cellar is demarcated by a wooden wall and a door fitted with a patent lock. A large number of boxes were discovered in this cellar.'"

Click-clack, clickety-clack.

"'The boxes contained:

33.5 kilos of gelignite,

57.3 kilos of other explosives, disguised inside plastic packaging for electric wires,

8 explosive devices with 14 kilos of gelignite in total,

4 canvas bags with a content of 35.9 kilos of gelignite,

412 timers (s–i–g–n–a–l r–e–l–a–y–s) with different time settings, viz. some for 40 minutes, some half an hour, and some 30 hours,

320 incendiary bombs (m–a–g–n–e–s–i–u–m t–o–r–c–h–e–s),

adaptors for incendiary devices consisting of magnesium nuts, magnesium gaskets, and rubber gaskets,

a ring of 41.15 meters of detonating fuse with a large detonator at each end,

8 rings of brown fuse, total length 55.3 meters,

4 cut pieces of fuse, each of ca 10 cm in length and equipped with a large detonator at one end and an igniter at the other,

2 cut pieces of the same type of fuse, but without detonators,

8 cut pieces of fuse of 60 cm in length with a detonator attached,

200 small detonators,

10 large detonators,

8 powerful magnets,

900 grams of potassium chlorate, 24 fountain pens filled with C–a–r–b–o–r–u–n–d–u–m, and 1.1 kilos of Carborundum.

"'The packaging for all of the above consisted of 14 wooden boxes, dimensions 56 x 31.5 cm.

"'The explosives and other sabotage materials have been photographed. All the photographs accompanying the report are to be found in Appendix 1.'"

Click-clack, clickety-clack.

"Well, that's it."

The Stockholmer pulled the sheet of paper out of the machine. The first evening of summer awaited them in the city outside.

"Well, I'll be! We've finished, haven't we?"

"Yes, that's damn well enough! But we're not going to forget our chap Rickman in a hurry."

They both knew his biography by heart. Born in Wimbledon. Jack-of-all-trades and broker. Business manager for Jack Hylton and his orchestra. Moved to Sweden. Periods in Gällivare, Kiruna, Oxelösund, with testimonials from the Grängesberg companies' representative in London. Author of a book about Swedish iron ore.

And then there was the Hotel Atlantic story.

It had started as a wet evening in the hotel bar. They were a rowdy crew. British flight engineers to a man. After the Atlantic, back to Biggs's house on Odengatan for a chaser.

They squinted at the photograph of Biggs. He really looked like someone they would like to have known. Life with him was never dull, that much they had worked out.

"He knows the whole city, that guy. At least enough people to get a gang together for a 'risky job.'"

"Ha-ha, damn right it was risky. The entire boot filled with plastic explosive. Out to Nyköping in the middle of the night, then down to the port in the small hours. Drunk as skunks, the whole gang."

It was the third and final attempt. It wasn't even mentioned in Rickman's interrogation, because he hadn't been present. Nor were Biggs or Elsa Johansson. The drunken flight engineers alone were wholly responsible for the fiasco.

Evidently it had all become quite solemn in the middle of the night, when Biggs had suddenly interrupted the merrymaking with a serious question: Are you prepared to do your bit for your country? Everyone had nodded in silence. Biggs carried on with something along the lines of saving the British people and their native land. Is there anyone who doesn't want in? he asked. There was nobody. It was three o'clock in the morning.

"They were going to get a thousand crowns up front. Then five hundred pounds when they got back to England."

"Good Lord! Much better paid than we are, for sitting here, sweating."

Together they closed the window and turned off the desk lamps. Outside, the park was silent.

◆ ◆ ◆

There wasn't much light finding its way into the cell through the tiny window. But in the hours when the darkness was least profound, he had gone through the transcripts and arranged them in piles on the floor next to his bunk. The entire report was here, with appendices and arrest warrants. He had tried to keep count of the days, but it was difficult to distinguish night from day and dusk from dawn in the faint half-light of the cell.

The interrogation in the kitchen on Frejgatan replayed in

his mind. Every detail was crystal clear. The commissioner's slightly pale face, the assistant's nervous twitching. The silences, the pauses. The suspicion and the linguistic misunderstandings. He remembered every word.

The boys had just left for school, so they were spared the sight of their father being taken away. Had Lucia broken down when the door closed?

How many weeks had passed since the tall, thin man from the police was at the door? He remembered the strangely muffled sound of the bell. Otto Danielsson, the same man who signed the report. The younger assistant had remained silent almost the whole time, just leaned against the kitchen counter, taking notes. It had all happened quietly and calmly.

He had no idea how long it would be before his sentence was passed. It was only when he was given the transcripts that it occurred to him there might be an end to it all. He was mystified that the interrogation report and all the appendices had been left with him. He hadn't noticed when they were brought in and couldn't understand what it might imply. If nothing else, it meant no one would be pleading his case.

It certainly wasn't easy to tell the days apart. In the mornings he was often woken by keys in the lock, the bolt being slammed up, and the rattle of the food trolley as it was rolled in. The short trip to the linen store with the bedding every morning was not unlike the same walk after supper every evening. Who knew how many days it had been since he came across Bermann Fischer in the pale light of the corridor?

His plea for help had not been heeded. Perhaps it wasn't within the publisher's power to provide any assistance. Perhaps he was still incarcerated. Or perhaps he was free and could tell his colleagues all about the darkness in the cell.

The black clouds inside him were choking everything. They filled his chest with a thick smoke of fear. He fretted about trifles and anguished over the most irrelevant things. Had the Weil family got their typewriter back? It was as if he found a crumb of spiritual calm when he concentrated on minutiae like this. But sooner or later the feeling of suffocation returned, and not the slightest glimmer of light passed through the clouds.

Nothing gave him more anxiety than the thought of Lucia's recurring breakdowns. In his mind he saw her repeatedly lose her balance and collapse. Her body at his feet, lifeless.

The remorse that had preyed on him in the last few days made these visions harder to bear. Her support had gone now; she was alone with the boys. Thoughts spiraled endlessly around and around. The same tentative phrases formed a kind of refrain that he repeated, over and over. Words of guilt and forgiveness. Of decisions that should never have been made, and steps that should never have been taken. Of shame and humility before the Lord. And of weakness. That only God can forgive.

To whom did he turn with this confession?

To myself. So began the letter written in his soul. A letter that took shape inside him and was rewritten every time he spoke inwardly to himself. A series of words that had no need of expression. No need of a voice to be heard. He crossed out, paraphrased, formulated his prayer. For wasn't it a prayer? Other voices intervened. He thought he could hear Josephson's endearing parting phrase. *Zay gezunt!* He works in mysterious ways.

He was a warm man, Josephson. But in the next moment it was the strict teacher of his childhood who demanded a commentary on the lines they had just read together. However hard he tried, the teacher was never satisfied, always insisting on a better interpretation of the same passage.

In this half-dreaming state, which could last for hours, there were moments when he could make out Lucia's gentle features at his side. He could feel her warmth, quite clearly. She was there, in the shadows. He turned to her, and she was going to listen. In the next instant he was alone in the darkness, and the pain was back with the same force. It all began again. The circle of words going around.

In the end sleep brought relief. And brighter dreams, of the sisters at Sophiahemmet. Everything was still now. The nurses' white cotton caps held in place by a velvet ribbon. Lucia was in good hands, in the serenity of the sisters' care. The skirts of blue, the plain blouses, the white collars, moving soundlessly around the bed where she lay. Soft light falling on them from the windows high above.

It was dawn by the time Immanuel found peace. Asleep on his bunk he was breathing evenly. He had no reason to feel so sure, but just before he fell asleep he had sensed that the time had come. He would not be in the cell for much longer. Not that the taciturn man with the food trolley had let slip anything of significance. In fact he said nothing, and of course he had no authority. He rattled in with his trolley. And after a while he came back for the plate, without a word.

Nevertheless, it was with a feeling of certainty that he had finally gone to sleep in the imperceptible light of dawn. He had left the food uneaten this morning and fallen back asleep when the door closed. He hadn't even woken when the porridge was taken away untouched.

His sleep was disturbed by new sounds intruding into his dreams. They intensified. It was no longer the distant tapping on a typewriter, not the sharp *click-clack, clickety-clack* he could catch when he held his ear to the cold plaster. It was something else, something louder, forcing its way in. Not even a sentence of death hammered out on a typewriter could sound like this, he thought.

It was the ring of singing metal. Was it the guard's keys in the lock or the crash of the bolt against the doorframe? No, the sounds had another depth entirely. It was possible to discern a sequence created by the notes. He recognized the simple melody being played by the distant carillon and hummed along.

"Sieh, wie lieblich und wie schön ist's . . ."

There was no doubt, he was awake, and it was the bells. He wasn't imagining it, it was the carillon in the German church St. Gertrude's. The tune being played was his father's hymn, the one published in *Der jüdische Kantor.* He remembered the handsome book that had always been under the grand piano at home, where he hid in the alcove with his brother.

Now the sound grew louder, it expanded. He closed his eyes and could see the movements of the boy in front of him. Up in the tower, close to heaven, he was performing his strange art. His father's music filled him, and he followed the jolting dance in his head.

"Sieh, wie lieblich und wie schön ist's . . ."

Something had changed. The melody was higher. An octave higher, that must be it. In that moment it was as if he were moving, up there in the tower. Between the steel strings and pedals and chiming bells. Everything was moving, and everything was ringing. For a second it was as if he were the one playing.

AFTERWORD

The box had been quite badly knocked about. I took it home with me to my apartment a few years ago. This was after my father had died and my mother was starting to clear the house where my sisters and I grew up. "Imm's posthumous papers" was written by hand on the lid. Imm was what my parents called my grandfather, and I knew the box contained documents that had belonged to him. Sometimes I would glance up at it, sitting there on a top shelf. For some reason over Christmas 2015 I lifted it down and began to look through the contents. I lost myself in letters and articles, verdicts and interrogation reports. I began to see the outline of a story that was anything but straightforward.

Immanuel, my grandfather, came to Sweden as a refugee in the autumn of 1939, with his wife, Lucia, and two teenage sons. He was a journalist. As the son of the cantor at the synagogue in Königsberg and a committed Social Democrat, he was no longer able to work for German newspapers. From the end of the 1920s he had been a correspondent in Warsaw. Just a few months before the Germans invaded Poland, he left via

Latvia and Helsinki. They crossed the Baltic Sea to Sweden by boat. In Stockholm he continued to write under the byline Dr. B. for the liberal Swiss newspaper *Basler Nachrichten*. He was also given work as an editor for a German exile publishing house, run by one of Germany's leading publishers, Gottfried Bermann Fischer. During the war years the company published many of the most significant writers banned by the National Socialists, including Thomas Mann and Stefan Zweig.

During those years Stockholm was home to numerous notable refugees from the German-speaking world. Some were in transit, others settled for life, like the author Peter Weiss. Lise Meitner, the important Austrian nuclear physicist, arrived in Sweden simultaneously with Bermann Fischer and became a close friend of the family. Bertolt Brecht arrived the following year with his wife, Helene Weigel, the legendary actress. Like the publisher, they left for the United States via Russia and Japan in 1940, the same year that the young Social Democrats Willy Brandt and Bruno Kreisky made Stockholm their home. The German-Jewish philosopher Ernst Cassirer had already escaped to Sweden in 1936 and left on the same boat to New York as linguist Roman Jakobson in May 1941, after the eastern route via Moscow and Yokohama had been closed. A German occupation of Sweden seemed likely to many, and emigration was an option considered by Jewish families in Sweden too, including the important publishers Bonnier. The fact that *Dagens Nyheter*, the most important Swedish newspaper, had Jewish owners did not exactly ease the government's relationship with Berlin. In spite of growing pressures, the Bonnier family never sold the newspaper and decided not to emigrate. As we know, Sweden remained neutral during the war and, unlike Denmark and Norway, managed to avoid occupation. The Wallenberg family, the country's most powerful industrialists, somehow succeeded in keeping both the British and the Germans satisfied. Modern assessment of Sweden's role during the Nazi era has focused on the compromises and negotiations required to keep the Germans happy, including the continuous shipping of iron ore. The critical debate is still very much alive: Was Swedish neutrality hypocritical?

During World War II Stockholm was home not only to interesting intellectuals but also to secret agents. Historians have referred to the city as a Nordic Casablanca. Through Bermann Fischer, Immanuel came into contact with a group of Englishmen based in Stockholm and producing anti-Nazi propaganda. What he was unaware of was that these same people were planning to sabotage the transport of Swedish iron ore. The order for the attack came from the very top. Winston Churchill, who until the spring of 1940 was First Lord of the Admiralty, was prepared to use violent means to halt the transport of iron to Germany. One Alfred Rickman, a man of many talents, had been commissioned to blow up the ore port in Oxelösund, but was exposed before the sabotage could be carried out.

On February 8, 1940, the Swedish postal service intercepted a letter that, on closer inspection, was found to contain a short message written in invisible ink. It revealed that the British Secret Service had a contact person in Stockholm named Rickman. It was this message that put the police on Rickman's trail, enabling them to arrest the whole team and confiscate the explosives. The significance of stopping the attempt has been discussed at length by military historians. If the attack had been carried out, neutral Sweden might have been dragged into the war. The letter written in invisible ink is sometimes mentioned as a curious feature in the affair.

The journalist who thus exposed the Englishman was my grandfather. It appeared that he was in contact with an agency in Berlin that procured articles for minor German-language newspapers in Poland. He was arrested and sentenced to eight months' imprisonment for spying for the Germans. The British would-be bombers received considerably longer prison sentences. The publisher Bermann Fischer was also arrested but was released after a few weeks. He was deported from Sweden and with his family managed to make the journey to New York via Russia, Japan, and California.

Those who have written about the Rickman affair have assumed that the letter writer was a German spy working for the German security service, or directly for the Gestapo. At first sight, this might seem likely. But anyone who is more familiar with the letter's author, the son of a famous Jewish composer and cantor, knows that it must all be more involved. When he was interrogated, Immanuel insisted that deportation to Germany would be equivalent to a death sentence. He was not a spy sent out by the Germans. He was deprived of his German citizenship and was stateless when he was released from prison. What followed was two years in a Swedish internment camp.

During interrogation by the Swedish police, Immanuel maintained that he had received the invisible ink from a man unknown to him, a representative of the correspondence bureau in Berlin to which the letter was addressed. This man asked him to use his normal news reports to pass secrets that might be of political interest to Germany, things that he learned as a journalist "behind the scenes." Immanuel claimed under questioning that he had used the ink only once, to write the letter that had been intercepted.

But the explanation my grandfather later gave, to clear

himself of the accusation he was a lackey for the National Socialists, was different. The editorial office in Berlin was actually a rallying point for opposition journalists whose chief ambition was to circumvent the Nazification of the German national press and enable neutral political reporting in German-language daily newspapers outside Germany. He hadn't wanted to reveal their real motives to the police, for they were in greater danger than he was. Indeed, they were soon to be closed down by the Nazis. Ilse Stübe and Rudolf von Scheliha were sentenced to death in 1942 for treason. Immanuel's brother was executed too. A curt three-line letter in the box states: "Your brother was arrested by the Gestapo in April 1942 and shot dead some weeks later." But who was Wolfgang Horst, the man who supplied the invisible ink to my grandfather? He is mentioned in the police investigation, but otherwise left no trace whatsoever.

My grandfather was sentenced to prison as a German spy. But Bermann Fischer and several other commentators were of the opinion that he was misled and didn't know that he was in fact leaking information to the Germans rather than to an underground resistance movement. The more I have tried to make sense of the train of events, the more unsure I am that things can be viewed in this black-and-white way. The refugee life to which Immanuel was trying to adapt was characterized by ambivalence and ambiguity. My story doesn't try to cast blame on him or exonerate him. The same applies to all the other figures who appear in the book. *Dr. B.* is a novel, an invention. But it has as its starting point the story I found in the documents in the box of posthumous papers.

The last time I met my grandfather, I was still a child. Older members of my family of course knew him better and are thus better able to comprehend his inner life and his moral choices.

It was never my intention to create a psychologically accurate portrait. In my account he is at the center of a labyrinth of astonishing interconnections and exposed to fiercely hostile powers. It was the complexity of these connections and the pressure that these forces must have exerted on him that fascinated me and made me write this novel, perhaps a portrait of the city of Stockholm at the beginning of World War II rather than of a journalist in exile. I have not searched international archives to gain a final understanding of all the ambiguities. But the unlikely connections and coincidences that form the basis of my story are undoubtedly real: my grandfather did interview the legendary Russian ambassador Kollontai, he did stay at the same hotel as infamous German spies, and the letter written in secret ink is as real as the innumerable articles signed "Dr. B." in that cardboard box.

After the war my grandfather left Sweden and went first to Warsaw, then Vienna, and in the 1950s to Munich. He became one of the chief editors for *Süddeutsche Zeitung*. There are some in my family who looked with suspicion on those who were willing to return to Germany after the Holocaust. How could Immanuel go back to a country whose people were guilty of such a crime? But my novel is not about this other life; it is about the life that ended in Stockholm. For my grandmother Lucia it was a time of terrible ordeal. She died of a stroke at the age of only forty-four.

By the time he was twenty-five Immanuel had already converted to Protestantism. There was nothing inherently unusual about that. The Jews' assimilation in Europe assumed many forms. By degrees they managed to win rights in society held previously only by Christians. Not all chose to convert, but many did, in order to fit in and to practice professions barred to

Jews. In Immanuel's case the decision was founded on religious conviction. As a young man he was a thinker who was searching for the right context for his faith. He admired German literature and from prison he sent long lists of the most important books he thought his sons should read. But was there also a streak of German patriotism in him? At the outbreak of World War I he volunteered for the German army. He mentioned this to his fellow student Walter Benjamin, who said that the war held no interest for him. Benjamin added that it would have been different if it had been a Jewish war.

In his autobiographical writings Immanuel never refers to his time as an editor at the publishing house in Stockholm. It is understandable that he might have preferred to forget that part of his life. In his autobiography he reviews the whole of German culture, but there is no mention of Bermann Fischer. A single frayed scrap of paper in the box is a reminder of that story. I believe it is a piece of the dust jacket from Stefan Zweig's last and best-known book, his *Schachnovelle* (*The Royal Game*, in English), published in Stockholm after the author's death. Zweig posted the manuscript to Bermann Fischer the day before he and his wife took their own lives in Brazil. The character in the book is imprisoned and, in his isolation, studies a book about famous chess games, thereby developing miraculous skills as a player. Bermann Fischer met Zweig in New York just before he undertook his last journey. Did the publisher tell him about the new editor, the one who ended up in prison and made sure the publisher himself was forced to experience a number of weeks locked up? The name of the chess-playing prisoner in Zweig's novella convinces me he did: that name is Dr. B.

Who was Zweig's Dr. B.? Some literary scholars have suggested that the author may have met someone on the boat to

Brazil who inspired him to create his character. Others emphasize the autobiographical features and see Dr. B. as Zweig's fictional alter ego. So, am I instead claiming that Zweig's protagonist is modeled on my grandfather? No, not really. Like most fictional characters Zweig's chess genius is a composite creature. Inspiration must have come from many sources. The experience of being locked up in a cell might have been something my grandfather contributed via Bermann Fischer. And perhaps also the name, Dr. B.: in itself a tiny piece of fiction, since my grandfather never had the title of doctor.

SOURCE NOTES

From the prologue, "The world was divided. There were places where Jews couldn't live. And there were places they couldn't enter" is a paraphrase of Chaim Weizmann's statement before the Peel Commission, 1936.

Readings from Alexandra Kollontai's manuscript in the chapter "Sunflowers" are based on her writings, including "Den nya kvinnan" [New woman], originally published in *Sovremenyi Mir* [Modern world] 9 (1913), Swedish translator unknown; and "Kvinnan och familjen" [Woman and the family], first published 1909, Swedish translation by Anita Göransson (Stockholm: Gidlund, 1976).

Passages from Kollontai's journal in the chapter "17 Villagatan" are quotations from *Aleksandra Kollontajs dagböcker, 1930–1940* [The diaries of Alexandra Kollontai, 1930–1940], Swedish translation by Lars Olsson (Stockholm: Albert Bonniers Förlag, 2008).

In the same chapter there are quotations from Kollontai's *Kvinnans ställning i den ekonomiska samhällsutveckingen* [The labor of women in the evolution of the economy], first published as a pamphlet in 1921, Swedish translation by Mauritz Persson (Stockholm: Sverdlov-Universitet, 1925).

In the chapter "The Opera Bar" is a quotation from Ernst Cassirer's *Drottning Christina och Descartes* [Queen Christina and Descartes], Swedish translation by Bengt Wall (Stockholm: Albert Bonniers Förlag, 1940).

In the chapter "Snow Crystals" there are quotations from Vitalis Pantenburg's *Rysslands grepp om Norden* [Russia's grip on the north], Swedish translator unknown (Malmö, Sweden: Dagens Böcker, 1940).

The chapter "Wagner Evening" contains quotations from Richard Wagner's article "Das Judenthum in der Musik" [Judaism in music], first published anonymously in Germany in 1850, Swedish translations the author's own.